ROCKY MOUNTAIN PROMISE

ROCKY MOUNTAIN PROMISE

MISTY M. BELLER

BETHANYHOUSE

a division of Baker Publishing Group
Minneapolis, Minnesota

© 2023 by Misty M. Beller

Published by Bethany House Publishers
Minneapolis, Minnesota
www.bethanyhouse.com

Bethany House Publishers is a division of
Baker Publishing Group, Grand Rapids, Michigan

Printed in the United States of America

Library of Congress Cataloging-in-Publication Data
Names: Beller, Misty M., author.
Title: Rocky Mountain promise / Misty M. Beller.
Description: Minneapolis, Minnesota : Bethany House Publishers, a division of Baker
    Publishing Group, 2023. | Series: Sisters of the Rockies ; 2
Identifiers: LCCN 2023026950 | ISBN 9780764241543 (paperback) | ISBN
    9780764242229 (casebound) | ISBN 9781493443741 (ebook)
Subjects: LCGFT: Christian fiction. | Romance fiction.
Classification: LCC PS3602.E45755 R58 2023 | DDC 813/.6—dc23/eng/20230620
LC record available at https://lccn.loc.gov/2023026950

Scripture quotations are from the King James Version of the Bible.

This is a work of fiction. Names, characters, incidents, and dialogues are products of the author's imagination and are not to be construed as real. Any resemblance to actual events or persons, living or dead, is entirely coincidental.

Author is represented by Books & Such Literary Agency.

Baker Publishing Group publications use paper produced from sustainable forestry practices and post-consumer waste whenever possible.

23 24 25 26 27 28 29   7 6 5 4 3 2 1

To my sweet daughter Laney, my inspiration for Lorelei.
I'm so proud of what a smart, fun, determined
young lady you're becoming!

Consider the lilies of the field, how they grow;
   they toil not, neither do they spin:
And yet I say unto you, that even Solomon in all
   his glory was not arrayed like one of these.
Wherefore, if God so clothe the grass of the field,
   which today is, and tomorrow is cast into the
   oven, shall he not much more clothe you, O
   ye of little faith?

Matthew 6:28b–30

ONE

Spring 1838
Green River Valley (Future Wyoming)

A knot of dread twisted Lorelei Collins's middle as she studied the dark hump in the prairie ahead. The mound wasn't the right color to be a rock. It could only be . . . a buffalo.

A very dead buffalo.

As much as she wanted to turn her mare, Annabelle, and gallop the other direction, she kept her horse pointed toward the motionless body. Drawn like an onlooker to a carriage accident.

Except she wasn't coming to gawk. She had to see if the animal still lived. See if she could do something to save it, or at least ease its misery in these final moments.

Annabelle pricked her ears and slowed as they neared the buffalo. But when the mare tried to halt, Lorelei nudged her forward. "I know, girl. I don't want to see it either. But we have to make certain."

The trampled grass around them told the story clearly.

A buffalo chase had occurred. Somehow the hunters must not have realized this animal had fallen. Or they planned to come back for it. Pursuers sometimes ran with the herd for miles, bringing down as many as they could. Her belly roiled at the thought, but she pushed the grotesque image from her mind. People had to eat, but she hated to think about the process of killing.

Her mission was to save—especially animals. She was the one who came along after the hunters and found the helpless, those not mortally wounded, or the innocent that had depended on those now lifeless.

She probably couldn't do anything here, except pray the hunters came back and put the meat to good use filling hungry bellies and using skins to keep cold bodies warm through the winter.

As she guided Annabelle around the form so she could see its head, keeping a half-dozen strides away, she could see the protruding stem of an arrow near the beast's heart. Two more just behind it had likely punctured a lung. There would be naught she could do to save this one, even if it did still breathe.

She reined her mare in and slipped to the ground, leaving her reins crossed over the horse's neck. "Whoa, girl." Annabelle would stay put until she returned or called for her.

Lorelei crept toward the lifeless form. These mammoth animals amazed her every time she drew near one. They possessed such massive heads, far larger than the cattle back in Virginia. And the hair . . . great curls so bushy and coarse. This must be a female, for she didn't have the thick neck and chest that bulls developed. Nor any horns.

She focused her attention on the animal's side, doing her

best to ignore the arrows and streams of blood dampening the hair. No rise and fall to show life.

Her own chest tightened. Why did God make a world where his creatures had to kill one another just to survive?

She moved to its shoulder and rested a hand there, stroking the matted curls. The body was still a little warm, which meant death hadn't come long before. The animal felt so solid under her palm, a beautiful creature. *Thank you for all you did while you lived.* Probably giving life to young and ensuring this great species carried on.

She glanced down the length of the cow's belly, toward her udder. The shadow beneath her leg hid a swollen teat. Panic pressed in Lorelei's chest. The buffalo nursed a calf? She straightened and lifted her gaze around the area. Had the little one been carried onward with the herd? Or worse yet, been trampled under hundreds of massive hooves?

As her eyes searched for a small, dark form hidden in the tall grass, she nearly skipped over the pale shape standing fifty strides away. Her mind struggled to decipher what her eyes took in. This couldn't be a buffalo calf. Buffalo always had dark hair—nearly black when they shed, or dirty brown when the sun faded the outer coat.

Yet the silhouette looked exactly like a buffalo calf, thicker through the neck than offspring of cattle.

And it was alive. The soft mournful bawl it released proved so.

This must be the poor orphan, which meant it wouldn't survive now without a mother. The thing trembled on spindly legs, and she guessed it couldn't be more than a week or so old. And was likely so confused about what was happening.

It released another bawl, and her chest ached.

She bent over the mother again, this time leaning toward the udder. If she got enough of the animal's scent on her, the babe might allow her to approach. He wasn't old enough to be overly fearful of strangers.

After standing, she kept herself low and her posture soft as she approached the little fellow. It *was* a fellow; one glance underneath made that easy to see.

When she came ten strides away, the calf backed up a step. She extended her hands out farther and gave a low *maah*, as close to the sound of a cow as she could manage.

The calf still kept a hesitant stance but didn't flee as she eased forward. Five steps to go, then four.

Please, God, let me catch it. The Lord had the power to do anything. *Let this be one of those miracles.*

When she was almost an arm's length away, she stopped walking and stretched her hand as far as she could reach. The little one must have smelled its mother's scent on her, for it reached out to touch her finger with its nose, then took a tentative step forward, nosing along to her palm with its wet muzzle. Her heart melted at the sweet touch.

She kept her other hand outstretched. She would only have one chance to grab the babe. Ever so slowly, she shifted her body forward and over so she could come around to the calf's side. He began licking her hand with his slimy tongue. Poor fellow must be hungry.

The animal stayed distracted long enough for her to place her hand over his back, securing him in place. He jerked at the unfamiliar touch, but she locked her arm behind him, just like she'd done so many times with the foals on their ranch. This calf was still small enough she could handle him easily as he fought.

But he didn't struggle long, and she crooned soft words as he settled into her hold. "That's right, fella. I know you're sad, but I'll take care of you. I'll make sure you have a chance to grow big and strong, with plenty of food and a safe place to roam. You'll miss your mama for a little while, but I'll make sure nothing bad happens to you."

And she would fulfill that promise. First, though, she had to find a way to get him up on her horse and back to the ranch.

TWO

That must be the ranch." Tanner Mason stared down from the mountain pass at the wide valley before them. Two structures had been built halfway across the open land, with several corrals attached to the one that appeared to be the barn. Beyond, a large herd of horses grazed peacefully.

"Pretty place to live." Wallace Burke, his partner in this venture, sounded a bit too wistful.

Tanner cut a sideways look at him. Wally met his gaze with a twitch of his mouth that looked almost embarrassed. "Kinda makes a man think about settling down out here."

A spurt of panic slipped through Tanner, but he worked for a casual grin. "You wouldn't be happy tied down to a farm and chores."

Wally turned back to the picturesque scene before them and breathed a long sigh. "You're right." Then he straightened and nudged his horse down the slope. "Let's go meet these neighbors and see their setup so I can remind myself all the reasons I don't want this."

Tanner nudged Domino to follow his friend and worked

to loosen the tension Wally's words had created in his shoulders. They'd just spent two months building a small fort and trading post. This business they were establishing on the western frontier would only work if he had someone keeping steady travel back and forth to the East to replenish their supplies. The traveling itch Wally carried in his veins made him the perfect person, but if he ever chose to settle down, Tanner would have to find another partner.

They were already down one man in their business threesome. George had taken ill right before they left St. Louis, but he hoped to come with Wally's next supply delivery. Until then, Tanner would be on his own manning the fort and trade room.

He could do it, though. He *would* do it.

No matter how much this endeavor required of him, he would make the business a success. As they reached the flat prairie land of the valley, they nudged their horses into a lope. This stretch would be perfect for a horse race. Or just a long hard run to release the frustrations of life.

As they drew near the ranch buildings, they slowed the horses back to walk. The structure on the right must be the house, for it had a slightly lower roof and a longer overhang across the front. It faced the barn and corrals, where a group of people stood beside the rails. They all turned toward Tanner and Wally as they approached.

Three men, and one of them . . . an Indian. Though they'd met several Natives since coming west to build the trading post, the sight of them still jarred him a little, as it probably did most newcomers to this area. Their dress and appearance were so different from the people back east. He would never show his surprise, of course.

His gaze caught on another figure inside the pen, and his breathing hitched. A woman. Her dark red dress seemed so unusual in this land that it should have jumped out at him first thing. She must be the rancher's wife. Perhaps she could be persuaded to bake a few treats he could sell at the post, especially if he supplied the flour and molasses. Homesick trappers would pay well for such goods.

One fellow stepped away from the fence as he and Wally rode into the ranch yard. Tanner studied the fellow, and his gaze tripped once more.

Not a man.

Another woman, but she wore men's clothing. The garments did little to disguise her form, though.

"I'll be." Those words mumbled under Wally's breath meant he'd realized that same truth.

Tanner looked back at the two by the fence to see if he'd missed any details there. Yup. The other one he'd thought to be a white man also appeared to be a woman wearing trousers and a man's felt hat.

The Indian? *He* was definitely a man. What in the great states of America was going on here?

He and Wally halted a respectable distance from the woman approaching them, who now stood with her hands braced at that narrow waist. After they dismounted, Tanner removed his hat. "Hello, ma'am. I'm Tanner Mason, and this is Wallace Burke. We're opening a trading post just two passes over, so I guess we'll be your new neighbors." The Indian and the other woman in trousers came to stand with her, and the lady in the dress now stood at the fence, arms on the rail.

The first woman spoke. "I'm Rosemary Collins. These

are my sisters, Faith and Lorelei"—she motioned first to the one beside her, then to the brown-haired beauty in the dress—"and this is our friend and business partner, White Horse." She nodded to the brave.

Tanner dipped his chin in greeting. "It's a pleasure to meet you all."

Her hand went back to her waist, a position that gave him the feeling she was accustomed to being in charge. Must be the oldest of the sisters. "We'd heard a trading post was being built. What sort of supplies will you have on hand? Will you trade for furs only? Will you accept special orders?"

He bit the inside of his lip to keep a sober face. No small talk with this one, just directness. But he'd long appreciated forthrightness of every kind.

He nodded to acknowledge the questions. "We plan to stock the necessary items the trappers need as well as trade goods for the Indians. And we'd be happy to special order anything you request." He glanced at Wally. "Mr. Burke will be traveling back and forth to St. Louis for supplies. As you can imagine, the trips won't be quick, but he'll be happy to bring back anything specific you need."

Her sharp stare swung from his face to Wally's, then back. He let his own focus shift to the woman and Indian beside her. Then a brief glance at the pretty one still inside the fence. She had an animal at her side. A light-colored calf.

The elder Miss Collins spoke again, forcing his attention back to her. "And what of payment? Will you only accept furs, or coin also?"

Ah, he'd forgotten to respond to that question. The answer must be important to her, or she wouldn't have asked again. Though he'd expected to receive furs from nearly everyone out here, he'd take whatever these women gave if it meant ensuring they'd be customers. With as many horses as he saw grazing, they must be selling to someone back east, which meant they likely had another way to get supplies. He'd have to earn their patronage by making things convenient for them, as long as he didn't sacrifice profit for the post. "We're happy to trade for either, ma'am."

"You don't have any milk for sale, do you? Cow's milk or anything else?" The voice called from the fence, and all of them turned to the woman in the dress. The calf stood at her side as she stroked its neck in a steady rhythm. They both studied him expectantly. The animal even let out a pitiful cry. It sounded odd for a calf, deeper and a little more strangled. Had it lost its mother? Maybe that milk cow Tanner had worked so hard to drag along had been worth the trouble after all.

"As it happens, we do have a cow who currently supplies about three gallons morning and eve. I'm planning to sell all but a quart each day."

A smile bloomed across her face, lighting her features like a ray of sunshine. When she spoke, her voice maintained the same sweet tone, though it nearly trembled with joy. "You have milk? Oh heavens, who would have believed it? Yes, we'll take every bit you'll sell us. No matter the cost."

"Lorelei." The older sister's voice held warning, then she spun to face him. "Your price does matter. We won't take a drop for more than two dollars per gallon."

Tanner fought to school his expression. That was the price back in Boston, but they couldn't even get milk in St. Louis for that, much less this land nearly two months' travel from any city. "Ten dollars for every gallon. I couldn't let it go for less."

She raised her brows. "You already have the cow, and the milk will spoil if you don't sell it. It's not as if it costs more to feed her on this rich prairie grass than it does back in the States."

He let the corners of his mouth tip in a friendly way as he dipped his chin to acknowledge the truth of her words. "You're right. But I suspect there aren't many milk cows in the area. It won't be hard to find men willing to buy at my price."

She snorted, but before she could answer, her sister called out. "Rosie, please."

His attention swung to the fence before he could catch himself. The woman looked desperate, her and that little calf.

A movement closer to him shifted his focus once more. The Indian took a half step forward. "I will trade. Five horses for the cow."

The older Miss Collins's gaze shot to the brave, and Tanner didn't have to look at her to feel the strength of her glare.

The other man must have felt it too, for he looked to her and attempted an explanation. "White buffalo is . . ." He seemed to be struggling for a word. "The people think have powers. Not see in many winters. Not ever sell or trade. Very . . ." Again, he struggled for a word.

"Special?" Miss Collins's voice was gentle as she spoke to the man, and it held something much closer to respect than the tone she'd used with Tanner.

The brave's brow still lined with uncertainty, so she spoke again. "Are there not many white buffalo in this area, then?"

He shook his head. "None. I see one when boy. No more."

Interesting. Tanner shifted his focus to the animal gnawing at Miss Lorelei's skirts as she continued to stroke it. So this wasn't a calf—not of the bovine variety, anyway. And if white buffalo were so rare, perhaps they could work out an arrangement agreeable to all.

He chose his words carefully. "I didn't realize that was a buffalo calf. It's an orphan, I assume?" He directed the question to Miss Lorelei.

She regarded him a bit warily. "I found it near its mother, who lay dead on the plain. I'm sure he needs to eat soon."

That seemed to be her way of saying Tanner had best get on with his suggestion. The little fellow bawled its agreement.

"Perhaps we could work something out. I'd be happy to buy the calf from you and feed him myself. Then he'd be close to the milk cow." The bargain would save these people the markup he'd have to charge for the milk also. And he could likely buy it for cheaper now than later after they'd spent so much in feeding the animal.

"No!" Miss Lorelei and White Horse spoke at the same time, which was probably why the word sounded so much like a shout.

The man shook his head. "Not trade white buffalo. Harm come if trade."

Tanner studied the man. The Indians wouldn't trade it at all? Did that mean they wouldn't trade to acquire it either? The last thing he needed was a buffalo on his hands that he'd invested a great deal in and couldn't recoup his costs.

His gaze wandered to Miss Lorelei—a mistake. She turned those pleading eyes on him. He'd trained himself in the Boston Day Police to look past womanly wiles or manly posturing to find the truth. But he couldn't manage to be indifferent to the desperation radiating from her.

"Perhaps we could settle somewhere in the middle. A gallon for six dollars. Would that be agreeable?"

Lorelei nodded, thankfulness evident in the release of her shoulders. "Yes. Thank you so much."

The sound of a throat clearing from the sister in front of him brought him back to reality. He'd much rather stay lost in the sweetness of the younger sister than face this older one's demands. She reminded him too much of Jessamine.

A reminder of his past that roiled distaste in his belly.

Yet he forced himself to face the woman dressed like a man.

"A single gallon for five dollars, but if we buy two gallons and three quarts every day, we expect a discount. We'll pay ten dollars for that amount."

He just barely bit back a sigh. Only a female would be as stubborn as this.

Clearly not every female, for Miss Lorelei's voice rang out with as much frustration as he felt. "I'll pay the difference, Rosie. Leave it be." Then she turned to him, and the ire leaked from her tone. "Thank you, Mr. Mason. Would you mind if one of us accompanies you back to your trading post now to purchase what you have?"

The calf bawled again, this time louder and more desperate. The sound touched his awareness, but not as much as the care in her voice and the tenderness in her expression when she stared down at the pitiful calf.

The quicker he got out of here, the better. He couldn't allow his emotions any more rein. He turned and mounted his horse. "I'll go get what I have and bring it back for you. Sounds like he needs it right away."

She smiled at him, and that sunray made all the effort seem worth it. Maybe if he was lucky, he would even get to help feed the little guy.

But after that, he couldn't let her distract him anymore. He had to get the trading post fully stocked so they could be ready for customers. He would make a success of the place or die trying.

THREE

S he had food for the babe.

For the first time, it seemed Lorelei might be able to keep this calf alive and thriving without exhausting every resource she had. She'd been preparing to go back out to the mother buffalo and milk its lifeless body when these new neighbors rode up. Since the mother's body had still been warm, the milk wouldn't have spoiled yet.

But now she didn't have to.

Thank you, Lord. His love toward these innocent creatures never ceased to overwhelm her. He'd certainly made this little fellow unique, according to White Horse.

Lorelei turned to the calf, who'd begun rooting in her skirts. "Patience, boy. Food will be here soon." She stepped sideways so she could stroke its neck without getting plastered with that slimy tongue. She'd have to wash this dress before she wore it again. Good thing she'd been wearing her best outfit to meet Mr. Mason. And Mr. Burke too, but it sounded like they wouldn't be seeing much of him.

"Now who's that coming?" Rosie's muttered words brought Lorelei's head up.

Her sister stared off in the direction their new neighbors had just ridden. Two horses descended the pass, riding toward them, different animals this time. They looked familiar . . . didn't they?

She raised a hand to shield her eyes from the sun. Yes. That was Dragoon's bay mare, Bessie, with him riding. And Ol' Henry beside him. She grinned wide. These were some of their first friends when she and her sisters had arrived at the rendezvous last summer. Ol' Henry and Dragoon had been lodge mates of Riley, who'd helped them with the search that brought them so far west.

And Riley was now her brother-in-law, married to her sister Juniper. The two of them had set off a month before to ride the backbone of the Rockies. Too bad he wasn't here now to see his friends, but he and June were probably having too much fun to miss them.

She glanced at her other two sisters. Their group didn't seem complete without Juniper—the four of them together. White Horse made a great friend and partner on the ranch, but not such a wonderful sister. She flicked a glance at him, his tall form and dark features, and allowed herself a small smile at her joke.

As the two men reached the level ground of the valley, Dragoon gave a whoop and pushed his mare into a gallop across the flatland. That little girl could run too. She'd proven her speed in the races at the rendezvous, and Dragoon had even allowed Lorelei to run her privately later on, since her sisters wouldn't let her ride in any of the official matches.

He reined in to let Bessie cool off at a walk before she reached them, which allowed Ol' Henry to catch up too.

Didn't Aesop write a fable about slow and steady winning the race?

Faith met the men first, showing as much excitement at the reunion as Dragoon. "Where did you guys come from? Did you see the men who're opening a trading post? Riley's not here. He and Juniper are off riding the mountains all summer."

Dragoon reined in his horse beside her with a chuckle and plopped his hat on her head, then dismounted. Ol' Henry moved a little slower as he climbed off his buckskin gelding.

Lorelei would have liked to slip through the fence rails and greet the men up close too, but this little fellow seemed calmer when she stayed with him. Surely these old friends would come say hello to her as part of their greetings.

Ol' Henry stood for a moment with his horse's reins in hand and swept his gaze around them all. "Woowee. If you gals ain't a sight for sore eyes. You too, White Horse." He gave the motion for *hello* in the sign language most of the tribes used. Though he knew White Horse understood English, it was a nice gesture of respect. "I sure am glad you've been here to keep these ladies out of trouble." His grin flashed against skin so deeply tanned it held a bluish tint.

Faith piped up again. "Where did you go all winter? Did you get lots of furs? Did you join a big group of trappers?"

Ol' Henry's grin deepened, and he walked to her, then wrapped his arm around her shoulders as they strolled toward Rosie and White Horse. Just like a grandpa taking an exuberant lad to his side. "The two of us found a nice little lake north of Lolo Pass that was chock-full o' beaver an' otter. We tucked furs away in a cache till rendezvous. Then, wouldn't you know it, we just met up with the fellows starting up a trading post. Looks like I won't have to wait for the meetup to get me some decent coffee." He chuckled as he released Faith's shoulders and gave her a pat on the back.

Even with the dozen strides separating Lorelei from the group, it wasn't hard to see how enamored her sister was with the life of adventure they led.

Dragoon propped his hands at his waist as he scanned the ranch yard, house first, then the barn. "Looks like you folks are settling in well." As his focus roamed the corral, it landed on her. "Miss Lorelei, I see you got another critter. Hope this one behaves better than that—" His words clipped short as the calf stepped into full view. His eyes widened, and he moved around the others to approach her, his jaw slackening as he came near.

Ol' Henry too had caught sight of the buffalo and followed behind Dragoon. He was the most seasoned mountain man she'd ever met, having lived more than two decades in this land, but even *he* looked in awe of the youngster beside her. The calf let out another bawl, as though realizing he was now the center of attention and taking the chance to voice his need for food.

"Bright stars in the sky," Dragoon breathed. "Miss Lorelei, is that what I think it is? Have you gone and found a white buffalo?"

Something about the awe in his tone, the near reverence in his voice, made gooseflesh prickle her skin even though the spring sun beat down unusually warm. She placed a hand on the calf's neck, tucking him a little behind her. "I wouldn't call it white, exactly. More like a rich cream color."

It was darker on its shoulders than its neck, but definitely closer to white than the coffee brown of its mother.

Rosie came to stand beside them. "White Horse said white buffalo are rare, that his people consider them sacred. That they have powers."

Ol' Henry straightened, the look in his eyes distant as he nudged up the front of his hat and wiped a sleeve across his brow. "I had a good friend among the Lakota. Spent more than one summer with 'em, and he told me the story. Let's see if I recall it."

Ol' Henry was one of their favorite storytellers around the campfire of a night. He had a way of drawing a tale out in a way that kept you leaning in for more. This time, though, his manner didn't take on as much drama as usual. Perhaps he wasn't embellishing any, just remembering.

"The story goes that one summer, all seven of the Lakota Sioux bands came together and camped, but the people were starving because they had no game. Two young fellers went out to look for food in the Black Hills."

His voice began to strengthen as he settled into the story. "As they were searching, they met a pretty young gal dressed in white. She said, 'Return to your people and tell 'em I'm coming.' Then, when she showed up at the Lakota camp, she brought a sacred pipe and taught them to pray and how to be proper Lakota.

"Before she left, she laid down on the ground and rolled four times. Each time she flipped over, she changed color, and on the last roll, she changed into a white buffalo calf. As she left, great herds of buffalo appeared in the camps. After that day, the Lakota held their pipe in honor, and buffalo were plentiful."

He seemed to come back from his memories. "So you see, the white buffalo is a sign of peace and plenty to the Natives. Not just the Lakota either—every tribe I've met that relies on the buffalo for food holds a white buffalo sacred." He looked to White Horse for confirmation.

The brave nodded, and Ol' Henry turned back to them. "I can't ever remember a white buffalo kept as a pet. I've only seen one or two skins my whole life, they're so rare. But once a man gets hold of one, he won't sell it. Not at all. Not a Native, nor a trapper. It's bad luck, you see. If you lose the buffalo, you lose the time of plenty, and you're destined for hardship."

"Do you really believe that?" Though Rosie spoke with the respect Ol' Henry had earned from them, a bit of skepticism laced her voice.

Ol' Henry shrugged. "Don't matter if I do or not. The facts just now are that Miss Lorelei be standin' here next to a white buffalo calf. I'm a bit curious how it all came to be."

When he offered a friendly grin, it was impossible for Lorelei not to return a smile. As she told the story of finding the calf and bringing it back to the ranch, both men listened with intense interest. And when she added the part about Mr. Mason having a milk cow and going to bring some back for them, Ol' Henry's brows shot up.

"You don't say. Well I . . . it's been . . ." He didn't seem to know how to finish the sentence.

Dragoon piped up with the missing words. "It's been longer than I can remember since I've had good cold milk to drink." He rubbed his hand over the grubby buckskin tunic that covered his belly. "Maybe you'd allow us each a sip afore we let this animal drink its fill?"

She hesitated. She shouldn't think twice about being generous with friends, but this poor calf was nearly half-starved. To these men, the milk would be a treat, but to the calf, it meant the difference between life or death.

But two sips out of nearly three gallons wouldn't make a difference. She worked to keep any ungracious thoughts from her expression. "Certainly. Now, while we wait, tell us everything that's happened since we last saw you."

As Tanner descended the pass again and the ranch spread out before him, his gaze roamed the figures crowded around the fence. Two more than before. A pair of new horses also.

His gut tightened, though he had no reason to think something was amiss. These must be hired hands. Three women and one brave couldn't handle all these horses on their own.

He had to keep Domino at a walk, even when they reached level ground, so the milk didn't slosh around too much inside its pouch. The sisters wouldn't appreciate it if he delivered butter. He shouldn't have offered to bring it at all—from here on out, they could come daily to get what they wanted. He'd even let them use the large leather pouch he'd stitched on the journey out here to transport large amounts.

But the ride only took an hour, even with him moving slowly. Less than that on the return trip, when he wouldn't have to worry about liquid sloshing around. Wally had stayed behind to help their chore boy, Kentucky, finish organizing the trade goods, so at least Tanner was the only one wasting time on the second trip.

Long before he entered the ranch yard, the pitiful bawling of the calf rang across the open land. He reined in by the barn and slipped off his gelding, then carried the flask of milk toward the group by the fence.

The pretty woman in the dark red dress stepped away from the group and waited for him to reach her, arms out in eager anticipation. Her smile didn't beam like a sunray this time. Lines of strain marked her eyes as she took the container from him. "Thank you. He's rather hungry."

"Sorry it took me so long." Though it hadn't really. He'd poured the milk from the bucket into this traveling pouch, then headed straight back.

A good businessman would have not relinquished his goods without receiving payment, but Lorelei and the calf both seemed desperate for the milk. She pulled the plug from the flask, then poured a little into a tin cup and handed it to one of the men leaning against the fence.

Tanner shot a look at the two newcomers, and recognition slid in. These were the trappers he and Wally had met after leaving the ranch the first time. The way the others crowded around them, they must not be strangers here.

Were they such honored guests they were granted this high-priced treat even before the frantic calf? A pain of envy poked his belly. Not for the milk, but for the favor they'd just been shown.

But then Lorelei bent over the calf and began murmuring as she drew him toward the flask. Tanner had planned for her to pour the liquid into a bucket, not feed directly from his container. Perhaps she didn't have a bucket. He'd have to clean the flask before he put any more milk in it, though.

Soon enough, the calf caught on and drank from the

small opening as though from its mother. Perhaps that had been the woman's intent all along. As the pint-sized buffalo guzzled the meal, Tanner's gaze lifted to her.

The sunray was back. Pleasure lit her face as she braced herself against the calf's hungry barrage. What was such a pretty thing doing here in this frontier wilderness? The unexpectedness of her presence must have been what drew him to her. He'd always been good at resisting the temptations of women back in Boston, but he'd let his guard down when he left St. Louis behind.

As the calf drank, he forced his gaze away from the woman. He scanned the rustic barn and cabin, then shifted his focus to the herd of horses in the distance. "Nice place you have here. A lot of horses too." He turned back to the people lining the fence. "Have you been here long?"

The elder sister straightened. "We came west last summer and built the ranch."

He raised his brows. "You brought the horses with you?" Maybe he was being nosy asking so many questions, but how could these three women have obtained so many animals? They must have come from the Indian. Perhaps that was how he'd become part of the business.

She shook her head, frown lines forming on her brow. "Some of them are descended from horses our father once bred. He owned a sizeable ranch in Virginia until a few years ago. The others we . . . acquired after we got here."

One of the trappers spoke up. "She means they took 'em back from a yellow-bellied thief when he turned his gun on the wrong gal."

He would have expected Miss Collins to aim her frown at the trapper and his impertinent comment, but instead her expression softened to a slight curve of her mouth. "What he means, Mr. Mason, is that after we came west, we found the horses that had once belonged to our father and also discovered a host of other mounts the man had stolen. We've returned as many to their rightful owners as we could locate, and those remaining are now part of our herd." She glanced to the brave. "White Horse has half ownership in everything. The two horses who produced part of the herd were gifts from our father to his mother."

Tanner couldn't help but stare as he took in the story. What a tale. Any women living and ranching in this mountain wilderness had to be tough, but these three appeared to possess a double portion of grit. They'd been through far more than he'd imagined.

Hopefully they wouldn't mind one more question. "So what do you do with them all? Sell them to the Indians?"

She shrugged. "Some. And trappers. But mostly we have a contract with the cavalry to supply a number of mounts each year."

Even more impressive. Grit and business savvy.

A noise from the calf drew his focus back to the animal as it gave a hard butt against Miss Lorelei's hand. She chuckled and straightened, then lifted the milk container out of its reach. She turned that brilliant smile to the group behind her, making him wish he didn't stand apart from the others. "I think he feels much better about life. Hopefully that will last him until we get more milk tomorrow."

She looked to Tanner, and the richness of those warm brown eyes pressed through him. "Will you be milking tonight as well as in the morning?"

Steady, Mason. You can't offer to ride the milk over in the dark. He swallowed to strengthen his defenses. "I milk her mornings and evenings. You're welcome to come purchase milk anytime." *But I can't deliver it again.* Hopefully she understood the unspoken message.

And he'd slipped the word *purchase* in too, which should remind her he needed to be paid for this order. His father would be proud. Though that no longer mattered. He was simply being a good businessman. Ensuring his trading post would be a success.

He had to, for it was his last chance to make something of himself.

FOUR

T he sound of the trading post door opening made Tanner spin to face the newcomers. He needed a dog, or something to announce when people approached. This place was too remote.

His years as one of the Boston Day Police had taught him not to turn his back on strangers, but he couldn't help that when he was here by himself. Since Wally and Kentucky had left with the wagon for St. Louis that morning, he was on his own now, at least until Wally returned in two months with George and another load of supplies.

A single man entered, removing his hat and blinking as he paused in the doorway and stared around the room. With the sun still streaming in behind him, the fellow's face was mostly shadowed, making it hard to see more than the bushy hair around his head.

Tanner left the bead necklaces he'd been sorting by color and moved to the trade counter. "How can I help you, sir?" Perhaps he should find a less patronizing way to greet customers. He still sounded like a youth working the counter at Mason's Mercantile. And he'd not been that for nearly a decade. Nor would he ever be again.

"Not sure yet." The voice made the newcomer sound not much older than a store clerk himself. He left the door open as he meandered into the room, but at least Tanner could make out his features now. The overgrown lad wore the buckskin trousers every man in these parts sported and a cloth shirt that looked new enough to have been bought at last year's rendezvous. Or more likely, this fellow had come west the summer before, just in time for winter trapping.

"Feel free to look around. Let me know if you have trade furs you want me to value."

The man swiveled to face him, then took two lanky steps—the kind that would cover a lot of ground hiking up and down mountains—and slapped a hand on the counter. "I heard you was openin' a trade shop. I told Skeet it couldn't be true. We near caught the scurvy all winter long, and now you show up and say we can buy goods anytime we please. But here ye are. Wait till I tell the rest of them. You'll have all o' Johnson's men here afore you can sneeze twice. Redding's too. We passed those boys about a week back on the Yellowstone. Leastways Skeet said it was the Yellowstone. Thought it was the Jefferson myself."

Keeping up with the man's ramble wasn't easy, especially with the sluggish way he drew out some of the words. But Tanner would need to pick up the skill quickly. A trading post centrally located like this one would be a hub of news.

And he would be the chief reporter. Somehow that hadn't occurred to him when he'd chosen this venture for his final chance. They'd find him far better at keeping a confidence than spilling gossip.

But he gave the man a friendly nod. "Tell them all we pay a fair price for every fur. And we're fully stocked with supplies and goods to trade with the Indians." He'd done a great deal of research before purchasing his inventory. Even spoke to Etienne Provost, one of the partners from last year's rendezvous.

The fellow turned and wandered to a row of shelves where Tanner had stacked clothing. As he looked his fill, he jabbered on about how long it had been since he'd seen red flannel. Not since coming west from Georgia last autumn, which fit the narrative Tanner had suspected.

Tanner kept himself behind the counter the entire time the fellow stayed, which allowed him to study the man. He'd spent the last decade developing his senses, making himself adept at reading people.

He would need a little more education in the nuances of these trappers. Though this fellow was young and probably still greener than most, the winter he'd survived in this harsh land showed in the lines around his eyes and the way he studied things. He was eager, but not foolhardy. Not much, anyway.

But he did love to talk. By the time the fellow had been there a quarter hour, Tanner had to work not to tune him out. Most of the trappers would likely be starved for conversation after going the winter with only a small group. Something else to prepare himself for.

"Did you hear about the white buffalo calf those women are raising north of here?"

Tanner blinked to sharpen his attention on the lad. His entire body tensed.

"We was already headed there to get a gander at the ladies, but two Snake Indians we met on the trail told us about it. They acted like it was somethin' mighty special. Like it meant gold would be fallin' from the skies soon enough. One o' the boys with us said the last white buffalo seen in this area was close to fifteen years ago. Soon as I get back to camp, we're headed to have a look at it. Maybe those gals will bake us a batch o' biscuits too while we're there." He accompanied the words with a low whistle, then flashed Tanner a grin. "Even if they're ugly as a hound dog, reckon I'd rather be watchin' them than twiddling my thumbs here. Right good to meet you, fella. Wha'dyou say your name was?"

"Mason. Tanner Mason." He barely ground out the words.

"Horace McGill. But folks call me Pole Bean." The kid offered a cheeky salute and a farewell, then turned and strode through the door, leaving it open once more.

Tanner closed the door and pulled the latchstring in, then placed the bar across to lock it closed. He scooped up his gun and shot bag, strode through the back door into the courtyard of the little fort they'd built, and covered the short distance to the room he'd built as a cabin. Inside, he shoved the board off the hole he'd dug in the ground to store cold foods and scooped up the flask of milk.

As he nudged the cover back in place, he was grateful he'd finished the hole in the storage room floor where he could keep extra rifles and the few other expensive goods they carried. Surely no one would break into the place in the couple hours he would be gone, but having those precious goods hidden away made him feel better.

White Horse had come for the milk yesterday, but it looked like Tanner would be delivering it again today. He couldn't let all those men converge on the Collins sisters to gawk at them and who knew what else, not without being there to step in if they needed help.

Maybe he shouldn't meddle. But he'd been in the business of protecting the innocent for too long to stand by now.

"I, um . . . think he's nearing a couple weeks old. I call him Curly because of this tuft where his horns will grow in." Lorelei fought her unease as she glanced down the row of trappers leaning against the corral rail. The fence would provide little protection if any of them wanted to get through to her. Or Curly.

These men had simply appeared. She'd been pouring water into the piggin pail when the low rumble of men's voices had sounded. She'd spun to find this entire pack—eight shaggy, filthy men—staring at her from atop their horses and mules. She'd barely kept in a scream.

So far they'd been polite enough, but they'd wasted no time in dismounting and lining the fence to ogle Curly—and her, but she was trying to ignore those looks.

At least Faith was hidden away in the house. Rosie and White Horse had gone to check the herd and likely wouldn't be back for an hour or two.

"He looks like any old calf back home. A mite older'n two weeks, though. Not sure what's so all-fired special about him."

"I heard the Indians will give nearly anythin' they have for one of these. Heard we can get a whole winter's worth of furs in trade."

"No." One of the older men in the group barked the word. Maybe he was the leader. "White buffalo can't be bought or sold. It belongs to all people, and wherever it stays, it brings good health and plenty."

One of the younger men shifted his focus to her. "If you're not already hitched, ma'am, I'd be awful proud to marry up with you. My name's Horace McGill, and I'm from Georgia, but I be plannin' to stay in these parts for now. I'd make an awful good man for you."

She nearly choked on the dusty air blowing in her open mouth as she stared at him. No hint of a grin to show he was jesting. He couldn't possibly be serious. Could he?

The sound of their front door closing jerked her attention over Mr. McGill's shoulder to the house.

She nearly groaned. *Go back in, Faithie. Stay far away from these men.*

But her sister marched toward them, dressed in her trousers. She and Rosie had taken to wearing them nearly all the time since pants were easier to work in. Lorelei couldn't bring herself to throw propriety to the wind so fully.

She had to get rid of this group before they started proposing marriage to her baby sister too.

Turning back to the strangers, she honed her focus on the one who'd made such a preposterous request. She would proceed under the assumption that he'd been jesting. Better yet, she'd ignore the absurd comment completely.

She shifted her gaze to sweep along the entire row. "Gentlemen, it was nice to meet you, but little Curly needs rest now. I'm sure you understand."

Several nodded, but the rest just eyed her. None of them turned to leave.

"Hello." Faith stopped behind the men, and every one of them spun to face her.

No. Lorelei had to grab their attention back. She raised her voice. "Sirs, good day to you all. It's time you leave."

A pounding of hooves from the south stopped any of them from obeying. Frustration sluiced through her, and maybe a touch of worry. What now?

She shielded her eyes from the sun to see better, and the familiar form eased the fear away.

Mr. Mason.

Why had he come back today? His horse covered the ground with a long stride, not the easy lope he and his partner had approached with before. Why the urgency?

He waited until nearly the last minute to slow, then leapt from his horse, rifle in hand. Had he been carrying a gun before? Probably in his scabbard, but definitely not in hand.

All the trappers studied him, and a few shifted away from the fence for a better look. A new tension thickened the air. Not quite animosity, but definitely wariness.

Mr. Mason stopped a few strides in front of the others, feet braced, shoulders squared as though facing an enemy.

Before he could speak, another voice rose from the trappers. "Well if it ain't the fellow from the trading post. Mason be your name, right?"

Horace McGill. His young, slightly high-pitched voice broke the tension. He stepped forward from the back of the group and stood to the side, partway between Mr. Mason and the others. "Fellas, this is the trader I was telling you about." Then to Mr. Mason. "This here is Johnson, the one in charge of our party. And there's Sloan and Timmons and Wahlberg and Linton . . ." She tried to follow along with the names as he pointed out each man, but she lost track.

Her gaze wandered to Mr. Mason, who was looking at

her instead of the men he was being introduced to. Their eyes locked, and the intensity in his focus didn't at all match the way he'd looked before. Neither the businessman nor the friendly neighbor.

The darkness sparking now looked protective. Determined. Almost feral.

Mr. McGill finished his introductions, and Mr. Mason's focus swung to the men. "I'm glad to find you all here together. You've likely looked your fill of this unusual buffalo Miss Collins has taken in. As you can see, the animal is quite young, and these women have their hands full. For that reason, they will not be accepting visitors. Please spread the word and give this place a wide berth yourselves. If any man has questions, you can send them to me at the trading post. These women are not to be bothered." His unspoken *do I make myself clear?* rang loudly in the silence.

The leader, Johnson, stepped forward. Not a big step, but enough to gain every eye among them. When he spoke, his voice drawled slowly, yet a seriousness hung in his tone. "I reckon you're trying to be neighborly. But I also reckon this ain't your place to butt in. Being a newcomer in these parts, you won't know that my boys are plenty respectful. They won't hurt these women or that calf. We just came to pay a visit and gander at this unusual fellow."

His posture relaxed, though his words seemed to grow even heavier. "I think you'll find a lot of the men in this part of the country will want to do the same. And one lone shopkeeper won't gainsay them. Not just white men neither. The Indians, they think it has special powers, do you know that? I can tell you now, it'll be best to let them look their fill before moving on. They won't mess with these gals as long as the white buffalo calf is here. Can't risk losing everything if they make it angry."

Lorelei didn't dare breathe as the man finally stopped speaking. A lot of men would come look at this calf? And Indians too? These men must be planning to tell anyone and everyone they met.

Which raised the question, how did this group hear? Mr. Mason and Mr. Burke were the only ones to know, except for Ol' Henry and Dragoon. And her sisters and White Horse. So one of them must have mentioned it. Perhaps only an innocent comment in passing, and the novelty or intrigue had made the news spread.

What would they do if a line of men began appearing at all hours of the day? Rosie would be beside herself. Probably wouldn't leave the ranch yard so she could stay here and defend them.

For that matter, White Horse might do the same. He wasn't as vocal about his protection, but he stayed close any time there was a sign of danger. His presence certainly made them feel safe too.

As Mr. Mason's did now.

He and Johnson studied each other, likely taking the other's measure. Johnson had called him a lone shopkeeper, which must feel like an insult to a man as virile as this rifle-wielding defender.

At last, Mr. Mason said, "I hope that's true." Then his gaze shifted to the rest of the men. "If you've looked your fill, you'll be ready to head on now."

A few voices murmured through the group, then most of the trappers turned and nodded toward her and Faith.

"Pleasure to meet you, ma'am."

"Nice little calf there."

"Sure am glad you ladies brought civilization to the West."

They finally meandered toward their mounts grazing on the other side of the barn. Mr. Mason didn't move from his position, but he did return the farewell nod from Johnson as the trapper followed his men.

The knot in her own belly still didn't ease.

FIVE

A s the trappers rode away from the ranch, Mr. Mason
finally turned and strode toward her and Faith.
Lorelei tried to read his serious expression. Maybe
. . . distracted? Concerned? Frustrated? Or something altogether different.

He didn't talk immediately, so she broke the tense silence.
"Thank you for speaking up for us."

His mouth pinched. "It doesn't sound like it did any good."
He eyed Curly. "I can't come riding over every time a fellow
shows up to gawk. You might *need* to sell him."

Her insides plummeted. Was he using this situation to
intimidate her into handing the calf over to him? Just when
she'd been thinking charitable thoughts about him. "We are
very capable of protecting ourselves. Thank you for your
interest in our welfare, but it isn't needed. A few visitors
coming to see the calf certainly isn't reason enough to hand
him over to the highest bidder."

His lips tightened again, as if he was preparing some
kind of retort. Better she send him on his way instead of
wasting time arguing.

She glanced toward his horse. "Did you have a purpose in coming other than to deliver milk?" The flask hung from his saddle, but he'd made it clear delivery wouldn't be a regular offering.

His posture stiffened, pulling her focus back to him. "I did. A gangly fellow not much older than a boy was in my post saying his whole group of trappers was headed to your ranch to look their fill of 'those pretty Collins sisters and their unusual buffalo calf.'" The way Mr. Mason said that last bit made it clear the words were a direct quote.

But he wasn't finished. "Where I come from, a decent man doesn't stand by and allow a group of ill-mannered ruffians to show up at a ladies' home uninvited and stand around ogling them. I didn't know how many there were, but I figured White Horse might need an extra gun hand." He glanced around. "Where is he, anyway? And your other sister?"

Though anger sluiced through her, she worked to hold herself steady. "I can assure you, Mr. Mason, my sisters and I are quite capable of protecting ourselves. We would not have come to this land nor built a ranch here if that wasn't the case. You need not concern yourself with us." But had he really closed his trade room and followed the men here? Out of concern for them? For her?

He must truly be a gentleman. Yet if so, why had he come to this land and set up a post to trade with trappers and Natives? Was he trying to civilize the place?

She tipped her head as she studied him. "Where exactly do you come from?" Perhaps she shouldn't be so curious. Her new brother-in-law had said a lot of men came to this land because they wanted a clean slate. But if Mr. Mason could interfere in *their* business, she could ask a few questions about his.

He regarded her too, his gaze turning almost hard again. "Boston. Why?"

Boston was an even larger city than Richmond, where she and her sisters had lived before coming west. She narrowed her eyes. "And what did you do in Boston?" Likely a gentleman of leisure. Or maybe the head of a prestigious business. Something about him bespoke refinement. His clothing perhaps, for his looks were rugged enough with his wind-ruffled dark curls and several days of scruff on his face.

A moment stretched as he didn't answer. Was there some cryptic reason he would refuse this simple question?

"Don't pry into a man's background. Folks who come west often want to leave their past behind." Her mind even replayed the words in Riley's voice.

Perhaps she should take back the question.

When he finally replied, his voice seemed quieter. "I was an officer for the Day Police."

She barely held in her gasp. No wonder protection came so naturally to him. It was in the span of his shoulders, the way he stood with his feet braced, an aura of confidence and determination surrounding him.

Her gaze slipped to the rifle. He must be well-practiced with a gun. Though the police officers who'd carried firing weapons back in Richmond had usually worn smaller pistols fastened at their side.

He stepped back, as though her scrutiny made him itch. "I brought today's milk. Nearly three gallons." He turned and strode to his horse to retrieve the pouch.

When he returned to them, Faith reached out to take the container.

As soon as he handed it over, he moved aside. He didn't meet either of their gazes but motioned to the flask. "The calf may not need all of that, but I thought you'd want the rest for butter or cooking or such. If you don't, I'll take it back to the post to sell. I'm sure any man who comes in would be happy for it." Then he finally did meet her gaze with a glare. "Unless I run them all off in a misguided effort to protect the stubborn neighbor women."

She could choose to be affronted by that comment, or she could take it with a bit of humor. He really seemed to be a good man. He just turned a bit grumpy when others didn't abide by his wishes.

Perhaps he'd never met women like her and her sisters. They'd grown up with more freedom than most ladies, roaming their father's ranch. At least until Mama died. Sadness still drenched Lorelei's spirit when she thought of that stormy afternoon just after her sixteenth birthday. Then Papa had sold everything and moved them into Richmond, and the city had always felt like a corset laced too tight. Coming west had been the breath of fresh air they'd all needed.

Maybe Mr. Mason was experiencing the same. Perhaps he'd not even realized how constricting Boston had been and he was still learning how to stretch his lungs among these majestic mountains and stretching plains.

She sent him a sweet smile. "Don't run your customers off, Mr. Mason. We really do need your trading post in this area. It will be wonderful to have a steady source for supplies." They already had a long list of things they planned to trade for during the summer rendezvous, but hopefully they could get most of it at his store instead. "Are you fully set up now?"

He gave a single nod. "Wally and Kentucky headed east with the wagon this morning."

Mr. Burke had left already? That meant Mr. Mason would be at the trading post by himself now. On the days he had no customers, he might become lonely. The thought tugged at her heart.

"When you have a free evening, come share a meal with us. We would appreciate company. Consider this an open invitation, whenever you're available."

His jaw dropped almost to his collar. She must have caught him off guard, as much as she'd surprised herself with the invitation. He'd probably think her completely unstable now. But she'd always had a soft spot for those left alone. Animal or human.

Curly must have smelled the milk, for he began to root through her skirts, butting against her leg.

Mr. Mason's gaze dropped to the calf. "Perhaps I will." Then he straightened, squaring his shoulders. "I should get back, but I need you to promise me something. If any man frightens you, even the smallest amount, come to me." He looked from her to Faith, then back to her, catching her gaze and holding it, his dark eyes intense.

She swallowed to bring moisture back to her dry mouth, at least enough to speak. "We will."

But could they? If danger found them, would they have a chance to ride all the way to his trading post for help?

That wouldn't happen, though. They'd never have to find out. Surely.

Tanner couldn't stop the worry swirling his thoughts as he sat at Elsa's side, the cow tied where he could view the front of the trade room as he tugged her udder to produce streams of milk. Three women living nearly alone in this wild land would lure danger no matter how much they kept to themselves. Adding in the draw of that white buffalo calf . . .

They would have all manner of scoundrels lurking night and day. White Horse's presence might help temper things, but he was only one man. And in some cases, having an Indian around might bring more trouble than help, depending on the opinions of the fellows who came.

And what of the times like yesterday when White Horse was out with the herd? The man couldn't be with all three women at the same time, not every minute of every day.

Tanner's chest burned the way it often did when his body tensed, so he forced himself to breathe out. This milk would help soothe the fire that sometimes rose up into his throat, but he'd have to finish milking before he indulged.

The steady crunch of Elsa's grazing accompanied the splash of liquid into the bucket. The cow had come from a Swedish farmer, named after the man's mother, and she'd proved herself a hardy animal and a high producer. Exactly as Tanner had hoped.

What would Miss Lorelei have done to feed her buffalo calf had he not had Elsa? The joy shining on her face when he'd said he owned a milk cow still warmed his insides, soothing the burn in his belly almost as well as cool milk did. She was one of the comeliest women of his acquaintance.

She looked similar enough to her sisters to know at a glance they were acquainted, but so much about her stood out from them—her willowy form made all the more graceful by the fact she'd been wearing a dress every time he saw her, not men's trousers like the others. The sweetness that nearly always marked her expression—except when she'd been telling him she and her sisters didn't need his protection. She'd certainly shown a stubborn streak then.

He allowed himself a grin at the memory.

But then Elsa's head rose from the grass, and he looked over his shoulder to what had drawn her attention.

His breath caught at the cluster of horses and riders approaching the front of the trading post. Their buckskins matched several of the trappers who'd come to trade, but the long black braids, some with feathers or other decorations woven in, distinguished them from his customers so far.

He gripped the bucket handle and stood in a smooth motion, keeping his shoulders set at an angle that would show both confidence and friendliness as he strode toward the newcomers. He searched for something in their appearance that would reveal what tribe they were from. No pompadours like the Crow. Nor bone necklaces or breastplates like the Sioux. These must be from a mountain tribe, which were harder to tell apart from one another.

It probably didn't matter which tribe they were from. If they'd come to the fort, it must be to trade. That was why he'd started this business, after all. A bit of confidence and carefulness would carry him through the exchange with no problem.

When he reached the men, he stopped and greeted them in the sign language he'd learned from Provost. The fact that most of the tribes in this area understood the hand talk would certainly make trading easier. Hopefully he'd learned enough to get started and could pick up more signs as he went along.

He needed to gain a few friends among the people in this area. Men who would spread good things about him and his post, and maybe teach him what else he needed to know about trading in this land. Perhaps these men could become that for him.

All six eyed him with wariness, but then one of those in front raised a hand in the same greeting Tanner had offered. He spoke several sounds Tanner couldn't decipher. But he pointed to a horse near the back of their group that held a pile of furs instead of a rider.

Tanner nodded and motioned for them to follow him as he started toward the front door to the trade room.

He'd managed the greeting. Now he just had to prove himself a shrewd but fair businessman.

SIX

Only three of the Natives dismounted and entered behind Tanner, leaving the door open wide. A glance through the frame showed the rest of the men still sitting atop their animals, and the packhorse still laden with furs. It made sense they would want to investigate the place before unloading.

He motioned around the room and formed the sign for *look*. "See all I have to trade for."

None of the men indicated whether or not they understood his words, but they spread out around the room to inspect the wares. He'd removed the lids from crates to show their contents, but he needed to build a great many more shelves and cubbies to display the goods better.

He carried the milk pail back behind the trade counter where it would be out of the way. While he watched the men, he tried to keep his posture relaxed so he wouldn't draw their attention. Best they focus on the goods for barter.

One of the three was the fellow who'd spoken outside, a brave with two quail feathers in each braid. He lifted some of the green flannel shirts and spoke to the older man who'd been browsing bead necklaces. The two exchanged lively banter, the leader even cracking a grin. The younger man left the stack of blankets and came over to see what they spoke of. He looked like he might not be more than twenty or so, his shoulders broad but not yet in his prime.

The three moved to a stack of hats, conversation continuing among them. At least they seemed to be enjoying themselves as they browsed. The youngster plopped one of the hats on his head and made a joke, drawing a smile from the elder. Too bad Tanner couldn't tell if they were making fun of the merchandise or discussing how grand they would look wearing it.

As they spent another quarter hour browsing the rest of the trade goods, they began piling a stack of supplies on the ground in the center of the room. Unfortunately, he and Wally had not put in a wood floor yet. Building the fort walls, the trade room, the supply room, and his own small living quarters had been priority. He'd planned to cut logs for flooring and shelves as he had time, but that certainly hadn't happened yet. Hopefully these men really would take the things now lying in the dirt.

The leader barked a few words to the younger man, who trotted outside. Then he turned to Tanner and motioned toward the pile that rose up nearly to his waist.

He made the sign for *trade*, then pointed out the door. He wanted to exchange all these goods for the pile of furs on that horse? That could be a fair barter, depending on the type and quality of the skins and how well they'd been tanned. It looked like there'd been ten or maybe twelve larger skins and a smaller stack of beaver hides.

The man pointed again and spoke in his tongue as the younger fellow entered with an armload.

Not a full load, though.

Tanner motioned for him to place them on the counter, then he helped lay the furs out flat. He ran his hands over the top one as the fellow stepped back. This looked like a wolfskin, and the hairs were all nice and tight, with none coming out under his touch. The underside was smooth, soft, and pliable. Whoever had tanned this hide did the job well. He moved it to the side so he could examine the next. As he did, he glanced at the three men watching him. They'd not brought in any more furs.

He made the sign for *more*, then motioned toward the packhorse outside. The Indian in charge shook his head and pointed to the three pelts. He spoke something and made a motion, neither of which Tanner could understand.

He pressed down the spurt of frustration. Trading could be an art in giving and taking, bluffing and being careful not to show one's true thoughts. Always having something in reserve and reading the other person's intent, far more than what they showed.

He would be good at this. He'd become a master at deciphering motivations and hidden intentions as well as hiding his own thoughts and emotions.

Best he examine the other two furs and value them all, then he could show which merchandise he would be willing to trade for these three skins. The fellow could bring in more furs for the rest of what he wanted.

The other two pelts showed the same quality workmanship as the first. He would be fair in his offer; a worker was worthy of his pay, after all. But he would not give away these supplies that they'd worked so hard to haul all the way from St. Louis.

He stepped around the counter and crouched beside the stack of goods on the floor. After laying several bundles aside, he pulled out a few of the things the men had selected first. A couple blankets, two knives, and several bead necklaces.

After grouping them together, he looked at the man and pointed to the much smaller pile, then to the furs on the counter. He made the motion for *trade*.

A scowl darkened the man's face, and he shook his head. He moved to the group Tanner had pushed aside, then removed the two felt hats and pushed the rest toward Tanner. He spoke a slew of words and a flurry of signs.

The only one Tanner could pick out was the sign for *trade*. He locked his jaw against another round of frustration. He had to be able to communicate with more than one word. He'd learned so many, but none appeared to apply here.

Still, the man's message seemed clear. He thought this entire cluster of trade goods was worth those three furs. They might possibly be worth the entire load on that horse, but Tanner needed to count and inspect them before he could be sure.

He gave a hard shake of his head and pointed firmly in the direction of the horse. "All the furs. I need to see them all." He rose to his feet and stepped back from the goods. He'd made his offer clear, and it was fair. Even if the fellow waited for the summer rendezvous, he wouldn't get better.

The brave glared at him, a look that—along with his strong frame and the weapons hanging from the sheath at his neck and the belt at his waist—would make any man shirk back. He spoke a slew of angry words and gave a quick wave of his hand, which sent the younger man trotting outside again. Then he leaned down and began gathering all the trade goods together.

Unease rippled through Tanner. It looked like the brave planned to walk out with them. Tanner alone, even with his rifle tucked behind the trade counter, would be no match for six braves if they were bent on taking these things.

For that matter, they could abscond with every piece in this entire room and leave him with tomahawks and knives poking from his chest if they really wanted to. Why had he thought running this post by himself a good idea? Maybe they should have waited until George recovered. Tanner had counted on each man's honor in the trade process. But he didn't know the people out here. Any of them could be scoundrels, and with enough against him at once, not even his sharpshooting skills could help him hold his own. But he'd wanted to get the fort up and running before the summer rendezvous brought more supplies that would compete against their business.

Now he had to handle things on his own.

He inched toward the trade counter so he could grab the rifle if he needed to. He would defend his property if it came to that, but first he would try to use words.

The man picked up as much as he could hold, then spoke to the elder with a nod of his head toward the rest on the ground.

Tanner tried once more, making his tone firm. "Stop. Leave those things and take your furs. If we can't agree on a trade—" But he cut off his words as the younger man appeared in the doorway, his face a deep shadow but the mountain of furs in his arms easy to see. Was that everything loaded on the packhorse?

He carried them in and heaved the stack onto the counter where he'd placed the others. That pile must weigh close to a hundred pounds.

The fellow in charge spoke a few sounds to the younger man, who swooped down and picked up the hats that had been set aside. Then the leader turned to Tanner and gave a satisfied nod. Once more, the man spoke to him, but as before, the language was indecipherable. And this time the fellow's arms were too full to make signs. Not that they would've helped much, it seemed.

All three men turned and strode out of the building. Tanner stayed where he was, watching the open doorway and listening for the sounds of their leaving. Perhaps he should go watch and make sure they didn't take the cow as part of the trade.

His gaze slipped to the stack of pelts. His first guess as to count and quality appeared to be correct. He would have taken a few more things out of the stack the Indians carried off to make the trade even. But he could live with this exchange.

He would have to.

As the sound of hoofbeats faded in the distance, he blew out a long breath. Somehow he had to shore up his gaps so he could better communicate with the Natives. If only he could special order a few more men just in case a group came bent on thieving.

But that wasn't an option. He would have to find a way to add to his defenses by himself.

SEVEN

L orelei pulled the extra dough away from the circle she'd cut. They didn't have a biscuit shaper in their small stock of cooking supplies, but she could carve a decent circle with a knife.

Just having biscuits would be a taste of heaven.

They'd not had flour since a few weeks after last summer's rendezvous, though she and her sisters had become adept at finding the edible roots and berries White Horse and Riley taught them to identify. They'd had plenty of meat.

Since Rosie and Faith had visited the trading post yesterday, they finally had a bit of flour. Coffee too. This morning's cup had been a bit of nectar straight from heaven, especially with a splash of milk mixed in. And she'd churned fresh butter to put on the biscuits.

Hopefully she could manage to bake them over the open fire in the hearth without turning the bottoms black. The last time she'd attempted such in the rendezvous camp, the insides had still been doughy though the bottoms were burned. At this point, she'd eat them even if they jiggled like pudding.

Hmmm. Now that she had milk, perhaps she could make a pudding, though she had no recipe for it. Would Rosie remember how? Her sister had never enjoyed time in the kitchen, though as the oldest, she'd spent longer there than the rest of them. Juniper had always been the best cook among them. Was she getting to use those skills as she and her husband trekked across the mountains? Or were they subsisting only on roasted meat and fresh berries?

As Lorelei moved from the work counter to the hearth, she glanced through one of the openings between logs they'd left unchinked to act as a narrow window. This particular gap showed a view of the barn . . . and two strange horses standing in front of it.

Her chest tightened as she moved to see better. Four horses in total. Two saddled and two heavy-laden with furs and packs. She shifted sideways for a glimpse of the corral where Curly stayed. Two men had draped themselves over the fence, watching the calf. No, three men. Which must mean there were more horses she couldn't see. Maybe more men too.

Had White Horse seen them? Rosemary and Faith were out working with the new colts, but they'd all decided White Horse should stay close to the house and barn in case more visitors came to see the calf. He'd been behind the barn splitting rails for more fence the last she'd seen him.

Should she go out and speak to these strangers who'd come to gawk at her young charge? Or watch from this protected spot? Maybe as long as they didn't climb through the fence, she could stay out of sight.

But she'd like to know exactly how many were there, and she couldn't tell for sure through this tiny window.

After brushing the flour from her hands, she stepped to the door and lifted the latch as soundlessly as she could manage. The leather hinges opened much more quietly than the metal version they'd had on the doors back in Richmond. She cracked the door just wide enough to get a clear view but hopefully not so much the men would notice her if they glanced this way.

Three men, the third one a slight distance from the other two. He held his mount and pack mule with him, the reins still in his hand. The horse eyed Curly with a suspicious look, nostrils flared, as though the mount might bolt any moment.

No wonder the man kept a grip on him. The pack mule stood with its head drooped, not even pricking a long ear toward the calf.

The murmur of the men's voices drifted across the yard, but she couldn't make out any words. Then the fellow in the middle straightened and lifted a gangly leg up to the middle rail.

Her body tensed. Surely he wouldn't climb the fence.

With a quick movement, he answered her question, hoisting himself up and swinging a foot over the rail.

She grabbed her rifle and swung the door wide, marching out to cover the distance between them with long strides. "Get out of that corral, sir." She had no time for pleasantries. Not until a fence separated him from her calf.

The men spun at her shout, and even over the distance, she couldn't miss the grins that split their beards.

Unease tried to press through her, but she didn't have the luxury of scurrying back to the house now. Where was White Horse?

She kept her stride purposeful as she charged forward. "Sir, that calf cannot be handled. Please climb back over the fence."

His smile turned into something more like a leer. Instead of retreating, he turned toward Curly. "I just wanna touch him. The Indians think he's got some kinda special powers. I'm hopin' they'll rub off on me."

The man's loud voice—or maybe the stranger himself—spooked the calf. Curly darted to the far corner and eyed him warily. The man merely turned the new direction and crouched a little lower as he stomped forward.

Lorelei reached the fence, but what should she do? Aim the rifle at him and command him to get out? Go into the corral and brace herself between him and the calf as she pointed the gun at him?

When he came within an arm's length of Curly, the calf bawled and darted down the fence line out of reach. Good fellow.

The man swore, then spread his arms wider and closed in on the calf with a determined step. She had to intervene before he actually caught Curly. He'd likely do so any second, for the little guy was too young to outwit a grown man for long.

She raised the gun to firing position and aimed it at the scoundrel who was closing in on her charge. "Back away from him, or I'll shoot."

The man glanced over his shoulder, and when he saw her gun, he finally ceased his advance. To her left, a chuckle rumbled from one of the men. She couldn't shift her focus to him, though. What if either of the bystanders tried to stop her? They would stick up for their friend, even though he was in the wrong. She couldn't fire and reload fast enough to take on all three at once.

Lord, protect me.

The man in the corral narrowed his eyes at her. "Aren't you a spiteful little thing? The buffalo ain't yours. He's a wild animal, belongs to the land. If I wanna touch him, I can do just that without permission from no skirt. You just point that gun somewhere's else." He turned back toward the calf and moved closer.

A weight pressed on her lungs. He wasn't going to stop unless she did something to make him. Could she really put a bullet in his flesh? She'd never shot a person before. Was she good enough aim to hit one of his legs so the wound wouldn't be mortal? Even if she didn't hit him, a near miss like that would certainly show him she spoke in earnest.

"I wouldn't do that, miss."

She glanced sideways at the man who spoke, and her heart hitched at the sight of his rifle pointed at her.

"Nook may be a might teched at times, but I can't stand by and let you burn a hole in his hide. Lay aside that gun, and once he's had his fill, we'll be on our way."

She forced a swallow, but it didn't dislodge the weight on her chest that kept her from breathing.

Another voice sounded from behind her. "You'd better lay aside your gun and get out of here. All three of you. Now."

Lorelei spun, her heart jumping at the familiarity in the tone. Riley. And Juniper.

Both her sister and brother-in-law held rifles pointed toward these trespassers. She'd not seen such a beautiful sight in a long time.

Breath finally reached her lungs as she turned back to the man in the pen. He'd caught the calf now, his arms locked around its front and rear in a tight hold. He turned Curly so the animal became a barrier in front of him. His fierce expression made the weight slam against her chest again.

"You'll have to shoot this calf before you shoot me. And if you send a bullet into this fellow, you'll have every Indian in the area down on your head."

Had this man taken leave of his last sense?

She steadied her rifle aimed at him and added as much strength to her voice as she could muster. "You've touched him. Now it's time to leave."

"Don't you worry. I'm goin'." He shuffled the calf sideways toward the gate. Did he plan to take Curly with him?

"Let the buffalo go." She had no problem infusing her voice with command this time.

Nook didn't answer, just kept guiding Curly across the corral, keeping himself bent low enough that none of them could get a shot without striking the calf.

His friends didn't move to help him, thank the Lord. They simply looked on with amused expressions.

She glanced back at Riley and Juniper. They still sat atop their horses, rifles trained on these men. They couldn't do a lot to stop the fellow from taking Curly out of the gate, though, not from that distance and with the calf in the way.

She would have to handle that part.

Keeping a tight grip on her gun, she moved around to meet the would-be thief.

He reached the gate at the same time she did, and his dark eyes peeked up over Curly's shoulders as their gazes met.

Something danced in his expression. A glimmer of excitement. Did he think this a game? He would soon learn she was quite serious when it came to protecting animals—from scoundrels or any other threat.

But then a motion by the calf's chest caught her notice. A pistol. Pointed at her.

Once more, her chest constricted as she stared down its barrel. Smaller than the other man's rifle but still pointed directly toward her. He was close enough that she made a sizable target.

Yet she couldn't get a clear shot at him without hitting the calf.

His voice called loud enough for all to hear. "I've got a pistol aimed at this li'l gal. And I don't mind pullin' the trigger if she don't get out of my way."

How had he gotten a gun out while holding so tight to Curly?

What should she do? Would he really pull the trigger? Shoot a woman? A glance at his eyes showed the thrill had been replaced by dark intention.

He *would* shoot her. Ol' Henry and White Horse must be right about the value of a white buffalo calf in this land. Clearly some men took the superstition so much to heart that they were willing to kill over it.

Another motion behind Nook caught her focus, and she lifted her gaze just enough to see it.

White Horse. He'd slipped through the fence rails and was stalking silently toward the man, tomahawk raised.

She barely bit back a scream, but the thief caught the change in her expression. He craned his neck, and at the sight of White Horse, a small cry slipped from him.

Still, he didn't release the calf. Instead, he tried to turn Curly. But when the buffalo wouldn't move fast enough, he shifted his hands so one held around the calf's side. He lifted his pistol in the other and aimed at White Horse.

Someone screamed. A gun exploded.

EIGHT

Chaos erupted as Curly butted and bawled, breaking free of the man's hold and scrambling toward the other side of the pen.

She grabbed for the gate latch. Had White Horse been hit? She couldn't see clearly through the rails.

When she jerked open the barrier, the sight that greeted her clogged her throat. White Horse knelt over the trapper. The stranger lay face up, his chest rising and falling in hard efforts, his mouth working open and shut like a fish. A dark, wet circle widened on his chest.

How had he been hit? White Horse hadn't had a gun at the ready. She could get answers later. For now, she moved out of the way as his friends scrambled through the gateway behind her.

If the wound was as bad as it looked, he likely had only a few moments left in this world. Her own chest burned, and her eyes stung. How had it come to this? To death, here on their doorstep?

She knelt by Nook's head as his friends gathered on either side. White Horse had stepped back to allow them room.

She reached to pull down the man's collar so they could find the wound, but the trapper who'd pointed a rifle at her earlier touched her hand to stay her.

"There's no help for him, ma'am. It'll just hurt worse."

She looked back at the face on the ground. He'd turned nearly as white as snow. He groaned, his mouth still working as he tried to find breath. Her own breath required effort. *Lord, help him.*

A gurgle sounded from his throat. His lungs must be filling with blood. *No.* A noise came from his mouth like he was trying to speak. She strained to make out words.

"Tell . . . Ma . . . love . . ." No more sounds came out, though his laboring grew worse. Tears clouded her vision, but finally his efforts stilled.

She wiped her eyes. The terror had eased out of his expression, leaving it dull. Lifeless.

One of his friends made the sign of the cross over his face and chest.

Lord, receive his spirit, please. She had no idea if the man had known the Savior. *Oh, Lord, how did it come to this?*

Hands gripped Lorelei's upper arms, lifting her, helping her stand. Riley.

She let him guide her to the gate, then awareness slipped in, and she looked over at the calf. "Curly." She couldn't leave him alone with these strangers, nor could they risk the gate staying open.

"I'll stay with these men and help. Go to your sister." Riley murmured just loud enough for the words to register through the numbness taking over her mind.

He gave her a gentle push, and she continued through the gate toward Juniper. Her sister stood with their horses, one hand gripping her saddle as though she needed the animal's solid presence to hold her upright. Watching a man die was no easy thing.

A new thought slipped in. Had Juniper been the one to pull the trigger? Unless the trapper's pistol had backfired on himself, it must have been her or Riley. That would explain the pallor in June's skin now.

When Lorelei reached her, the comfort of seeing the sister she'd missed so much swept through her. She moved in for a hug, and Juniper wrapped her tight. Her sister felt smaller in the embrace than she had only two months before. Had the journey been that hard? Is that why they'd returned early?

Those answers too would have to wait for later. Tears blurred her vision completely, and at last she pulled back and wiped her eyes on her shoulder, sniffing away some of the mess from her face.

Juniper reached a hand to her cheek, worry darkening her green eyes. "Lor, are you hurt? What did they do to you?"

She shook her head and swallowed the knot in her throat. "Nothing. I'm fine." She sniffed again and cleared her throat, then glanced toward the men. "Why are you and Riley back so soon?"

Juniper took her hand and squeezed it. "That can wait. For now, why don't we go inside? Riley and White Horse will handle these men and see that the one receives burial."

Oh, that would be wonderful, to leave those hard details to someone else. But first . . . "Let me move Curly to the barn so he'll be out of the way."

Juniper's and Riley's horses needed to be unsaddled too.

By the time they had all the animals settled, Rosemary and Faith had come galloping in from the herd. No surprise they'd heard the gunshot and feared the worst.

Then came the decision on where to lay the trapper to rest. Hopefully it would be a long time before they had another body to bury in this land, but if they planned for this ranch to be their permanent homestead, they should give some thought as to where to place the cemetery.

A little section on one side of the valley nearest the hills received the most votes, so the men carried the body there and began digging. White Horse loosened the trappers' saddles and hobbled their horses to graze, but he didn't remove the saddles completely. Everyone was ready for the remaining two strangers to move on, including the men themselves.

Once they'd dug the grave deep enough and lowered Nook in, Lorelei stood with the others around the opening as Riley prayed. Her heart ached for the senseless loss. This never should have happened. *Lord, why?*

When the prayer ended, they stood in silence another moment. One of Nook's friends, the one who'd first pointed a gun at her, shook his head and cleared his throat. "Sure is a shame. Nook was a good feller for the most part. Liked ta have fun. Guess he carried the fun a bit too far this time."

Fun? That seemed the unlikeliest word to describe what had happened in that corral.

As the men covered the grave, Juniper turned the direction of the house and started that way. Riley moved to her side, and the way he scrutinized her seemed more intense than a normal look between a husband and wife. Twin lines formed between his brows. Juniper must have been the one to shoot the man. How hard would it be for her sister to face the impact of her actions?

But she'd done the right thing. He'd been pointing a gun at Lorelei first, then White Horse. He had to be stopped. At that range, he would have killed White Horse.

Juniper's tender heart would still grieve, though.

Riley touched her sister's arm, then slid his hand around her back. "Let's get you inside."

Lorelei moved to June's other side. "Yes, let's go in. We have cool buttermilk now. And so much to tell you." Hopefully news about the trading post and all the other changes would help distract her sister.

Lorelei sent Riley a smile to tell him they would take good care of Juniper. But either he didn't understand, or he wasn't ready to relinquish his bride yet. The two had only been married six months.

The five of them walked toward the house as Faith began to pepper their sister and Riley with questions. "How far did you make it? Why did you turn back so soon? Did you stay at the top of the mountains the entire time, or did you have to ride down into valleys? Did you find enough food to eat along the way? Was there snow on the mountains still? The farthest range we can see from here still has snow. Did you find any sign of Steps Right?"

At that last question, Riley shook his head and shot a glance back at White Horse. "No one had seen or heard of her." Steps Right was the Peigan woman the four of them had come west to find last year, but instead they'd met White Horse, her son. Steps Right had been sent away from her tribe, and White Horse was convinced she was hiding out somewhere in the mountains. Their search for her had slowed through the winter as they built the ranch, and then the foals started coming as soon as the weather warmed. There had been a hope Riley and Juniper would meet someone on their journey who'd seen or heard of her.

As they walked, Riley answered a few of Faith's other questions, though still no word about why they'd set aside their quest so early. This expedition had been a dream of his, and Juniper had been beside herself with excitement about the journey before they left.

Maybe the travel had been harder than they expected. Riley had been concerned about the two of them going on without a larger group of seasoned mountain men. He'd thought perhaps they might find more companions along the way, but that didn't appear to be the case.

When they entered the cabin, the dimness of the room was a stark contrast to the bright sunshine outside. Juniper didn't even pause to take in the space but moved toward the line of mattresses they stacked along the far wall during the day. Since it was just the three women who slept in here, they hadn't bothered to build walls yet. White Horse stayed in his own lodge out beside the barn.

Riley seemed to understand his wife's intent, for his long strides moved ahead. He picked up the nearest mattress and laid it flat before his wife sank down onto it. He sent an uneasy smile toward the rest of them. "You don't mind if she rests here for a minute, do you?"

Rosemary moved into action first, striding to Juniper's side. "Of course not." As she sank onto the edge of the mattress, her voice gentled. "June, what's wrong. Are you ill?"

Lorelei glanced at Faith, who looked just as concerned as she felt. Was Juniper's weakness from more than the events outside? Her belly twisted as this entirely new worry took root.

Juniper motioned for them all to gather around, as though she had an announcement to make. The knot in Lorelei's middle balled tighter as she and Faith stepped forward to join Rosie, kneeling beside Juniper's mattress. Riley positioned himself on the other side.

Juniper's skin had paled even more than before, but a soft smile curved her mouth as she reached for her husband's hand. Her gaze swung from Rosie to Lorelei, then over to Faith. "We have good news."

Lorelei tried to breathe out the tension inside her, but couldn't manage a full exhale. Her sister didn't look well. How could that be good?

As if to prove that concern true, a flash of panic crossed June's expression. She clapped her free hand over her mouth and turned, rolling onto her side.

Riley sprang to his feet and leapt toward the kettle sitting on the hearth, the one with the leftover coffee they'd brewed that morning.

As he scooped the container up, sounds from the bed jerked Lorelei's attention back to Juniper. She twisted so her head hung off the edge, and her body now convulsed.

Helplessness washed through Lorelei as she moved to Juniper's head. What could she do? Rosie was already sitting there, rubbing Juniper's back and murmuring quietly.

Riley moved to kneel at her sister's side, coffee sloshing out of the kettle as he tucked it beneath her face.

She spewed the contents of her belly into the container. Once. Then again. More convulsions racked her shoulders, then a third time she heaved into the kettle. Not nearly as much as before, though.

As Juniper hovered over the dish, Rosemary continued to rub her back, and Riley held the stray wisps of her hair away from her face. Helplessness mixed with fear in Lorelei's chest. Something must be terribly wrong with Juniper. A cool wet cloth would help, and some water to sip.

As she moved to gather those things, Rosie's voice sounded from the bed. "What is wrong with her, Riley?" Her tone said she would be delayed no longer.

Lorelei scooped a cup in the clean water, then turned back to the group so she could hear his answer.

Riley still crouched at Juniper's head, but he turned to look at the three of them. "A baby. We're going to have a baby."

A gasp slipped out from Lorelei. Her mind worked to make sense of the words. Juniper was with child? Already? No wonder they'd returned early.

But this sickness . . . Their family had known expectant mothers who suffered from nausea, but what Juniper had just experienced was more extreme than usual. She looked near death, especially now that she'd sunk back against the mattress. June worked for a smile, though it trembled.

Lorelei moved around to the side of the bed not quite so occupied and sank down beside her sister. "Would you like a drink of cool water? And here's a wet rag."

Juniper's weak smile turned on her as she took the cup and sat up enough for a small sip.

Neither Rosie nor Faith had spoken yet, but Faith now broke the quiet, her voice far softer and more reverent than usual. "A baby. That's so exciting, June. When is it coming? Do you know?"

Juniper lay back on the mattress and Lorelei took the cup, then handed the cloth for her sister to wipe the perspiration from her face and neck. "I think sometime in October or thereabouts."

A baby. Her mind still struggled to imagine her sister, the one who'd never even liked to hold their neighbor's children, now expecting her own. Sure, Juniper had helped take care of her and Faith when they were younger. But she was only three years older than Lorelei. Seeing her married had been a little jarring. But a baby seemed far more different.

"Are you certain that's all it is?" Rosie's quiet voice held gravity, though that wasn't much different from her normal tone. "There's not something else wrong?"

The question brought back Lorelei's suspicion from before. "What about—" How could she say this politely? "—the shooting. That man. I know it must have been hard to pull the trigger, but you might have saved White Horse's life."

Juniper's eyes met hers, confusion clouding them.

"I shot him." Riley's deep voice plunged into the quiet. "I regret it, but he was pointing a gun at you, and he didn't seem in his right mind. I couldn't let him take one of your lives."

Juniper took her husband's hand as her eyes glassed over. "I'm so sorry, love. You had to make an awful choice, but you protected our family."

Then her eyes rounded as she turned to Lorelei. "Oh, Lor. You thought . . . ?" Juniper's other hand reached for her fingers, and she squeezed, her grip cold. "That man. He could have done awful things to you." Her voice quavered. "I can only hope he knew the Lord. That he's not now . . ."

Riley touched his wife's shoulder, and she sniffed, then dabbed at her eyes. "I can't seem to stop crying these days."

"I guess you really must be with child." The dryness in Rosie's tone was a stark difference from Juniper's weepy words. "Mama cried every day when she was expecting Lor and Faith." Rosie pushed up from the mattress. "You'd best get used to it, Riley. June, I'm going to make some tea and mix up a stew for you. You need some fattening up if you're eating for two. Faith, go empty that kettle and rinse it out, then fill it half-full with fresh water. Lorelei, finish up those biscuits. That may be the only thing Juniper can keep down for a while."

The smile that curved Juniper's mouth looked less forced now as she watched their oldest sister stride to the fire. Then she slid a look to Lorelei. "I see not much has changed around here. I'm sorry we had to end our adventure so soon, but it's good to be home."

NINE

As the clack of hooves on rocks drifted from the other side of the cliff ahead, Tanner straightened in his saddle, adjusting his grip on the rifle resting across his lap. It made him far more comfortable having the Hawken out of its scabbard and at the ready.

Low voices joined the noise of the horses. The cadence sounded like English, but he couldn't make out words. Then the tones fell silent, and the first horse appeared around the curve in the trail.

A trapper, about fortyish years old. That was Duvall, the fellow who'd come by the trading post that morning with his two companions. His packhorse came next, then a second man. Crompton. The youngest in the group, a fellow named Nook, must be behind him.

He raised a hand in greeting. They should recognize him, though this setting was different from the dimness of the trade room. But no sign of recognition crossed either man's expression. There was no third man either.

Wasn't this Duvall and Crompton? He scanned the features once more. Yes, for sure. The same curl at the ends of Duvall's mustache, and Crompton wore the neckerchief he'd purchased in the store.

As the men reached him, he moved his mount to the left so they could pass. "Hello." He nodded in greeting.

Duvall shot a look at him and gave a sharp dip of his chin but spoke no words. Crompton only eyed him warily as he passed.

Tanner kept his mount moving forward, but he couldn't help a glance back at the two. Could he possibly have mixed up two strangers with the men who'd come to the post that morning? Yet even strangers would have offered a friendly greeting. In this land where one might go for days without meeting another person, a chance to say hello wouldn't be passed by.

And where was the younger man? Nook had been especially talkative, droning on about where they'd traveled and what they'd seen along the way. Tanner had to force himself to listen as he studied the mannerisms of all three. He much preferred to watch instead of converse, but talking was the way he would learn this country and its people.

When the fellow started jawing on about the white buffalo calf, as most everyone who came by the store did, Tanner had warned them away, just like he'd done with all the others.

"There's an Indian there who guards it ferociously. It's not worth your scalp to try to see the animal."

It wasn't fair to White Horse to speak such an injustice, but that was the only thing he could think of that might put enough fear into these curious trappers to keep them away from the Collins sisters' home. He had a feeling White Horse wouldn't mind the words if they accomplished that goal. He should let him know the next time he saw the man, though.

And that would likely be in a few minutes.

His middle tightened as, once more, all the possible reasons why no one had come to get the milk today played through his mind. Was one of the women injured? Sick?

Miss Rosemary was usually the one to ride over for it. Perhaps she simply wasn't feeling well, and the rest of them hadn't managed to break away from chores yet. But dusk had long settled, and the calf would be ready for a feeding soon.

He'd fully expected to meet Rosemary on her way for the milk. Yet he passed no one except those two trappers who'd acted so peculiarly. And why were they headed back toward the trading post—away from the Collins ranch? Should he return to the fort to see if they needed to purchase something else?

He couldn't bring himself to turn around. Something didn't feel right, and his gut said all might not be well at the Collins ranch. He squeezed Domino faster as they rounded the last curve and the valley stretched before them.

No rider traveled the open land, and as far as he could tell, all looked peaceful around the ranch buildings. The calf wasn't in the corral next to the barn. Perhaps they'd had extra milk from yesterday and, with Rosemary sick, they'd decided to wait until morning to come for more. Yet even as he tried to convince his mind that scenario was plausible, his gut clenched tighter.

As soon as his horse descended the rocky slope to level ground, he pushed the gelding into a canter. When he reined down to a walk at the edge of the ranch yard, the door to the house opened and Miss Rosemary stepped out.

Not sick. Tension thrummed tighter through his entire body. Was something even worse wrong?

As he leapt to the ground, another man stepped from the house, about Miss Rosemary's age and dressed like a trapper, though he wore no beard.

Tanner kept his rifle in hand and left his horse to stand as he moved forward. Miss Rosemary didn't look worried, so maybe she and her sisters weren't being held hostage by this stranger. The fellow eyed Tanner as though he thought *Tanner* might be the threat.

That would be the case only if this man intended to harm the sisters.

Why would they have let him in the house? Rosemary possessed a great deal of wariness and a decent amount of common sense. She wouldn't invite a strange man in. He must've forced his way. Tanner adjusted his grip on the rifle so he could raise and aim in a heartbeat if he needed to.

"Mr. Mason. I guess we forgot to come for the milk today. Thank you for bringing it." Her voice sounded direct as it always did, but not thick with tension. Yet they'd forgotten about the milk? Perhaps he'd only known Miss Lorelei a short time, but he couldn't imagine her ever forgetting something so vital to the care of her young charge.

"Is everything all right here?" He shot a look at the man so Miss Rosemary would take his meaning.

Her brow wrinkled, and she glanced at the fellow. The sight of him didn't ease her expression. "My sister and her husband have returned from a journey into the mountains. And more has happened. A man was killed over that white buffalo."

Tanner's jaw went slack. "Killed? Who? Are any of you hurt?"

His gaze shot to the corral again. Two horses stood near the barn, heads drooped as they dozed. All seemed quiet.

The others must be in the house then. Miss Lorelei and Miss Faith and perhaps White Horse. And the other sister? He rested his focus on the man once more. "You're the brother-in-law?" No wonder he acted as though he belonged here.

He gave a single, decisive nod. "Riley Turner. You're from the new trading post?"

"I am. Tanner Mason. My partner has gone back for more supplies." He should take this chance to shake the man's hand, to prove himself friendly and encourage him to bring his furs to the post.

But his business was not his uppermost concern right now. He turned back to Miss Rosemary. "Are any of you hurt? What did that man do?" He had to bite his tongue to keep from asking specifically about Miss Lorelei. Knowing her, she might well have placed herself between the stranger and the calf.

She shook her head. "We're all well. It's just . . . been a troubling day." She looked past him to his horse. "Did you bring the milk?"

He nodded, but his body didn't want to turn and retreat long enough to gather it.

"Bring the flask inside, please. The girls have the evening meal ready. You should eat with us." As she turned and strode toward the house, an odd sensation swept over him, like the ground shifted beneath his feet.

He glanced at Riley Turner, who was still watching him.

Not so much wariness now in his eyes. Mostly curiosity, it seemed.

After retrieving the pouch of milk from his saddle and settling his horse where the animal could graze, Tanner started toward the house.

The door opened before he reached it, and his heart pulsed faster as he searched to see who met him at the entrance. Miss Faith. He managed to keep from showing his disappointment.

"Come in." She nodded to the man just behind her. "You met Riley, I take it. Come meet Juniper. They brought news."

News? Even more than the fact that a man was killed here?

As his eyes adjusted to the lanterns lighting the inside, his gaze swept the room until it found Miss Lorelei. She sat on a mattress pushed against the far wall. The woman beside must be her sister, who was stretched out on the bed as though she were ill.

Lorelei met his gaze with a gentle smile and motioned for him to approach, though she made no move to rise. He stepped nearer but stopped far enough away to remain respectable. Hopefully. He'd never been inside a house with no interior walls to hide where the women slept. They had no privacy from visitors, though they likely didn't invite others inside often.

Hopefully.

Miss Lorelei's gentle voice drew his focus from his thoughts. "Mr. Mason, I'm honored to introduce our sister, Mrs. Riley Turner. Though I'm sure you could call her Juniper, if you like."

It didn't at all feel proper to call her by her given name, so he only nodded and said, "It's a pleasure to meet you."

Mrs. Turner offered a smile, though her face looked pale. "My sisters are thankful you've become our neighbor."

Lorelei sat straighter as her focus honed on the flask hanging from his shoulder. "Oh my." She rose in a fluid motion and stepped to him, reaching out. "I can't believe I forgot."

He gave her a light smile. "Sounds like you've had a lot of distractions today."

She looked past him toward the hearth, where her other two sisters knelt. "Rosie, I'm going to feed Curly before we eat."

Her eldest sister straightened and swiped stray hairs from her cheek. "Our meal is ready. I don't suppose you'd let us eat before him."

Lorelei shook her head. "He'll gulp this down quickly. And this way he won't cry all the way through our meal. Feel free to begin without me."

"We'll wait." Rosemary's words came out on a sigh.

But as Lorelei opened the door and stepped into the fading daylight, a prickle of unease slipped through him. Was it safe for her to go out alone after dark fell? Hadn't whatever happened today proven the danger that came with unexpected visitors?

He glanced around the room. Riley had knelt beside his wife, and Rosemary and Faith bent over the fire again. Maybe White Horse was outside, but he might have retired to his lodge.

He strode to the door. "I'll see if she needs help."

No one tried to stop him, and he didn't wait long to give them another chance before slipping out the doorway.

TEN

Tanner followed Lorelei outside, and the cool evening air of the open plains settled around him, soothing some of the worry from his spirit. Lorelei had already reached the barn, and as she slipped inside, the bawling they'd heard before shifted into a long pitiful cry. As soon as the sound faded, the tinkle of Lorelei's voice rose in its wake.

The melody drew him toward the barn, and he pulled open the door. Her voice murmured from one of the stalls that lined the right side, mixed with splashing as the calf slurped.

"I'm sorry I've neglected you this afternoon, especially after your fright. It's just that Juniper's home, and she needed me more than you did for a while. It's hard to believe, really. That I'll be an aunt."

Realization slipped through Tanner. That must be why her sister looked so ill. His cousin Cameron's wife had suffered from sickness while she carried their son. The few times Tanner had seen her, she'd looked pale and fragile.

"I don't know what to do. About you, I mean." Her voice

had turned sad. Did she realize Tanner had entered the barn? She must have seen the moonlight when he opened the door—dim though it be.

"I'm not going to let you starve, never fear. I won't let one of those unscrupulous men take you either. But I can't bring danger to my sisters, especially with Juniper's condition. I simply can't. If something happened to the baby . . . or to any of them . . ."

He was a cad to continue listening, for she must not realize he stood there. He took a step forward and cleared his throat, not loud enough to startle her but just to make his presence known.

"Who is it?" Her voice rang sharp with an edge of fear.

You really are a cad. He should've known she'd be frightened if she couldn't see who was there. She had no way of knowing it was him. "It's me. Tanner." He stepped to the stall door where she could see him.

What a sight she made. Such a fetching image as she bent to hold a bucket low enough for the calf to reach. She had to brace her feet because of the animal's tenaciousness as he gulped down his meal.

Tanner searched for something to say that might pass for casual conversation. "He's grown since I last saw him. And no wonder, with the way he drinks that milk."

Her mouth curved in a sweet smile as she looked down at her charge. "I'm glad he's healthy." Then she turned to Tanner. "And I'm especially thankful for your milk that keeps him so. I'm still amazed you brought a cow just at the time our need was most dire. The Lord's hand at work, no doubt. It would have been much harder to care for him any other way."

Tanner raised his brows. "How else would you have done it?" The calf wouldn't be able to eat grass at this age.

Lorelei pressed her lips together. "We have a few mares who've foaled already. I probably would have tried to milk them, or maybe even tried to get one to nurse him as a surrogate."

Tanner bit back a laugh. She might think he was laughing at her, but it was more the idea of the horse nursing a buffalo calf. "That would be a trick."

She shrugged, and her cheeks appled. "I would have tried if I couldn't find another way." She lifted her gaze to meet his again. "I'm thankful I didn't have to."

The way she loved this calf . . . Though he didn't quite understand it, her dedication made him respect her.

Which brought him to the question he'd not gotten an answer to. "What happened today? Your sister said a man died?" He tried to keep his voice steady. To keep out any sign of the tension lodged in his throat.

Sadness washed over her expression, and she looked down at the calf again. She didn't speak for a long minute. "Everything happened so fast. I'm still not sure how the situation reached that point. Three men were here. Trappers. One of them climbed into the corral before I could stop him, then he wouldn't come out. He caught Curly and was trying to get him out through the gate. When I tried to scare him with my rifle, he pulled out a pistol and tucked down behind the calf. I didn't know what to do, then White Horse showed up and the man turned the gun on him. I think he would've killed him. But he didn't." Her voice trailed off, and the pain there squeezed his throat.

"Who shot the trapper?" Hopefully it wasn't Lorelei.

That kind of weight was smothering, even when there was no way to avoid it. He knew the fact well.

"Riley." The name came out as little more than a murmur.

Tanner eased out a breath. At least *she* didn't have that burden.

He let silence settle as his thoughts whirled. This had to stop. Men were so unpredictable when they'd gone for months or even years without seeing women, and the lore surrounding white buffalo added so much more likelihood of danger. Now that the brother-in-law was here, he could help protect the place. But he'd been here earlier, and a man had still died.

That buffalo simply couldn't stay on here at the ranch and endanger these women. What could he say to convince Lorelei to let it go? It sounded as if she now realized the danger. Perhaps she would be satisfied to find a safe home for the animal.

He toed the ground in front of the stall's opening. "I think we should move him to the fort. I'll keep watch over him night and day, and maybe he would nurse directly from my cow. That way he won't bring any more danger to you and your family."

She opened her mouth, probably to object, but he raised his hand to stay her. "He'll still be yours, unless you'd rather I buy him outright. If you want to keep ownership, I'll just take care of him. You can pay me for the milk, and we'll call it even. Or don't pay anything at all. We'll just call it a good turn from a neighbor." He'd rather lose the profits at this point, so long as he could draw the danger away from these sisters.

When he finally allowed her room to speak, she gave a

slight lift of her mouth. "I appreciate what you're attempting. I do."

His gut tightened as he waited for the refusal that would come next.

She exhaled a breath that sounded like it weighed a thousand pounds. "I just can't stomach the idea of sending him away when he's still so young. Anything could happen to him. What if he needs me and I'm not there?" She raised her gaze to Tanner's with that final question, and the turmoil in her eyes made him want to step forward. To promise her he would make it all right.

He couldn't promise that, but what he could commit to . . . "If anything happens to him, I'll come for you straightaway."

The calf had finished his meal and was noisily licking the bottom of the pail. Lorelei didn't seem to notice as she studied Tanner. The pain marking her expression showed the depth of her anguish. "If he's hurt or sick, you won't be able to leave him. Do you have any veterinary experience?"

He scrounged for anything he could offer that would relieve her angst. "I watched our dog deliver puppies when I was a boy."

Her face shifted to a doubtful expression. "Were there complications?"

At least she was trying to give him a chance to prove his ability. "Not that I can recall. The sight of blood doesn't bother me, though. I've always been able to keep a clear head in dire situations."

She managed another weak lift of her lips. "I suppose that's something. I've been nursing injured animals since I was a girl. My father always let me help him tend the sick or wounded horses on our ranch."

Another of those monumental sighs leaked from her. "I suppose I need to think on it. I know I can't put my family in danger any longer. I never dreamed a simple buffalo calf could draw so much attention, especially out here when there are thousands and thousands of them."

She released one hand from the bucket and scrubbed the curly hair on the animal's forehead. "You don't mean to cause trouble, do you, fella? You're just a sweet boy."

That singsong tone did something to his insides. Made his chest lighter. Made him want to step forward and stroke the hair from her face. Would it be soft? Those smooth brown tendrils looked like rich tea and probably felt like velvet. Or maybe the finest rabbit fur.

She slipped the pail from the calf's mouth, and its bawling complaint broke the trance Tanner had somehow slipped into. He stepped away from the opening so she could move out of the enclosure, then he lifted the logs into place to close the calf inside.

He followed her through the open barn door. Darkness had fallen outside, not so much that they couldn't easily see the path to the house, but enough that a few stars winked down at them. Walking beside her felt a little like escorting her across one of Boston's many pleasure grounds.

Not that he'd ever taken a woman for a stroll across the green. Once, he'd saved a gray-haired matron from a pickpocket and escorted her back to her party, where she should have stayed to begin with. But that was back in the days when he'd walked the constable's beat.

Now his life looked very different, yet the woman beside him had turned out to be the greatest surprise of all.

"No, silly. Leave your hoof in the water. That's the only way you'll get better." Lorelei kept one hand firmly holding the calf's hoof in the salt water while she stroked him with her other. White Horse stood on the animal's other side, his strong arms holding the calf still.

Curly let out a complaining bawl but didn't try to move this time. She sent White Horse a smile. "Thank you for helping me with this. It would be a lot harder if I had to do it by myself."

Yesterday morning, Curly had begun limping, and by midday he could barely put weight on the left front leg. She'd helped cure abscesses in horses before and was fairly certain that was his problem now. Unfortunately, the remedy included soaking the hoof in salt water three times a day and keeping the hoof wrapped so it would stay clean the rest of the time. The warmth in the sole meant the abscess would likely rupture at any time. The sooner the better, for that was part of the healing process, but they'd still need to continue these treatments for at least another week.

White Horse merely grunted his response, but they'd been working together so much of late that she could easily fill in his words in her mind. This time he likely meant he was happy to help.

His awe toward the calf had gradually shifted into a kind of tender reverence. The two of them still stayed close to the ranch buildings while Rosie and Faith spent most of the day with the horses. Riley and Juniper were here too, but June rarely ventured out of the house. When her sickness was the worst, she rested. Otherwise, she'd taken to preparing meals and catching up on washing and mending. Riley tried to make himself useful around the place, but he usually kept close to Juniper to help with whatever task she began.

A shift in White Horse's demeanor broke through Lorelei's thoughts. He'd straightened and now stared through the open barn door. She looked the same way, but could see nothing out of the ordinary. Only wide blue sky and unending grassland.

Then Riley called from outside the barn, his tone low and urgent. "White Horse."

Lorelei pushed to her feet as the brave left the calf and slipped to the barn opening. He disappeared outside without a word, leaving her with a knot of panic twisting her gut. Should she stay with Curly or see what was happening?

The latter. She had to know what threat faced them now. She scooped up the pail of salt water and carried it with her, lest Curly try to drink it, even though he had a bucket of fresh water in his stall. She could come back to clean and wrap the hoof later.

When she reached the barn doorway, the sight halted her midstep. A vast line of Natives rode through their valley along the river, a line that stretched nearly from one end to the other. She couldn't even see the tail end from this viewpoint.

There must be at least a hundred. Nay, two or three hundred. An entire Native city, from the looks of things. Many of the horses carried high loads of furs and packs, and some dragged lodgepoles behind them.

She scanned the yard for White Horse and Riley. The two stood to her left beside the barn, as though trying to hide in the building's shadow. She sat down the pail of salt water and closed the door behind her, then shifted over beside White Horse.

"What are they doing?" She kept her voice low so it didn't carry over the open space.

"Moving to new camp." White Horse matched her quiet tone.

"What tribe are they?" She couldn't find any distinguishing marks, but he'd likely spotted some.

"Sioux."

White Horse was Peigan Blackfoot. Were they at odds with the Sioux? She couldn't recall him saying much about the tribe, so hopefully not.

The front of the parade had halted near the end of the valley, and the leaders appeared to be speaking among themselves.

"Where do you think they're going?" The line would have to spread nearly single file to ride through the mountain pass. That was the only way out of the valley unless they crossed the river. With the spring thaw flowing down from the mountains, the water level was at its highest since they'd first arrived here last autumn. Crossing could be treacherous with all these children and supplies. Yet crossing the pass would be a challenge for some of the horses that carried long lodgepoles.

"I think they camp here."

As White Horse's words sank through her, Lorelei began

to understand. Even now, the middle sections of the group had reached the front and had also halted, spreading wide in a large rectangle. Many of the people were pointing, as though laying out where lodges should be erected.

And why not? This valley stretched long and had plenty of water and grass. The land was protected on all four sides by mountains, though the wind still had plenty of room to sweep through. At least the peaks protected them from the worst snowstorms.

A bawling from behind her snagged her attention. *The calf.* Did they know about Curly? Had he been part of the incentive for them to move their village to this place?

What would this mean for her family and their own massive herd? Right now, they were keeping the horses mostly at the far end of the valley with rope fencing they'd made, moving them every few weeks to new grass so there would always be fresh grazing. Now the new herd with this village would eat the grass she and her sisters had been saving.

And were these strangers a danger to them? She knew well that each person should be taken as an individual, not an entire race of people marked as dangerous or not. Yet in a group this size, at least a few bad apples existed— unscrupulous men or wily women who would cause trouble.

And what of Curly? Even if these Sioux didn't yet know of him, she couldn't hide him in the barn forever. Hadn't the story White Horse told them of the white-buffalo-calf woman originated with the Sioux tribe? They might come night and day to gawk at, or even worship, the calf.

Lord, no. The urge to hoist him up on her mare's back

and take him to Tanner's trading post screamed within her.

But the idea tore at her heart. Maybe that was the right answer for later but not so soon. It would be too hard to let him go, plus there was the added complication of the hoof infection. Could there be another solution?

ELEVEN

Lorelei stared out at the Indian band gathering by the river and voiced the question spinning inside her. "What should we do?" She turned to White Horse and Riley for an answer.

Someone should ride to the herd to get Rosie and Faith. Why hadn't her sisters come back to the house already? The line of travelers would have passed right by them. A new fear clutched her chest. Had something happened to either woman? Maybe they were simply securing the horses before they rode to the house. *Lord, keep them safe.*

She'd been sending a lot of those desperate pleas heavenward lately but hadn't spent quiet time in prayer in a while. There was always so much to do, especially since Curly came. She usually managed to fit in her morning Bible reading, but one of her sisters or the animals often kept her distracted or cut the time short. *I'm sorry, Lord. I'll mend my ways soon.*

A motion to her left jerked her focus that way. Rosemary and Faith rode toward them at a steady trot. They looked unscathed, though their expressions were hard and grim. After they reined in and dismounted, her sisters stood on Riley's other side, all of them still watching the newcomers.

"How many do you think there are?" Faith's voice held more awe than fear.

Riley might have been waiting for White Horse to answer, but when he didn't speak, Riley said, "I'd say close to three hundred, counting the children. More than that number in horses."

"What should we do?" Rosie asked the same question Lorelei had voiced a few minutes before.

Riley looked to White Horse. "Should we go meet them?"

The brave gave a slow nod, but his jaw flexed tighter than usual. "We see if they offer peace pipe." Then he turned to Lorelei. "Do not bring buffalo calf from barn."

Her middle twisted, but she nodded. "I'll keep the door shut."

Riley turned to the house. "Juniper smoked that deer meat this morning. I'll get some for us to take as a gift."

Within a few minutes, Riley and White Horse strode across the open land to the place where the newcomers were already hoisting lodgepoles and tethering them together at the top. Juniper had come out to stand with the three of them as the men left. Her face looked pale and pinched, like she was in the midst of a miserable spell. Hopefully coming outside wouldn't make her sickness worse.

From this distance, Lorelei couldn't tell what was happening with the men after they reached the Sioux leaders. It seemed their reception wasn't unfriendly, but she couldn't see expressions or hand motions that might give an idea of what was being said.

The four of them remained quiet as they watched. At least until Rosie turned to her. "Lor, I think it's time the buffalo calf goes."

The words landed like a stone in her belly. She gave her sister a pained look. "Where, Rosie? He's just a baby. He couldn't survive on grass, even if we turned him out into a buffalo herd. And if that abscess isn't treated properly, he could go completely lame. Then he'd be a prime target for any wolf."

Juniper reached over and slipped a hand around Lorelei's back. "I know, honey. But it's drawing an awful lot of attention that might not be safe for us. Didn't you say Mr. Mason from the trading post offered to buy him? He has the milk right there to feed him, and he'd probably be thankful for the people coming to gawk. They might trade in his store while there."

The very idea she'd been contemplating, except she couldn't simply send the calf by himself. Not with this abscess. Not with Tanner the only one there. When he was busy trading, how would he protect Curly? Maybe he would have a secure pen to keep the calf, but what if curious visitors tried to get through the fence as they did here?

Could she possibly go with Curly? But it would be scandalous for her to stay there alone with an unmarried man. Even if she traveled back and forth daily, there would be so much unchaperoned time in each other's company. The rules in this mountain wilderness were different from back in Virginia, but that would still be frowned upon.

Who could come with her? Riley and Juniper? The accommodations there weren't as comfortable as the cabin they'd spent all winter making into a home, but perhaps if they brought a mattress for Juniper?

She sighed. What was she thinking? She wanted to get the calf *away* from her sisters so its visitors wouldn't put them in danger. That ruled out Rosemary and Faith too. Riley wouldn't leave Juniper's side.

White Horse? Her gaze landed on the man in the distance. His arms moved, probably speaking to their new neighbors using the hand talk.

Did Tanner know how to speak that language? Maybe having someone capable like White Horse around would be an aid to him. And White Horse had been her partner in caring for Curly.

White Horse would protect her—he'd proven that. His stepping in during that awful debacle two days before had been one of many times White Horse helped when they needed the weight of a man's presence. Or simply an extra set of capable hands. In so many ways, he felt like the older brother they'd never had, even though he was Native.

Should she voice the idea to her sisters now? Or wait until White Horse came back and ask him first? She had a feeling he would agree to the idea. It simply made sense to move the calf, and he would come along if she asked him. Perhaps the two of them together would stand a better chance of convincing her sisters and Riley.

But it seemed she wouldn't have the chance right away, for when Riley and White Horse returned, they brought with them five Sioux braves.

The men didn't speak to one another as they approached, though White Horse's face looked a bit stony. When they drew near the barn, Riley's voice sounded tight. "Calling

Bird and these others would like to see the calf. Can we move him to the corral?"

He and White Horse must be trying to oblige the chief and leaders of the tribe. To start out on friendly terms. A wise move, but her jaw clenched tight as she guided the calf out of the barn and led him toward the corral, placing her hands at his chest and rump. They did this every morning, so Curly didn't object or try to pull away. She still hadn't wrapped the abscessed hoof. But now that would have to wait until after their visitors left.

She stayed in the corral with the calf as Rosie closed the gate behind her. None of the others followed her in. Probably her family wanted to stay out where they could be useful if something unexpected occurred.

The Sioux men murmured among themselves, their voices rising higher as their hands motioned toward the calf, then the sky.

After what felt like hours—though might have only been a quarter hour—the men finally left. The air seemed to cloud with the angst they all breathed out as they gathered by the fence.

Lorelei glanced from Riley to White Horse. "Can I take him back to the barn?" It would probably be better to get the calf out of sight again, though he couldn't spend days without end inside that dark place.

Riley nodded. "I think that's best for now. They seemed friendly enough, but I got the feeling we'll have a long line of visitors once they set up their lodges. Let's put him away, then we'll talk about what to do."

She wrapped her arms around Curly and led him to the gate, which Rosie opened again for her to guide the calf through. As she passed White Horse, she glanced up at him. "Could you come help me wrap his hoof?"

Inside the barn, she quickly dipped the abscessed hoof in the salt water again to wash away dirt, then wrapped leather around the hoof and tied it in place with a string. She stood and eyed White Horse. "I need your help."

He regarded her, waiting for more. He didn't look worried, though. That was good.

"Mr. Mason offered to let us keep Curly at his trading post. I think we need to do that, especially if he'd let him stay in the courtyard inside the walls. But he won't be able to take care of him alone." She motioned to the injured foot. "I need to go along to tend this hoof and anything else that comes up. I know my sisters won't let me stay there by myself. If you go too, they might agree. You can help protect Curly and maybe be of service to Tanner if he needs an interpreter for trading. Will you come?"

His dark eyes studied her with an intensity that made her itch, but she held the look. She could nearly see his mind turning with possible scenarios and potential dangers.

She couldn't help drawing on his affection for Curly. "We need to protect him. He's a special calf, and I think this is the best way."

His throat worked, then he gave a single faint nod, almost as though he dreaded saying yes. Did he think this was a bad idea? Should she press for his true opinion or accept this agreement and run with it?

He stepped back, allowing her to take the calf into the stall like she usually did, but also ending the conversation, it seemed.

She let out a breath. At least he'd agreed.

After they settled the calf and left the barn, all of them headed toward the house. Once inside, Riley and White Horse both took up positions where they could peer through openings between logs and see anyone approaching.

The steady murmur of voices, intermingled with horse nickers and the calls of children, drifted easily into the cabin, overpowering the low crackle of the fire.

Juniper sank onto the mattress they kept laid out for her, and Faith plopped down beside her. Rosie planted herself near White Horse, where she too would be able to sneak glances through his opening in the wall.

Lorelei glanced around for something to do. No one occupied the chairs by the table, but she wasn't quite ready to sit. She moved to the fireplace and added another log, shifting the charred stubs so they would burn more fully.

She needed to be the first to speak, to give out her idea. Straightening, she turned to face the group. "Did Calling Bird and the others give you an idea if they came to this valley because of Curly? Or did they simply find this place and think it looked like a good camp?" She was pretty sure she knew the answer, and it would be a good segue into her proposal.

Riley looked at White Horse. "They knew about the calf. They asked about him when we first greeted them. They didn't say they came here because of him, but that was the feeling I got. What do you think, White Horse?"

He nodded. "Is same feeling."

She let out a breath. "Then we need to move him. Do you think if he's not here on the ranch anymore, then all those people might move on?"

Riley's expression turned uncertain, and once more he

looked at White Horse. "I don't know. That's an awful lot of families, animals, and belongings to pack up and travel with. White Horse might have a better sense."

They turned to the brave, but he didn't answer at first. In truth, he looked conflicted. Finally, he shook his head. "I do not think they stay. They come for good favor of white buffalo calf."

Riley studied him. "You think they'd leave even after they set up homes?"

White Horse gave something like a shrug. "We do not know until we see. That is what I think."

Her chest tightened. "Then we need to move fast. Right now. Tanner said we could take the calf to his post. It's best for the Indians to see us move him, right? That way they know to pack things up and travel on."

"Lorelei. What are you planning?" Rosemary gave her an intense stare. This would have to be handled carefully.

She gentled her tone, the way she would speak to a wary colt. "Curly needs to leave. His presence is putting us in danger." She slid a deliberate look toward Juniper. "We can't risk anything happening. But Curly still needs special care. His leg will have to be soaked for at least another week, and he's still so young. If this mass of people picks up and moves to the nearest flat spot they can find beside his post, he'll need someone to watch over the calf while he handles the store."

"Get on with it, Lor. Say what you mean." Rosie nearly growled the words.

She took in a breath for courage. "White Horse should go with Curly as a sort of guard. And I'll go to take care of the calf."

Juniper had lifted a cup of water to her mouth but now sprayed droplets in a half circle around herself. "You what?"

"Lorelei." Rosie had that tone she used when she was trying to be patient with silliness. "You're not going to the trading post. Not to stay there."

Lorelei smoothed her skirt to give herself a moment before replying. What could she do to help them understand? This was the right course, she could feel it deep inside. "It's the best way. No matter where Curly goes, he'll bring visitors from every direction. We have to shift that attention away from our ranch. But he's just a calf—a very special calf that's important to so many people. More people than I ever imagined possible. He must be cared for properly. Protected and nurtured." A new thought slipped in. "If something bad were to happen to him, the tribes in the area might even grow angry, mightn't they?" She looked to White Horse for support.

He wore an expression that said he'd rather not get drawn into this discussion. Just like a man.

"What do you think about this idea?" Rosie turned the question on him too.

White Horse's mouth pinched. But he said, "I will go."

Rosie studied him a long moment, and he met her look. It seemed almost like something passed between them, though Lorelei couldn't tell what. They'd all come to trust White Horse so completely over the winter they'd spent with him building this ranch. He certainly wasn't how she would picture an older brother in their family, but he filled the role perfectly. His age was even right, just a year or two older than Rosemary. In the prime of his strength. He would protect her and Curly from any threat at Tanner's trading post.

Rosie turned back to Lorelei. "But what about Mr. Mason? It's not seemly for you to stay on the premises with an unmarried man. I'm assuming you plan to sleep in a different building than him, but it's still not done."

Lorelei motioned to White Horse. "I'll have a chaperone. That's what makes it perfect." The argument could certainly be made that she would be at the trading post with *two* unmarried men, but not if they really chose to think of White Horse as a brother.

Rosemary rolled her eyes, but Riley spoke before she could respond. "I, um, suppose Juniper and I could go with her."

He looked to his wife for agreement, or maybe to get her opinion, for he didn't sound very certain.

Lorelei straightened. "That's what I *don't* want. I'm trying to draw the danger away from June. She can't come, and you need to be here with her and the baby." She would scrap this whole plan if they tried to travel that path.

Juniper reached for her husband's hand, but neither of them pushed the idea further.

Lorelei turned back to Rosemary. Hers would be the opinion that bore the most weight as the leader of her family. Faith hadn't spoken up, which was a bit of a surprise for their impulsive sister. Lorelei had expected her to be most open to the idea. In fact, she'd been hoping for a bit of support from that corner.

A glance toward Faith showed she bit her lower lip. Did she think this a bad decision too? Good thing she'd not voiced an opinion then.

"Lorelei." Juniper's soft voice turned their focus to her. "What do you plan to do with the calf once he grows bigger?

Release him back into a herd? We can't keep a full-grown buffalo bull here on the ranch."

The swirl of uncertainty she'd been keeping down tried to rise. This was a question she'd avoided, even in her thoughts. "I . . ." She finally sent a pleading look around the room. "I don't know yet. All I know is we have to protect him now." She took a breath for courage. "I saw God's hand in this from the very beginning. How I found Curly just at the right time, how I was able to catch him in the wild. Then Tanner showed up exactly when we needed him—with a milk cow, no less. What are the chances he would have brought a milk cow all the way from St. Louis?"

She focused on Juniper, who'd asked the question. "I don't know what God's plans are for Curly. All I know is we need to take the next step before us. It's not safe for him or for us to keep him at the ranch, but the Lord has provided a neighbor who's willing to provide shelter for him. It's time we accept that help."

Juniper nodded, her eyes shining a little, as if she approved of the answer. Then she looked to Rosie, and Lorelei held her breath as their eldest sister met her gaze. If Rosemary said no, should she let the idea go? How could she?

Rosie finally gave a single nod. "Maybe we could try it. As long as Mr. Mason is agreeable and we can find suitable quarters for you in a different building from him."

Her mind whirled with Rosie's first statement, so she could barely keep up with the string of words that followed. She forced herself to refocus.

"I'll be riding over every day to make sure things are in good order and see if you need anything." Rosie's voice grew stern. "If I think for a moment you're in danger, either from that man or from people coming after the calf, I'll bring you home then and there. Do you understand? The calf can stay and fend for itself. It's not nearly as important to me as you are."

Lorelei fought hard to hold in a grin as she nodded. "This is the best plan. I'm sure of it."

TWELVE

Tanner stood in the center of the fort's courtyard and eyed the darker sky in the direction of the Collins ranch. Was that more than just a cookfire? It certainly seemed like it, but did the sight of smoke warrant riding over there to make sure no buildings had caught flame? Yes.

Though he was doing his best not to be a nosy neighbor, especially since their brother-in-law had come, he couldn't stand the thought of those women in peril and him standing here watching the sky.

He strode to the supply building where he kept Domino's bridle, then snatched the leather from its hook and slipped outside the fort wall. His first whistle made his gelding's head pull up from the grass, and his second started the horse toward him with a steady stride.

Just as Tanner met the animal at the rope fence, Domino's attention jerked to the side. Tanner followed his gaze.

Horses appeared through the pass.

He tensed and touched his hand to the butt of the pistol

tucked into his waistband. Why had he not thought to bring his rifle?

But as soon as the riders came into view, the knot in his belly relaxed, even as a new pressure weighed his chest.

Lorelei, with the calf draped across her saddle. Rosemary rode on one side of her, and White Horse on the other.

He left his gelding and started toward them. The only thing that kept him to a walk was the fact that no panic marked their features. Why had only these three come? If fire had injured anyone, they wouldn't be riding at a calm walk.

When he reached Lorelei's horse, she halted. Her expression looked worried, but also a little . . . hesitant?

The weight in his chest pressed harder. "What's wrong? What happened?"

He glanced at Rosemary, then White Horse, but both were looking at Lorelei to answer.

When she spoke, her voice sounded overly bright. "We've had some new visitors. An entire Sioux village has set up camp along the riverbank behind our house."

The pressure in his chest rose up to his throat, nearly choking the air out of him.

Before he could manage an answer, she continued. "We were hoping if we move Curly away from the ranch, they might decide to stop setting up house and move to a different camp."

His mind whirled with the possible outcomes of taking the calf from their ranch. She must be bringing the little fellow to him. That would likely bring the entire village here. He could handle that, though. He'd have steady trading for weeks, no doubt.

But could he protect the calf and carry on business at

the same time? He'd find a way. Maybe if he kept the calf in one of the buildings during the day and let him graze in the courtyard at night.

Lorelei shifted on her horse. "You offered to let Curly come to your trading post. Is that—"

He gave a strong nod. "Yes." He could figure out the logistics later. For now, he had to set her mind at ease and help the calf settle in.

Turning, he waved for them to follow. "Bring him closer to the fort."

Elsa mooed as they approached, and the calf bleated out a response. Would it be possible to get the little fellow nursing from her? Did they even want that? It might be harder for Tanner to get his pint of milk each day. A burn rose in his throat just thinking about not having the soothing liquid.

One step at a time.

Once they reached the gate into the little fort, he reached up to take the buffalo calf and carry him inside. No need to bring the horses in too.

Lorelei gave him a grim smile as he wrapped his arms around the youngster and slid him down. The little guy would be too large to carry soon. The calf bawled in complaint of the jostling, but once Tanner set him on the ground, he spread his wobbly legs.

In fact, one of those legs had a piece of leather wrapped around the hoof. "What's wrong with him?" He glanced back at Lorelei.

She dismounted and moved to the calf's other side. "The hoof is abscessed. It has to be soaked in salt water two or three times daily and kept clean." As she spoke, she stroked Curly's neck, then scratched the knot of hair between his ears. The sweet smile brightening her face nearly distracted Tanner from the meaning of her words.

Soaked twice a day? On top of everything else he had to manage around here? He really would need to find a young trapper willing to settle down and help as shopkeeper. At least for a time. He could worry about payment cutting into profits later.

Lorelei was speaking again, so he forced his attention onto her words. "That's why White Horse and I have come too. We'll stay and help with the calf. White Horse could help translate if you'd like. Whatever you need." Her voice took on that same apprehensive tone her expression had carried moments before.

She wanted to stay . . . here? With the calf? His mind stuttered over the idea. Where would she sleep? Surely not with the calf. His own quarters would be the only decent shelter. He could bed down in the trade room. That would be far enough away for propriety, but he could still hear if she called out because of danger.

And White Horse?

He studied the man who'd come to stand beside Miss Rosemary in front of the calf. He looked every part the defender and protector. Here to guard both the calf and Lorelei. Tanner had known these women trusted the brave or they wouldn't allow him to live on their property and be a partner in their business. But even to the point that they relied on him to guard their sister's virtue?

His own protective instincts rose up. That seemed a role that should be given to blood kin, or at least an actual relative. Why wasn't Riley here to protect his sister-in-law? His wife's health must be poorer than Tanner had realized.

No matter. Lorelei would need no protection from him. And he'd exhaust his last breath to defend her from any other threat.

He gave a firm nod. "You're welcome to my quarters. I'll sleep in the trade room. The calf can stay inside fort walls, and we can move things around in the storeroom if he needs a place inside." He looked to Rosemary. "Will you be staying too?" That might make things a bit more proper.

She studied him, her gaze sharp enough to make even the most seasoned detective squirm. At last, she spoke in a terse voice. "I need to sleep at the ranch. But I'll be over here daily. We've brought food for them to eat, but anything they need from your store, we'll settle up each week."

Tanner nodded. "I imagine any help White Horse can offer as an interpreter will more than cover supplies they need. And they're welcome to my food." They were welcome to anything he had if it kept Lorelei safe, especially if White Horse occasionally helped translate for him.

"We pay our own way, Mr. Mason. We won't be beholden to you." Rosemary's voice took on the sharp command of an army officer. And something in her expression looked like she wanted to say more.

He waited. Best she get out everything that bothered her.

"Just so you know, Mr. Mason, we are placing a great deal of trust in you. You've been a good neighbor so far, stepping in to help and showing yourself to be a man of decent character. If that changes . . . If you do anything to break that trust or endanger my sister, even unintentionally, I can assure you retribution will be swift and complete."

He fought hard not to crack a grin. He didn't question for a second whether this feisty sister could accomplish every word of her threat, but she clearly didn't realize the lengths he would go to protect the charges placed in his care.

"I accept the responsibility and will do my utmost to prove worthy of your trust." He extended a hand to her.

She gripped his palm and shook. "See that you do."

Lorelei opened her eyes to darkness.

Not complete black but a murky light that showed unfamiliar surroundings.

Tanner's cabin.

She gripped her blanket and sat up as memory flooded back. He'd insisted she sleep in the single room where he normally lived at the corner of the fort, opposite the trade room. The fire had gone out in the night, leaving only the glimmer of hot coals. She'd meant to add wood at some point, but she must have slept the entire night through, something she rarely did even at home, surrounded by her sisters. Perhaps this stack of furs Tanner used as a bed was far better than her mattress stuffed with prairie grass.

When she slipped from her blankets, her stocking feet landed on hard-packed earth. She did miss the wood floor, but this wasn't so bad.

After pulling on her boots, she stoked the coals and added two seasoned logs, then headed to the door leading to the courtyard. Dim light peeked through the log walls, so White Horse was likely awake already. He'd slept in the storage room at the other corner on this end of the rectangle formed by the walls.

As she stepped outside, she paused a moment to let her eyes adjust. To the east, the sun had brightened the sky, but hadn't risen high enough to paint the clouds with lovely colors.

Movement across the small open area caught her focus. Tanner stood in front of the trade room, his hand on Curly's neck as the calf nuzzled his leg.

He caught her gaze, even over the distance of twenty strides, and the corners of his mouth tipped up. Goodness, he was a handsome man. She'd noticed that fact before but not paused to fully appreciate the view he made.

He started toward her, and something about his ambling step made her heart pick up speed. Curly hobbled after him, but Tanner's gaze stayed fixed on her.

As he neared, the awareness of her state prickled through her. She'd slept in her dress as a matter of practicality, but she must look as crumpled as wadded paper. She hadn't even stopped to clear the morning bitterness from her breath. She slid a hand up to swipe down the stray hairs that must be poking out all around her head. There was nothing she could do about the messiness of her braid at the moment. Tomorrow, she would make sure she tidied her appearance before stepping outside.

Tanner halted a few steps from her, and the flash of teeth revealed by his grin made the stubble on his face stand out even more. Not-quite-put-together was a good look for him. Even better than the polished façade he usually showed. Definitely more intimate.

Perhaps *that* wasn't good, but just now, she couldn't bring herself to wish for a change.

"Did you sleep well?" His voice rumbled with a faint sleep-roughened edge.

She nodded and did her best to quell the heat rising up

her neck. "Remarkably well. I'm afraid you might not be able to say the same, though."

He shrugged one shoulder. "Not at all. I made a new stack of furs and couldn't tell the difference." His gaze slipped from hers, either because he was being more gallant than truthful, or perhaps because unmarried men and women didn't discuss sleeping arrangements in polite society.

Time they speak of something else.

She nodded toward Curly, who'd settled at Tanner's side again, this time licking his trousers instead of merely nuzzling. "He's accustomed to eating only once a day in the afternoon, but he may make a pest of himself if he smells milk on you."

The corners of Tanner's mouth tipped up again as he flicked a glance at the calf. "Last night's milking is ready for him if you want to split his feedings now that he's here. I'll stoke the fire and get coffee brewing, then milk Elsa again."

She should prepare the morning meal for them. And the coffee. As long as she was here, the least she could do was take over the tasks a woman usually handled. "I can brew coffee. I brought smoked meat I can warm to break our fast, as well as biscuits." They were two days old, but when warmed and with a dash of the butter she'd churned when she baked them, they tasted like a little slice of heaven.

She never would have served dry biscuits to guests back in Virginia, but after going through most of the winter without flour, even *seven*-day-old biscuits would seem like a luxury. Of course, no form of bread would last seven days around their place. Too many eager hands.

Tanner's eyes lit. "Sounds perfect. I might be able to come

up with a rind of cheese too, that you can use at your discretion."

Her belly jumped at the word *cheese*, her mouth nearly salivating at just the thought. "I haven't had cheese since we left St. Louis last spring. I'll use it sparingly."

He chuckled as he turned away. "Use as much as you like. I'll bring in more wood, then carry over more supplies for you."

She slipped inside and did her best to set both her bedding and her appearance to rights before he knocked with the load of firewood.

His presence filled the small room, though she gave him plenty of clearance as he dropped the load beside the hearth and added two more logs to the small blaze she'd nurtured.

The supplies he returned with a few minutes later included far more than a rind of cheese. A sack of dried apples, ham salted and wrapped in paper, and even a sleeve of crackers.

She nearly giggled as the aroma wafted around her. "Ham? I haven't had ham since before the cheese. And apples! Wait till I tell Faith. She's been craving apple pie ever since her birthday."

Tanner seemed amused as he watched her. "If we have everything you need, make her one. Would your sisters like to come over for the evening meal, do you think?"

Lightness bubbled inside her, spilling out in a grin impossible to contain. "That would be wonderful."

Curly's mournful cry drifted from outside, breaking through her haze of pleasure.

Tanner turned toward the door, but stepped to the left of it and dropped to his knees. "I keep cold stuffs down here. Mostly just the milk." After pushing a crate aside, he pulled a cloth-covered pail from a hole in the floor. "Let me scoop a cupful out, then you can feed him the rest if you want. Or save it for tonight, either way. I'm going out to milk Elsa now."

He'd barely closed the door when the thud of hooves sounded on the ground outside the fort. Had White Horse gone for a ride?

She moved to one of the wider cracks between logs and peered out. Rosie was dismounting at the gate. She must've left the ranch at first light to be here so early. Maybe once she saw everything was going smoothly, she wouldn't feel the need to linger during every moment of daylight hours.

Lorelei moved the kettle to a better position among the logs, then turned to go out and greet her sister.

The murmur of voices already drifted from the courtyard, and when Lorelei opened the door, Rosie was speaking to both Tanner and White Horse. Her brow furrowed with worry. Or maybe just intensity, but either way, the sight tightened something in Lorelei's middle.

What had happened now?

THIRTEEN

L orelei joined the group as Rosie was saying something about the Sioux village.

When Tanner answered, his voice no longer held that sleep-roughened edge. Only tension. "How far behind do you think they are?"

"They were already packed up and starting out when I left the ranch, but I traveled faster than they'll be able to."

Tanner glanced toward the rising sun. "They could start to arrive by midmorning, then."

"Maybe early. Move faster than you think." White Horse's tone held its normal calm strength. No sign of worry there.

Lorelei turned to her sister. "Is it the entire village? Are they moving, or are they coming to cause trouble?"

Rosie's mouth took a grim line. "Looks like all the lodges are down. I think everyone's coming here."

Well, that was good. "Do they look angry? Do you think they intend trouble?"

Rosie shrugged and threw out her hands. "I don't know.

But all three hundred or so of them will likely set up camp right in front of the fort." She motioned toward the small, hilly valley in front of the trading post.

Lorelei eased out a long breath, then placed a hand on her sister's arm. "We expected that. That's why we moved Curly, to encourage our new neighbors to travel away from the ranch. We don't need that potential danger around Juniper and the baby. And now their horses won't eat the grass we've been saving for our herd. This is good."

Rosie didn't speak immediately, but the way her jaw flexed and her nose flared, she must have been trying to rein in her emotions.

She gave a short nod. "I'm just not sure I like you being here with so much happening in the area." And without Rosie staying on site every minute, no doubt. Their oldest sister worked so hard to keep them all safe. Releasing control like this must be tying knots of her insides.

Lorelei glanced around the three of them. "Is there anything we should do to prepare for their coming?" If not, she would take Rosie inside and feed her. The aroma of salted pork would soothe her sister's worries if anything could.

White Horse shook his head. "I watch and signal when they come."

Tanner propped his hands at his waist. "I'm ready for visitors any time. I'll get the animals fed and the cow milked now."

Lorelei nodded. "Good." She reached for her sister's hand. "Give Mr. Mason your horse and come with me. Do I have a treat for you."

Lorelei waited in the shade of the trade room's back doorway as she listened through the slats for the voices inside. Such a steady flow of men had come from the Sioux camp to trade these last two days, she'd barely seen Tanner.

White Horse, on the other hand, seemed to be everywhere. Helping Tanner in the trade room, standing guard in what had become his favorite position in one of the front corners of the fort walls. From there, he could see the entire village and any who approached the trading post from the left or right as well as a full view inside the courtyard.

So far, the Natives had been very little trouble. Nearly every time she stepped outside, she could see eyes peering between logs in the fort walls, and sometimes fingers poking through as they called to Curly. He mostly dozed right outside the door of her little house, and she usually kept it open, for light and fresh air—and also to keep an eye on the calf and the happenings outside. She tried to speak with their curious visitors, but none of them seemed to understand English. Her knowledge of their signs had proven woefully lacking.

Aside from the inability to communicate, she had never expected this arrangement would be so peaceful. She'd churned more butter and done a fair amount of cooking, sending heaping plates for Tanner and White Horse. She'd kept Curly's hoof doctored and clean, and wiped down the walls of the cabin.

There wasn't really anything out of order there that needed tending. Tanner's belongings all seemed fairly new, even the barrel of clothing pushed against the corner that he used as a seat and table combined. He must have purchased most of this before he left Boston. Or maybe in St. Louis, for that was usually the place people outfitted themselves before going west.

The unfamiliar voices on the other side of the door faded away, and she listened another moment to be sure the customers had left. Since she had more time than usual on her hands, she'd attempted something special this afternoon. Something she never would've imagined she could make over an open fire. But with the supplies on hand and her special day coming so soon . . . Well, she would know from Tanner's and White Horse's reactions if the attempt was worth eating or not.

She pulled the latchstring just enough to release the door, then eased it open a crack. Tanner's silhouetted form stood behind the counter, looking down at something. He'd not heard her yet, and the last thing she wanted to do was startle him. The front door stood open, but no one else seemed to be in the room. White Horse must have escorted the customers out.

"Tanner?" She kept her voice quiet in case someone was present she couldn't see.

He jerked his head up. "Lorelei." He glanced around the room to make sure no customers remained, then strode toward her.

She pushed the door open fully, then stepped inside. "I brought you both the evening meal. You've been working so late, and I didn't want you to go hungry."

As he reached her, his attention locked on the food. "I've never eaten so well as since you came here. I've wanted to come by to thank you, but by the time all the customers left last night, it was far too late to come calling on a lady."

Good thing the lighting in here wasn't strong enough for

him to see her blush. Her little dirt-floor cabin on the other end of the courtyard was a far cry from the morning parlor back in their Richmond townhouse.

Tanner wasn't looking at her anyway, for his eyes were still fixed on the food as he took one of the plates. "That looks like corn bread, but there wasn't cornmeal in the cabin." He lifted his eyes in question. "Did you find it in the storage room?"

The heat spread to her ears as she shook her head. "It's cream cake. I'm not sure it's any good, though. I hope I haven't wasted all the ingredients trying to bake it over an open fire. I've only made it in a cookstove oven before."

His eyes rounded, but she couldn't tell if it was from frustration for her possible waste or anticipation of sampling the treat. He glanced down at the plate in her hands. "Is that yours?"

"For White Horse. When I bake, I sample too much, then I'm never hungry for the actual meal." And the knot in her middle had stolen the rest of her appetite anyway.

Tanner glanced toward the open front door. "He's walking our visitors back to their camp. I think he's telling them we're closed for the night too." His mouth curved in a wry smile, then he lifted the plate. "Do I have to wait for him before I dig in?"

His eagerness made it easy to smile. "Nay. Eat when you like."

His eyes lit as he reached for the square of cream cake. "May I start with dessert?"

"Absolutely." His little-boy excitement was so much fun to watch. She should temper his expectations, though. "It likely won't be as good as you're expecting. The bottom came out a little black. And I couldn't get the inside as done as I wanted."

He lifted the slice with his hand. "I'll have to ask Wally to bring a cookstove with his next load." Then his eyes drifted shut as he bit into the cake.

She held her breath, especially as his eyes stayed closed while he chewed. Did it taste so foul he couldn't look at her?

Then one eye opened to catch her staring, and a smile spread to the corners of his mouth. "Best I've ever eaten."

He was teasing now. She shook her head and looked away but still couldn't fight the tug of a smile. "You don't mean that."

"It's definitely the best thing I've eaten since coming west." Humor laced his voice. "Seriously, it's wonderful. I've never had cream cake, but I think this could easily become my favorite treat." He took another hearty bite, and not even the crunching of the blackened bottom seemed to get in the way of his obvious enjoyment.

Warmth slipped through her. "It's my favorite too. My sister Juniper always makes it on my birthday. I didn't think we'd get to have it this year, mostly because we had no flour or sugar or milk." She sent him a thankful smile. "But I also wasn't certain it would bake correctly without a real oven."

He'd nearly downed the whole square of cake now and swallowed his bite before speaking. "When is your birthday?"

"The sixth of May." Would he realize that date was coming quite soon? Even if he did, her birthday would hardly be a significant event for him. He had his hands full with his business and now with the onslaught of customers they'd brought to his doorstep.

He slid a look at her. "Monday?"

She nodded. "If we kept track of the days correctly." As she shifted her gaze around the room, the heaping pile of furs against the back wall was hard to miss. "The Sioux have been good to trade with?"

He grimaced as he picked up a piece of smoked deer meat. "Some of them expect more for their furs than is fair, and they get a bit grumpy when I disagree. It's hard to find the balance at times between fair trade and good business decisions."

She raised her brows at him. "Aren't they the same?"

"Not always. Sometimes I need to accept a less-than-equal exchange to keep that customer from spreading untrue rumors about our store. And sometimes I do it as a matter of safety. But usually I need to hold fast to my scruples about what's fair to both sides. It takes a bit of discernment to know which tactic to take in each situation."

He spoke the words casually, as though the ideas were a matter of course. Yet that kind of innate wisdom didn't come naturally to most men.

"Have you always been a merchant?" she asked. "Is that what you did back in Boston before joining the Day Police?"

His mouth formed a thin line. "No, but my father has always been a merchant. He was founder and president of the great Mason Mercantile chain. I suppose it's in my blood."

Mason Mercantile. She'd heard of them. In fact, she, Papa, and Faith had visited one when they traveled with him to Washington City. It was a great big structure with two levels that took up nearly a whole block. Most men might have spoken those words with pride, but Tanner's voice held an edge of bitterness. What was the story there? How far did she dare press? "But you . . . didn't work for him?"

He shrugged. "I did for a time. Clerk and delivery boy while I was studying at university. I thought I should learn the business from the bottom to the top."

Something about his practiced indifference made her chest ache. There must be pain in that part of his life. Did she dare ask more? She couldn't seem to stop herself. "What made you change your mind?"

Again a shrug. That movement was feeling like a protective action. A way to hide how he really felt. "My father brought in my cousin to be his successor. I realized that had been his plan all along. There was no need for me to learn the mercantile business."

Though even the bitter edge had been excised from his casual tone, the words made her want to reach out and hug him. "I'm so sorry." That paltry statement could do nothing to ease the pain of what must have felt like a betrayal.

He picked up a biscuit, and his voice shifted to a forced lighter tone. "It turned out to be for the best. I joined the Boston Day Police and eventually made detective. That was much more satisfying work than pulling orders from shelves." Though his defensive façade was still firmly in place, something in that final statement rang true. He made a savvy businessman, but that same intuition and quick mind would make him an excellent detective.

She gave him a soft smile. "I'll bet you were very good at solving mysteries and protecting people."

A shadow crossed his face. Had she pushed too far, or did a memory haunt him? Would he speak of it without prodding?

He didn't say anything at first, but he didn't take another bite either. Maybe if she stayed still and quiet, like she did with a frightened creature, he would trust her.

His Adam's apple bobbed. "You might say I was too good at those things. I uncovered a scheme to defraud my father's company of most of its working capital. I successfully brought the players to trial, but during the proceedings, I discovered the man who'd orchestrated it all." He finally sent a glance her way. "An inside man. My cousin Cameron."

She sucked in a breath. The man his father had chosen over Tanner to be his successor had proven a criminal? How must that have made Tanner feel?

As tears welled in her eyes, she pressed a hand to his arm. "Oh, Tanner. What did your father say? I'll bet he was so grateful."

Tanner looked down at her hand, then up to her face. Every line of his features had pulled so tight, he looked like a stone statue. "He asked how I could dare destroy the empire he'd built by running its name through the muck. He said he never wanted to see me again."

Her throat closed, and she couldn't draw breath as pain washed through her. She nearly stepped into his arms. This man deserved far more than a hug to alleviate his pain, but that was all she could offer. Instead, she managed to squeeze out a few words. "Oh, Tanner."

His mouth pulled into a mirthless smile. "He didn't mean that last part. He often said things like that in a fit of ire. But I took him at his words. I left Boston and my job behind. I sold the five percent portion of Mason Mercantile my father had given me on my eighteenth birthday and used it to fund this trading post. Wally and our other partner, George, agreed to join me in the venture, and we started preparations."

He shrugged. "I'm glad things worked out the way they did. I like it much better here than in Boston." Then he bit into the biscuit, probably as much to end the conversation as to finish the meal.

She couldn't blame him. Her insides still felt numb from his story. He'd been through so much. Had been spurned by his family. By his father, the man who should have been his strongest supporter. And yet he'd turned and made the best of his circumstances, starting out on this new venture he was already proving very competent at.

The quiet was beginning to feel heavy. She should find something lighter to say. She glanced toward the still-empty doorway. "Do you think White Horse stayed to take his meal in the Sioux camp?" She was half jesting, but the thought wasn't impossible. Perhaps he'd made friends there. He was a grown man and could come and go as he liked.

Tanner shook his head as he swallowed his bite. "He might be circling the perimeter of the fort to make sure all is as it should be. He's never far. Speaking of discernment, his intuition is better than any man I've known. He has an uncanny way of appearing exactly when my sign language skills are failing me."

She smiled. "He's a good man. We were lucky to find him, even though we still haven't located his mother."

"His mother?"

Lorelei hesitated. Was there any reason she shouldn't tell Tanner about Steps Right? No. In fact, maybe he could help listen for any news of her from those who came into the trade room.

"More than twenty years ago, our father came west to trap for a season, and a Peigan Blackfoot woman named Steps Right saved his life. As Papa was dying, he made us promise to bring back a necklace of blue crystal beads that belonged to her. That's why my sisters and I came west to the rendezvous last summer.

"We never found Steps Right. Actually, there seemed to be quite a mystery around her disappearance. But we did find White Horse, her son. His mother had been sent away from their village, and he'd settled her in a cave in the mountains. But then she disappeared. We still don't know where she is, though White Horse is certain she's alive and will send word to him when she's ready to be found."

That familiar unrest stirred in her soul. Was it really all right to leave an elderly woman to survive in the mountains by herself? Even one as capable as White Horse said his mother was? It seemed they should be searching for her, not waiting idly for news.

Tanner regarded her. "Do you think she's safe?"

He must have been listening to her thoughts. "White Horse seems to think so, and he knows her better than any of us. Would you keep her in mind, though, as you hear trappers talking? We met a man last autumn who said he'd been nursed back to health by an Indian woman in a cave near here. That's why we built the ranch where we did, so we could seek her out. We haven't found another sign of her, even though Riley and Juniper searched more and asked about her on their travels."

Tanner gave a firm nod. "I will."

As he took another bite of the tough bear steak, quiet settled between them. But after he swallowed, he spoke once more. "So, cream cake on your birthday . . . Do you have any other traditions for your special day?"

She bit her lip to keep from smiling. Why had he returned to this topic? "Not really. My father used to take me riding. One time we found a nest of newborn baby bunnies. We didn't touch them, of course, but he let me stay and watch as long as I wanted."

Another memory slipped in. "That was the first year Juniper made cream cake, I think. Our mother had taken Rosie away for medical treatments, so I think Juniper was trying to do something special to keep me from missing them. She invited all the ranch hands and even the neighbors. We had so many people, there wasn't room for everyone in our kitchen, so most ate outside. That really was a grand day."

Tanner's eyes had softened as he watched her. "It sounds like it. How old were you?"

"Turning five, I think." She tried to keep her voice casual, as though that memory wasn't one of her very favorites.

A shadow darkened the doorway, and they both turned that direction as White Horse entered. She greeted him with a smile and held up the plate in her hands. "Are you hungry?"

He stepped forward to join them and took the food she handed over. But the way his gaze shifted between her and Tanner showed he was trying to decide whether anything untoward had happened here.

Have no fear, dear brother. As much as she admired Mr.

Mason, she wasn't the sort to catch his eye. Besides, they had a great deal more important things to worry about than matters of the heart.

Like protecting a calf and her family, and staying alive in this land always so full of surprises.

FOURTEEN

T anner chewed his bite of smoked meat as he watched Lorelei refold one of the trade blankets. It seemed the only time he saw her since the Sioux village arrived was in this trade room, and he was usually eating. Business had been so busy these days—he'd lost track of how many had passed. Five, maybe?

Today seemed to be slower, though, so maybe their neighbors had traded most of their furs now. So slow that Lorelei had ventured in to bring the midday meal instead of sending it with White Horse. She'd been careful to stay out of sight when people came to the post, though he wasn't sure if that was because she didn't want to disturb his business or she didn't want others to know she was staying here. Perhaps both.

"Shall I bring more of these from the storage room?" She laid her hand on the top blanket of the stack.

He shook his head and swallowed his bite. "That's the last of them."

She frowned at the cloth beneath her palm. "This won't last very long."

"Nope." They'd brought as much as they could carry on the two wagons, and he'd figured so many goods would last until Wally came back with another load.

But he hadn't calculated an entire tribe setting up camp in front of the store. Blankets, rifles, gunpowder, and bullets were usually the first to go—that, and coffee for the trappers. He tried to limit the rifles to one per man. A fellow shouldn't need more than that, and this way the supplies would stretch further.

"How long before Mr. Burke returns with more goods?" She glanced around at the shelves Tanner had been building. They already looked quite barren.

"At least three months, I'd say. Likely not any sooner than that."

She raised her brows as she nodded. "Looks like you might have some days off before he comes."

A smile tugged at his mouth, as it did so often when she was around. "It seems you understand the situation quite well."

"What kind of situation is that?" A rough voice rumbled as a shadow filled the doorway.

Tanner straightened and set the plate on the trade counter behind him. How had he not heard the man approach? Usually White Horse alerted him even before Tanner caught approaching sounds. Maybe he was relying too much on the brave and letting his own senses dull.

Lorelei had stepped away from the blankets and moved next to Tanner. She probably wanted to slip behind him and slide out the back door. He moved to the side to allow her space for that very thing as he called out to the customer. "Come in."

The man obeyed, stepping in and away from the doorway so Tanner could see him better. As two more fellows followed him inside, the first one's gaze followed Lorelei. "There she is." His voice boomed across the small room, and Lorelei paused midstep as she glanced back at him. "We heard from the Sioux there's a lady at the trading fort."

She gave him a weak smile. "Hello, gentlemen. Welcome." Then she lifted the door latch and slipped away before anyone could answer.

Tanner breathed out his relief and turned to face the three men who now stood in the entry.

"She one of those Collins sisters?" The fellow eyed him.

Tanner only nodded. No need for these men to know more than that. "Come in and look around. I'm Tanner Mason. Anything in particular you came for?"

"Bullets and gunpowder. And guns too, if you've got them. Prefer rifles, but I'll take fusees if that's all you have." The burly man scanned Tanner's wares as he turned in a slow circle. Something about the assessing way he studied everything made Tanner's chest tighten. Or maybe it was the fact the fellow seemed so hungry for weapons.

The other two had moved to opposite sides of the store, the skinny fellow browsing the blankets Lorelei had just folded, and the bald man bending over and reading the labels on the salt barrels. He looked like he could use a pair of spectacles, but that was one thing Tanner didn't have to sell.

He addressed the one who'd been doing all the talking. "I do have bullets and gunpowder, and one rifle." He actually had more rifles, but that was all these men would get from him.

"We'll take them all. Anderson, go bring in the furs off

that mule." He thumbed over his shoulder, and the skinny man left the blankets to follow his boss's bidding.

"Our policy is one barrel of gunpowder and one box of bullets for each group. So you're welcome to that." Tanner kept his voice calm and pleasant.

The man reacted just as he'd suspected. He stiffened, gaining a good two inches to his height, and his eyes flashed a steely blue as he turned a hard glare on Tanner. "We'll need more than that. We're tradin' you a year's worth of furs. We need a year's worth of supplies."

Tanner added a hint of a conciliatory lift to his mouth. "I won't charge you more than the powder and bullets are worth. You'll have furs left over for the rendezvous and can get the rest of what you need then. We've so many people come through here, I've had to ration things. I'm sure you can well believe that."

The man's nostrils flared, and underneath that mass of scraggly beard, his jaw looked to be locked solid. He stared hard at Tanner for a long moment, but Tanner did not look away. He'd not give this man the power to rile him.

Finally, the fellow gave the appearance of softening. "I wasn't needin' them for myself. We're headed across the mountains to the Nez Perce and Salish, and those folks are always eager for trade goods like rifles an' beads an' colored fabric. Anythin' they can't make themselves. I'll pay you a fair trade for more guns."

Tanner did his best to keep a glare out of his expression. "Like I said, we have barely enough for the people who come in here to trade. It's not easy hauling it up from St. Louis." Let the man gather his own supply train if he wanted to become a trader.

The man's mouth pinched as he turned to his bald companion. "Quigley, tell Anderson to only bring in ten hides from those buffalo cows. Then the two of you load up the powder and shot. Be quick about it."

As that man disappeared out the door, the boss turned back to Tanner. "I'll see that rifle now. You'll find those hides more than fair trade for what little you're offering."

Nothing in Tanner's gut liked this man, nor trusted him. The last thing he wanted was to show him where he kept a few rifles behind the counter. His main stock stayed in the hidden compartment in the storage room, but each morning he brought out enough for that day.

Ten quality buffalo pelts would be an even exchange for what this man offered, but how could he distract the stranger while he pulled out the gun?

He motioned to the boxes of beads. "You might want to peruse the trade goods while I go bring the rifle."

The man slid a look where Tanner pointed, then ambled that direction.

Just to throw him off the scent, Tanner moved to the back corner where he piled the furs he traded each day before he moved them to the storage room at night. This corner was dark enough that the fellow wouldn't be able to see exactly what he was doing.

After pretending to reach for a rifle, he kept his back mostly turned to the man as he moved quickly to the counter, slipped a Hawken off the stack, and laid it atop the counter. "This is the latest model Hawken makes, and you'll find the accuracy superior to anything you've shot before, even at long range."

The man turned back to him, his gaze honed on the rifle.

As he strode to the counter, his two sidekicks carried in armloads of furs.

The exchange didn't take long, as the buffalo hides were decent quality and had been handled reasonably well. The leader, who one of the men called Purcey, softened his manner a little, though he still eyed Tanner with a hard look.

Finally, the group left, and Tanner stepped to the door to watch them mount up. The last thing they needed was for those three to catch sight of the buffalo calf and cause more trouble.

But the men rode westward, skirting the Sioux village on their way into the heart of the mountains.

The knot in his gut finally eased. Now he could turn his attention to what really mattered. Preparing his surprise for the morrow.

Even before she opened her eyes, the sense of something wonderful crept through Lorelei.

Warmth. And that smell. Coffee?

She slid her eyes open and glanced around. This was definitely Tanner's cabin. She hadn't risen in the night to add wood to the fire, yet flames danced in the hearth. The pot sat in the coals at the edge of the blaze where she brewed coffee, but she certainly hadn't filled it. Tanner must've done so.

Then her sleeping mind finally sharpened. Her birthday.

She pushed her warm blankets down and sat up, glancing once more around the room to make sure she was alone. Had Tanner remembered this was her special day and come in quietly while she slept to ensure she woke to a warm room and such a delicious scent? Or maybe he wanted coffee himself, and it had been kind of him not to wake her.

For just a moment, though, she would let herself believe the former. This was her birthday, after all. She could enjoy a little fancy if it didn't bother anyone else.

After rebraiding her hair and filling a cup with the warm brew, she wrapped a shawl around herself and stepped outside. The mornings still carried enough of a nip, and she'd learned to be prepared.

She'd slept longer than usual, for the sun had risen farther up the eastern sky, lighting the courtyard fully. Curly toddled to her and greeted her with a lick to her skirt as she rubbed his mussed forelock.

A moo sounded from outside fort walls. Was Tanner out milking the cow?

She started that direction and peered out the gate. Elsa stood tied, and Tanner settled on a log near her tail, his back to Lorelei. He must have heard her, for he turned from his work, and the smile that spread across his features warmed her even more than the coffee. Even more than Curly's enthusiastic greeting as he nuzzled her skirts again.

"I don't have your food yet," she murmured softly to the calf as she pushed his head away and stepped outside, latching the gate behind her.

"Happy birthday." Tanner's voice rumbled with that delicious edge it carried in the mornings. Every time, it drew a smile from her, and his words even more so now.

"Thank you." She came to stand beside the cow and raised her cup. "It was nice to wake to brewed coffee. I'm assuming I have you to thank?" White Horse didn't drink the stuff, so there really wasn't a question. Unless one of her sisters had come over early, but they had their own chores back at the ranch.

Not since that first day had Rosie appeared before the noon meal. She'd been faithful to come daily, though, and it was nice to visit for an hour or so. It was also nice Rosie seemed satisfied with the arrangement.

Tanner's mouth curved as he turned back to his milking, but he didn't answer. The sound of liquid swishing into the pail took over, which meant she should probably begin her morning tasks. She took a sip of the coffee, giving herself a moment to appreciate the breadth of Tanner's shoulders and the way they tapered to a lean waist. His hands worked the cow as though he'd milked hundreds of times before.

"Your sisters said they'd be here midmorning."

She blinked to shift her thoughts from him to his present words. "Rosemary?" Maybe Faith was also coming to tell her happy birthday. That would be thoughtful of them. Poor Juniper. Maybe Lorelei could ride back with the girls to visit with June too.

"All three of them, if Mrs. Turner is feeling up to it. And her husband allows it, I suppose. She said nothing would keep her away, but he didn't look as certain."

Lorelei's heart leapt. "Really? I should prepare something special for the midday meal." Maybe he wouldn't mind her using flour for fresh biscuits. And ham with them. The girls would think it such a treat.

Tanner flicked a glance up at her, then returned his focus to his work. "I think they have plans for the food. Miss Faith gave me a list of what to have ready. Said they'd do all the rest."

His tone grabbed her focus even before his words did.

"Gave you a list to have ready for what?" Suddenly, he looked far too innocent. Feigned innocence. What were he and her sisters up to?

He didn't look her way again. "You'll have to ask them to be certain, but I think they have something planned that includes a ride into the mountains. Maybe looking for baby bunnies." Now he slid a glance her way, the corners of his mouth twitching.

He remembered. That simple comment about the birthday when Papa spent the day with her. Had he sought out her sisters to re-create the experience with her? Or did one of the girls plan this outing? Either way, how special to be remembered so well.

FIFTEEN

Tanner's body tightened as his eyes sprang open in the darkness. What sound had awakened him? Even as his eyes scanned the shadows of the trade room, his mind registered that no daylight penetrated the cracks in the walls.

A flash of motion jerked his attention toward the path from the front door, and the shadowy form approaching made his insides twist even as he reached for the rifle he kept near his bed pallet. That couldn't be Lorelei or White Horse, not coming through the front door.

Had someone from the Sioux camp sneaked in for free supplies? Or was this a stranger?

He eased the rifle into firing position as soundlessly as he could while the man approached another three steps. Now Tanner could see the outline to know where to aim. "Who's there?" The form looked burly enough to be a shaggy-haired trapper.

The figure froze, and only the faint sound of breathing laced the air. Silence stretched. Would the intruder not answer? He must know Tanner had seen and heard him.

Just in case, he strengthened his voice. "Speak up, or I'll send a bullet through you. I can see you well."

A click sounded in the stillness. That had to be the rear set trigger of a rifle locking into place. Then a growl rumbled through the space between them. "Just comin' to get what you were holdin' back."

Purcey.

Apparently, he'd not been satisfied with the ration of bullets and powder he'd left with. This corner of the room where Tanner slept was also the place he'd pretended to get the rifle from.

Where were the man's compatriots? No one else appeared to be in the room, but they might be standing guard outside. This fellow must not have expected Tanner to be sleeping here.

Anger sluiced through Tanner's chest, and he tightened his hold on his gun. "You've taken all you're going to get. Leave now if you value your life."

Tanner had shot a few men in the line of duty protecting Boston's citizens, but that life was behind him. The last thing he wanted was to drag those miserable feelings to this place.

"Just need a few more rifles, and I'll be on my way. I know you've got 'em." The man moved forward, his steps soundless.

Tanner adjusted his aim. The room was too dark to reliably shoot a limb or some other place that would simply wound him. Putting a bullet in the man would probably end his life.

Did he dare risk letting the man come close enough to club him with the butt of the rifle? Surely the fellow wouldn't be foolish enough to approach farther. And if Tanner let him go with only a warning, Purcey seemed like the kind to hold a grudge—and most likely retaliate.

But if he ended his life, would his friends come back for revenge? They seemed more like paid lackeys when they came into the trade room yesterday, but he didn't know any of them well enough to be sure.

Maybe he could find another way out of this. He had to try.

Tanner leveled his voice. "There's nothing here worth dying over. You can turn around and walk back out that door, and as long as you don't plant a foot in my trade room again, I'll let you live. But if you take one more step forward, this rifle is aimed at your heart."

The shadow stilled. A silence stretched that lacked even the sound of breathing. "I'll leave, but you'd best watch your back. I'll get what I want. I always do."

The dark outline backed toward the door, not turning away from Tanner even as he reached the opening and slipped outside.

Tanner sprang to his feet and lunged to one of the larger cracks in the wall where he could see who accompanied the man—and make sure they all left. They might have seen Curly through the fort walls when they were there in daylight, and the last thing he needed was them trying to steal the calf to trade to the Natives. They might get a year's worth of supplies for that white buffalo.

With no moon to speak of outside, it was hard to determine how many horses stood in front of the fort. But he made out the burly figure mounting one of the animals. The man bit out a low command, then the group started out at a trot.

As the animals straggled into a line, Tanner could finally make out the forms of people atop the animals.

Four riders. Yet there had only been three when they came to trade yesterday. Was it not the same group? The voice had sounded like Purcey. His instincts had told him this was the same, and that feeling usually wasn't wrong. They must have added another to their number.

As he leaned to better watch them disappear down the southward trail, the clouds shifted enough to allow a ray of moonlight. The brightness allowed him a better view of the person bringing up the rear of the group.

Long dark hair flowed behind a lithe body. Definitely not one of the men who'd come into the trade room.

Why would a woman travel with scoundrels such as these? It wasn't uncommon, though, for trappers to take Native wives. Poor girl.

At least the thieves were leaving. Hopefully he'd gotten his point across and they wouldn't be back. In the morning, he should tell White Horse and Lorelei about the break-in so they could be on their guard.

And from here on out, he'd sleep lightly. Just in case.

"Someone should build a tearoom in this wilderness."

The sound of the polished accent reached Lorelei's ears long before the man's words could be identified.

She studied White Horse, who'd moved to peer out the open doorway of the trade room. He didn't look worried, only alert, as he watched whoever was approaching. At least one was an Englishman, from the accent.

A glance over her shoulder at the rear door showed Tanner

still hadn't returned from the storage room. She'd brought the midday meal for the men and planned to eat with them both, but Tanner had said he needed to retrieve a load of supplies while he finally had a lull in customers.

Should she go get him? If these were Natives or even seasoned trappers, she wouldn't hesitate to leave White Horse to manage for a few minutes. But an Englishman? Perhaps she should stay here and send White Horse to the storage room. But the thought of being alone with strange men clenched her insides in a knot. Just because at least one accent sounded like the newcomers haled from across the ocean didn't mean they were gentlemen.

She moved the plate of meat and cheese to the shelf below the trade counter and stepped forward to stand beside White Horse. She could at least offer a proper greeting. Tanner had said he would only be gone a few minutes, and his keen hearing would likely alert him to the sound of new voices.

Four men halted their horses at the hitching rail, but two of them immediately snagged her gaze, with their cravats and morning coats, not to mention tall riding boots. She slid a look over the other two. One looked like all the other trappers in the area, maybe a guide these men had hired. The fourth dressed like a servant, in simple trousers and dark woolen shirt. What in the world were any of them doing in this part of the country?

The man in the trousers slid to the ground and moved to the horses ridden by the dapper pair. Neither gentleman dismounted; they just sat eyeing the trading post, their faces easily revealing their opinions. The man on the right peered at the place down the length of his nose. A nose wrinkled in clear distaste.

But the gent on the left moistened his lips with his tongue, scanning the trade room with a longing look. He murmured to his companion, but his voice carried loud enough for Lorelei to make out the words. "If we are to find a cup of tea in this wilderness, this appears to be a likely place."

The moment the snooty fellow caught sight of her, his eyes flashed wide, then narrowed as a slow smile spread over his face. He reached up and removed the bowler from atop his head as his friend glanced her way too. The smile that lit that one's eyes made them crinkle at the edges. This fellow's manner seemed as genial as his friend's was distasteful.

Still, she was representing Tanner, so she had to be her most welcoming self. "Greetings, gentlemen. Welcome to our trading post."

The man with the kind eyes dismounted in a quick motion and left his horse in the care of the servant before striding toward her. He halted a few steps away and removed his hat, bowing low. "Madam, it is a pleasure to make your acquaintance, I'm sure."

As he straightened, he caught sight of White Horse, who stood to the side of the doorway in the shadows. His eyes widened just as his friend's had when he'd first seen her.

She motioned quickly. "Allow me to introduce White Horse, a trusted friend."

The other gentleman approached behind the first and stopped at his side. "I'm Lord Henry Brevard, Viscount of Draconshire. And this is Lord Fitzgerald, Baron of Wilton-on-Sea." His eyes scanned the interior behind her. "Is Mr. Mason available to do business?"

Lord Fitzgerald gave her another of those friendly smiles,

this one tinged with apology for his friend's brusque and almost-dismissive manner. "We were overjoyed to find a shop out in the midst of this field. As you can imagine, we've the need for a great many things after traveling so far."

She stepped back and to the side, motioning for them to enter. "Please, come in. Feel free to browse the shelves while I call Mr. Mason." She glanced past the men to make it clear her welcome extended to all.

The buckskin-clad fellow still sat atop his mule, wrists crossed and resting on the front of his saddle. He gave her a nod to acknowledge her offer, but didn't seem in a hurry to dismount. Perhaps he'd already been put in place by these two lords.

While the two Englishmen strolled in and began to peruse the section where she'd just reorganized trade beads, she moved to the rear door and pushed it open enough to poke her head out.

Tanner strode across the open area, and when he saw her, his mouth curved in a grin. He must've caught her expression, though, for the smile slipped away, and his step lengthened. She worked to remove any trace of worry from her look. Having customers was a good thing. She simply didn't feel as comfortable without Tanner there.

When he reached her, his gaze searched her face as he stepped into the doorway. He moved in close enough that she could hear the whisper under his breath. "What's wrong?"

She shook her head and worked for a smile. "Nothing. You have customers. Two Englishmen, and a servant and guide outside."

For a heartbeat, his eyes still searched her face. Barely more than a handsbreadth separated them, which meant she had to tip her chin upward to look at him. This would be the perfect position for him to lean his mouth down and . . .

She blinked to clear away that impulse, and the action seemed to propel him forward. He touched her upper arm as he slid past her, then turned to greet his guests.

"Gentlemen, welcome to our trading post."

As the viscount and baron introduced themselves, Lorelei's mind tugged back to the feeling of Tanner so close. What would he have done if she'd lifted up on her toes and pressed her lips to his? Not in that setting certainly, with two strangers and her honorary brother looking on.

But if they ever found themselves alone . . . and in the same nearness . . . what would he do? Did he feel any attraction toward her at all? There were times it seemed he did. Times he'd meet her gaze and not look away. But then his eyes would shutter, as though he put up a barrier between them.

Did he think her too young and naïve? He was likely a good seven or eight years older than she was, but that was a common age difference. He'd clearly experienced much of the world, though—far more than she had. He might want a lady more sophisticated.

But if by a remote chance that *wasn't* the case, did he hold himself back because he thought she wasn't interested? Initiating a kiss would certainly tear down that wall.

But to do something so bold . . .

No. If he felt anything toward her, he'd have to take the first step.

Conversation between the men had ceased, and she tugged herself from those thoughts long enough to see what was happening. Their visitors were again perusing trade goods, but this time they sorted food supplies.

Tanner gave her a soft smile, and his voice gentled when he spoke to her. "I left something for you on the table in the cabin."

Her heart leapt. Something from the supply room? Perhaps he was only giving her an escape from the presence of these strangers.

She nodded with her own smile of thanks. "There's food on the shelf." She nodded toward the plate she'd tucked under the counter.

He mouthed *thank you*, then she turned to go. As she slipped out the door, she glanced back into the room once more. Tanner still watched her with the warmth in his gaze that always made her feel seen and appreciated.

But Lord Fitzgerald also studied her. She gave the man a polite nod, and he returned the gesture. At least it wasn't the snooty Lord Brevard.

Then she backed into the safety of the courtyard and closed the door.

SIXTEEN

T he thunder of hoofbeats made Tanner's body tense. He dropped the knife handles he'd been sorting and strode to the trade room door. The late afternoon sun glared in his eyes as he stepped outside, but he turned northward toward the oncoming riders.

Two horsemen, riding through the pass that led toward the Collins' ranch. The sharp sun wouldn't let him make out more than that, but the knot in his belly pulled tighter.

White Horse was already running toward the newcomers, so Tanner lengthened his stride as he studied the riders.

Rosemary. And her brother-in-law, Riley. He rode a bit behind her, as though not able to keep up.

As White Horse reached the pair, Rosemary barely slowed her horse, only acknowledging the man with the motion of her hand. She seemed to be aimed toward Tanner.

Behind her, Riley slowed his horse to a walk and spoke to the brave.

"Rosie? What's wrong?"

He jerked a glance back at the sound of Lorelei's voice, just behind and to his right.

Rosemary reined in hard in front of them and jumped to the ground. Anger clouded her face as she marched the final steps to stand in front of him and Lorelei. The fierce glare she aimed at him made him nearly step back. The worry that had knotted his insides shifted into something a little too close to dread. What had happened? Had he done something wrong?

"I want to know"—she nearly spat the words at him, then turned almost the same look on her sister—"why the English lords who showed up at our ranch were talking about the proprietor of the trading shop and his lovely *wife*." She put so much emphasis on that last word, she practically shouted it.

Riley finally stepped up to her side, his voice a welcome moderating tone. "We assume there's been a misunderstanding. But we'd like to know what gave them that assumption." As level as his tone was, the look he sent Tanner was far from even-keeled.

That dread that had begun to rise in his belly spread up into his chest, wrapping around his lungs and making it hard to breathe. He cleared his throat.

The gasp that slipped from Lorelei didn't help matters. He couldn't bring himself to look at her as he addressed the pair eyeing him.

"I never said such." The words sounded like a flimsy excuse even in his own ears.

Rosemary's brows raised. "Then why would they think it?" The sharpness in her voice felt like a gun leveled on him. *Tell me everything or I'll pull the trigger.*

He heaved out a breath. They were on the same side here. He might as well explain what he'd been thinking.

"Lorelei was in the trade room with White Horse when the men arrived. I'd gone to gather a load of supplies from the storage building. I guess they introduced themselves to her and were quite impressed by her"—he slid a look at Lorelei—"loveliness." Would she be insulted by him stating it so bluntly? If only he could've told her this in a different setting.

He adjusted his focus back to her glaring sister. "When I returned to the trade room, she left. While the men did their shopping, practically the only things they talked about were how much they missed a good pot of tea and how impressed they were to find such a woman in this land of ruffians."

Rosemary's piercing look didn't change much, but Riley's seemed a bit more focused on each word. Not quite as skeptical.

Best he finish the explanation, but he had to be careful how he stated this next part. The last thing he wanted was to hurt Lorelei with these words. "The more they spoke of her, the more . . . *crass* their comments became. Not so much Lord Fitzgerald, but that viscount is a pompous cad. When he spoke a particularly vulgar statement, I stopped him and made it clear I wouldn't allow such talk. They could either get on with their trading or leave. That silenced them about Lorelei, and they did gather their things, pay for them, and had their valet pack everything quickly enough."

Rosemary still stared at him, brows raised with her arms crossed. Clearly, she expected more in the story. Time to tell this last part.

He cleared his throat again. "As the men were leaving, Lord Fitzgerald turned to me. He congratulated me on my lovely wife and said to give Mrs. Mason his regards." He slid another look toward Lorelei. She was watching him too, but he didn't have time to gauge her reaction to what he'd just said.

"And you didn't correct him?" Rosemary's voice still rang firm but no longer held him at gunpoint.

He shook his head. "After the way they'd spoken of her, I felt it would be wiser for them to think her attached, to give her the protection of my name, so to speak. Now that they've traded, they'll leave the area, and we shouldn't see them again. Men like that probably won't stay long in this land. They'll be headed east toward a ship bound for England in two months, I'd wager."

He shifted his focus to Riley. The man appeared to be considering his words. From everything he'd seen of Lorelei's brother-in-law so far, he seemed to be levelheaded, with a decent amount of wisdom and a good knowledge of this country.

Rosemary didn't seem quite as inclined toward thoughtfulness, for she turned to White Horse. "And where were you when those men said all those foul things about my sister?"

Frustration prickled through Tanner's chest. Perhaps he'd implied the men had said more than he'd actually allowed them to. Best he correct that notion. The last thing he wanted was Lorelei thinking he would let any man speak ill of her without shutting down the conversation at the first untoward remark.

But he let White Horse answer first. The man met Rosemary's look solidly. "When Lorelei go out back door, I go to front. I walk around walls to see if some look through them."

Lorelei spoke up then. "He's right. White Horse is always

so good to stand guard wherever Curly and I are. The Sioux village isn't nearly as curious now as they were those first few days. But I'm glad White Horse is there when someone comes to watch us."

That explanation seemed to satisfy her sister, for Rosemary turned back to Tanner.

Now was his time to clarify that other misunderstanding. "Just so I make myself clear, I didn't let those men carry on with saying anything unkind about Lorelei. Their first comments were complimentary." Too much so for his own liking. He'd had to rein in his impulse to stop them even then. "The first word that turned vulgar was the moment I told them to gather their things and leave."

Rosemary's lips had formed a thin line. "Thank you for straightening that out, Mr. Mason. It's too bad you didn't feel that same need for clarity when they assumed the two of you were man and wife."

What should he say to that? In truth, he still felt his way had been best. Those men would never see Lorelei again, in all likelihood. On the other hand, if they thought her unattached, they might have lingered in the area to enjoy the presence of such a lovely lady. She would have been forced to endure their attentions and Tanner would've had to be much firmer with them. This way, they wouldn't have to deal with any of that.

"Actually," Riley spoke up, his voice still thoughtful, "I think Tanner might have chosen the right tack in this situation."

Rosemary spun to face him, her hands bracing more firmly across her chest.

He raised a hand to stay her rebuttal. "I've told you before, ladies in this country can raise quite a stir. I don't know if those two Englishmen would do more than make themselves a nuisance to Lorelei, but Tanner was able to get them to move on without causing trouble. In my book, he handled the matter well." He turned the questioning look to Lorelei. "As long as you don't mind the misunderstanding. If you feel your reputation, or . . . I don't know . . ." He seemed to struggle to finish the thought.

Lorelei spoke quickly, her voice soft. "I don't mind." She didn't look at him, and from those few words, it was impossible to tell what she really thought of the situation. Was the idea of others thinking she was married to him repulsive to her? She gave no sign of that, but likely the entire situation made her very uncomfortable.

He'd have to apologize later when he could speak privately with her. When the overbearing anger of her sister didn't nearly squeeze the breath from his throat.

Rosemary let out a sound that seemed half grunt, half groan. She dropped her hands to her side and turned to stare into the distance. Her face was turned toward the Sioux camp, but she seemed to look beyond the lodges.

He held his tongue, as the rest of them did. Rosemary had much to consider, her sister's reputation being a valid concern.

As it was to him.

But Lorelei's safety was even more important. He'd been able to ensure her protection, both from physical danger and from the annoyance of a couple of Englishmen. Rosemary would see that as she thought through the situation more clearly.

She turned back to them, her gaze scanning from him to

her sister to White Horse to Riley. "I suppose what's done is done. The question is"—she turned her focus sharply on Tanner—"should this ever happen again?"

He had to be careful how he answered. But he had to be truthful too. "In a similar situation, if I feel it's the best way to protect Lorelei, I think allowing that misunderstanding might be best. As long as it doesn't endanger her reputation, of course. If a man plans to stay in these parts, we'll be honest with him and make it clear none of the Collins sisters are to be bothered."

Rosemary stiffened at those last words. She certainly took her duties as a protective older sister seriously and didn't like any insinuation she wasn't up to the task.

He turned to Lorelei for distraction. "But I suppose the decision is ultimately yours. If you wish me not to allow such a misunderstanding, I'll make our lack of connection clear."

She met his gaze, bashfulness glimmering in her brown eyes. Her cheeks had flushed a pretty pink, but she didn't shy away from the directness of his focus. "I'm thankful any time I don't have to deal with overzealous suitors. And I trust your judgment."

Did that mean she didn't mind the thought of being associated so closely with him? He studied her a moment longer but couldn't tell. He forced himself to look away from her. To face her sister once more.

Rosemary studied him as Lorelei had, and her expression proved far easier to read. That shrewd look was taking his measure, determining whether she could trust his assessments or whether he would twist a situation for his own benefit. No mere words on his part could answer that question. Only his actions.

Hopefully he'd already shown he would act in their best interest. That would have to be enough.

And if it wasn't . . . Well, this wouldn't be the first time he'd done his very best and been found lacking.

At last, Rosemary growled out an answer. "I suppose. Only when you think the man might be a threat or a nuisance to Lorelei. And you're to tell the rest of us anytime you have to use the ruse." She turned to her sister. "You'd better take care to stay out of sight. Don't go into the trade room."

A twinge worked its way through his chest. He'd come to look forward to Lorelei's visits when he didn't have customers.

Beside him, Lorelei stiffened. The quietness from a moment before was replaced by firm determination. "I'll go where I need to, Rosie. But have no fear, I won't put myself in harm's way if I can help it."

"Lorelei." Rosemary sounded just like a frustrated older sister.

He had to bite back a grin at the way Lorelei pushed back at the smothering protection of her family. Despite her sweet temperament, Lorelei Collins possessed a determined streak he'd do well not to underestimate.

SEVENTEEN

Was he doing the right thing?

Tanner led the hobbling man named Adams around the outside of the fort wall to the gate beside the cabin that had become far more Lorelei's quarters than his own.

After Rosemary's stern command yesterday for Lorelei not to come into the trade room, he hadn't dared call for her and White Horse to come speak to this fellow inside. But the news he had to share might be of value, and they would have questions for him Tanner might not think of. Letting him speak with the two of them outside seemed like the best choice.

He opened the gate and poked his head inside. Lorelei and White Horse were working with Curly, doctoring the abscessed hoof.

They looked up at the sound of the gate creaking, and he motioned them over. "I have someone you'll want to speak to." He wouldn't allow any stranger inside these walls, not even a man who seemed as friendly and innocent as this old codger.

Lorelei rose from where she knelt by the calf's injured hoof, and she and White Horse strode toward Tanner. He stepped back outside the gate and turned to Adams. "I appreciate you taking time to tell more of what you saw. Hopefully it will help us find our friend."

The man tipped up the front of his wide-brimmed hat. "Tickled to be of service, if I can. It was the strangest thing, that cave decked out just like a house."

Tanner raised a staying hand to pause the man before he rambled through the story again. Better to let Lorelei and White Horse hear all the details.

The gate beside him swung open, and White Horse stepped out first, followed by Lorelei. Both their gazes caught on Adams, then Lorelei's focus swung to Tanner with a question in her eyes. Despite the pretend-marriage debacle from yesterday, her look held a measure of trust. Did she wonder if he'd also allowed this man to think they were husband and wife?

Tanner hadn't yet managed a chance to speak with her alone, since her sister stayed until well after dark the night before. But he had to find that moment today. The last thing he wanted was for her to feel uncomfortable being here.

Just now, though, they had a far different conversation to carry out.

He turned to encompass all three of them. "Mr. Adams and his companions came to trade, and he mentioned a cave they found in the mountains not far from here." He motioned for the man to take over the story, and Adams jumped in with an enthusiastic nod.

"The boys and me was trappin' down along a little creek in this skinny valley, and I'd been eyein' the trail up one of the slopes where the mountain goats go off in the afternoon. The sunsets this time of year are somethin' wonderful to behold, but the peaks all around us didn't allow for much view. I got it in my head to climb that mountain goat trail one eve and watch the sunset."

He grabbed the brim of his hat and swiped it off his head, revealing a matted mess of wiry brown hair. He slapped the hat against his leg. "Right up there near the top, the trail passed right by this skinny little hole in the rock. Well, I gots curious and peeked inside. It was deeper'n I expected, so I lit a twig from my pipe, and the spark showed a sight I never would've imagined. The place was a cave, as long as from here to that corner." He motioned to the far end of Lorelei's quarters. "But skinnier, and not even tall enough for me to stand straight." That was saying something, for the wiry fellow only came up to Tanner's chin.

Adams's voice took on the excitement of before. "The thing that were the most curious was how the place was empty. Ashes and a few dead coals showed where a bunch of fires had been laid at the far end, and a stack of branches aside it looked ready for another. Someone had stacked up furs in a nice little bed nearby. What's more, two mountain goat hides were stretched out on frames that could be moved around. One looked dry enough to be taken down and worked over, but the other felt nearly fresh."

Lorelei and White Horse both listened intently, their rapt attention seeming to give the man fresh vigor for the story.

"I found a storehouse o' food wrapped up in leather bundles, and a piggin of water. Plus all these little satchels of dried leaves crunched up small, and roots and dried berries. Looked like the doings of a female, but I couldn't tell whether she be from the tribes, or an ol' mountain healer like I used to know back in Kentucky."

"Did you meet her?" Lorelei's voice strained with hope. The sound made Tanner's own body want to charge into the mountains and find this Native woman himself to bring back to her.

The man shook his head. "I waited till after dark, but no one ever came. Climbed up two more times after that while we stayed camped in that valley but never did see her. Looked like someone had been there both times I went. Charlie an' Gabe both meandered that trail lookin' for her too. Gabe swore he saw a woman with long white braids standin' up near the top one time. She had a light shinin' all around her like an angel. Or maybe like a ghost. Charlie wouldn't go back up after that, but I planned to. 'Ceptin Hezekiah Leflin's group came through about that time and said a new tradin' post had opened. We was fresh out o' tannin' salt, so we packed up and headed this way."

The man nodded to show the end of the story, but then his gaze took on a faraway look. "It sure was strange, seein' that place made up jest like a little house, but I'm half-inclined to believe Charlie. Only a specter woulda been able to hide away like that. Charlie can be silent as a warrior sneakin' up on an enemy camp, and he still didn't catch sight o' her, 'cept that one time she looked like she was glowin.'"

Tanner's gut twisted. Could the fellow be a few pennies short of a dollar? He'd not thought about that when he brought the man to Lorelei and White Horse. Hopefully he wasn't giving them false hope.

Lorelei's voice pulled him from that thought. "Did you

see any clothing there? Something that would tell us for sure whether the occupant was a man or a woman?"

Adams shook his head. "I didn't riffle through the things, 'cept to peek inside a few o' those pouches. Mostly looking for salt, actually, seein' as we were so low." He glanced at Tanner and rushed on. "I'dda left somethin' for a fair trade. I wouldn'ta just stole someone else's supplies. Didn't find none nohow."

White Horse spoke now, the deep rumble of his voice drawing their attention. "How far is this mountain?"

Adams pointed beyond the Sioux camp. "About two peaks over. You can't see it from here, but there's a little creek that flows and a line o' cedars at the bottom of the mountain. You can't miss the goat trail climbin' up."

A shout came from the front of the trade room, where the man's friends were loading supplies on their horses, and he glanced that direction. Then he gave Lorelei an apologetic look. "Reckon I better go get m' things or they'll be leavin' me." He backed up two steps. "It was right nice to meet you folks."

He nodded to Tanner. "Glad to have you and your missus here, Mason." Then he glanced at White Horse. "You too, young fella. You'ns take care." With a wave, he spun and half hobbled, half trotted around to the front of the fort.

Silence settled in his wake, but Tanner didn't have time to talk yet. He motioned to the gate. "I need to get into the trade room and keep an eye on things until they leave." He didn't want to miss the conversation about the man's story if he could help it, though. As he stepped through the gate, he motioned for them to follow him. "Will you come into the trade room to talk?"

He made sure his gaze encompassed White Horse and Lorelei both, but just in case she no longer felt comfortable there, he added, "Or if you'd rather not, we can just go to the back door so I can hear if I'm needed inside."

Lorelei fell into step behind him. "We can come into the trade room to make our plan."

Relief slipped through him, though perhaps he shouldn't be so eager for her to go against her sister's wishes. At least he could make sure she wasn't in the building before he allowed any customers inside.

As the three of them filed into the trade room, he moved to his favorite peephole in the front wall. The trappers had loaded their supplies, and Adams was just climbing aboard his mule. The group would be riding out soon. He'd wait until they left to open the trade room door again. For now, they needed privacy.

He turned to Lorelei and White Horse.

The brave met his gaze squarely. "I go to find the woman. She is my mother. I know this." He pressed a hand to his chest over his heart. Then he glanced at Lorelei. "My mother has root for Juniper's sickness. Help with baby."

Lorelei straightened, her voice growing hopeful. "She has an herb that will help my sister?"

White Horse nodded, then turned back to Tanner. For a long moment, their gazes held, the brave's eyes questioning whether Tanner felt capable of looking after things in White Horse's absence. Not once in the week and a half since he and Lorelei had come to the post had White Horse left. Not even to hunt.

Tanner nodded. "I think you should go. I'll stay near your lookout spot every chance I get."

"Should I go with you?" Lorelei turned a worried look to the brave.

He shook his head. "I return by morning. If I find her, I will bring the root back, then take you and your sisters to her."

She nodded, but lines formed across her brow to show something like worry, or maybe disappointment. She'd said she and her sisters came west to find this woman.

"If your mother will come back here with you, it would be an honor to have her as a guest," Tanner offered. Whatever he could do to help unite them, he would.

White Horse nodded, and once more his gaze held Tanner's. The man's eyes turned harder than before, and they seemed to hold a warning. Tanner guessed this had nothing to do with his mother—likely more to do with conducting himself with propriety around Lorelei.

Tanner gave a tiny nod, just enough to make it clear he would do everything in his power to protect this woman, even from himself.

White Horse seemed to accept the response, for he finally looked away. But then he turned to Lorelei. "Your sister is wise. Do not come to trade room."

Perhaps the brave hadn't accepted Tanner's answer as well as he'd thought.

But the advice was smart, considering the two of them would be alone here. The last thing he wanted was to tarnish Lorelei's reputation, even among her family and close friends. Nor did he want to plant a question in their minds about whether he'd acted as a gentleman.

Lorelei gave a nod. "I'll pack food for you to take."

As the two left the trade room, Tanner set to rights the things the men had sorted through, then peeked once more through the front crack. The trappers had gone, leaving only the Sioux village stretching out in the valley below. They no longer came often to the trading post, not even to ogle the calf.

But they didn't seem like they planned to leave anytime soon either. It must be inconvenient to carry water as far as they had to, and there wouldn't be grazing for their horses much longer. Surely then they would move on.

He turned and headed toward the courtyard to see if White Horse needed any supplies. After the brave left, maybe Tanner could finally find the chance to broach the subject with Lorelei of him pretending they were married. Even Adams had assumed as much, though Tanner hadn't realized it until the final farewell.

White Horse was speaking to Lorelei by the gate, a satchel tucked under one arm, and a bow and quiver draped over his shoulder. When Tanner approached, the man turned and raised a hand in farewell. "*Kitatama'sino.* Until we meet again."

Tanner raised his own hand in reply. "Kitatama'sino." White Horse had been teaching him more of the sign language, but he should ask the man to also share words of the Blackfoot tongue. He needed to learn as many languages as he could, and he should take this opportunity to do so.

White Horse's mouth tipped on one side as he nodded, apparently approving of Tanner's effort with the word. Tanner couldn't help his own grin. White Horse had become a good friend these past weeks. The trade room would be lonely without him.

He said he'd be back tomorrow morning. But in this land, nothing was ever quite so certain.

Tanner stood with Lorelei as White Horse approached his stallion, slipped the rawhide strap he used as a bridle around the lower half of its jaw, then slid up onto the animal's bare back and nudged him forward.

Lorelei raised a hand to wave as she called out, "Be careful."

White Horse nodded, then nudged his horse into a trot.

They watched until he disappeared over the rise of the hill, then Lorelei turned with a sigh. "We didn't get to finish wrapping Curly's hoof." She glanced at him. "I don't suppose you have a minute to hold him for me, do you? He'll become rather contrary without White Horse to keep him steady."

A weight lifted off his chest at the chance to help her, even with something small. He turned and strolled beside her toward where the calf was licking the pail she used to soak its foot. "You mean he doesn't obey instantly when you whisper in his ear?"

She rolled her eyes at him, but then a grin tugged her mouth. "Only the littlest ones comply that easily. The older they get, the harder they are to manage. I hear it's the same with people."

He couldn't help but chuckle. A caring heart and a sharp wit. How had no man found a way to woo her yet? If Tanner were good enough for her, he would have already set himself to that challenge.

But she'd seen his many flaws. She would never look twice at him as a suitor. Only her kindness made her accept him as a friend.

The calf mooed as they approached, then trotted to meet Lorelei. He allowed her to rub his head once, then began nuzzling her skirts.

She smiled. "That's enough, silly."

He butted harder, seeking out a meal, no doubt, and the effort earned a giggle from her. A pure musical sound that drew Tanner closer. How could he pull that laugh from her again?

She turned to him then, a smile still lighting both her voice and her expression. "If you can stand on his other side and wrap your arms around to hold him, I'll get a bit more water to wash the hoof before I wrap it."

He did as she said, and watching her work gave him an excellent chance to look his fill without making her self-conscious.

All too soon, she straightened and gathered her supplies. "The abscess is nearly healed. I think we'll do this two more days, then be finished."

"That's good." He should find something more intelligent to say.

She started to rise, but Curly wiggled at the same moment, knocking her off-balance. Tanner released the animal and reached to catch her hand.

She gave him a wobbly smile as she stood and brushed her free hand against her skirts. "Thank you."

The warmth of her palm in his was making his hand sweat and his heart beat faster. In proper society, they should never touch without one or both of them wearing gloves. But out here?

Out here they were dangerously close. It wouldn't be so bad if she didn't stare at him with those wide brown eyes, which were as captivating as a doe's, but not quite holding the same innocence. Her gaze showed not only her sweetness but also her intelligence. This woman possessed both head and heart, and the combination had his own head and body in an uproar.

He swallowed to quiet his insides, then forced himself to release her hand.

She didn't move away, though. Didn't step back as she should have. He should be the one to put space between them.

But when her gaze slid down his face and hovered on his mouth, the pulse that had been pounding in his chest nearly cut off his breathing.

Could she possibly . . . ? No. She could have no desire for a kiss from him. No one willingly chose him.

But his body had already taken the idea and run with it. The distance between them closed. Had she risen up on her toes to meet him?

Great sun in the sky, she had. He cupped her elbows in his palms and let his mouth hover over hers for a heartbeat, just in case she changed her mind.

When her lips reached up to his, fire sluiced through him.

EIGHTEEN

A flame burned in Lorelei's chest, igniting a longing only Tanner's kiss could quell. She'd never
believed a man's touch could stir her so. Never
fathomed his mouth would be so . . . gentle, yet intense. So
all-consuming. The confidence he usually carried in his
bearing seemed to have given way to uncertainty. Was this
his first kiss? Surely not a man like him, attractive in every
possible way.

Could he tell this was *her* first kiss? Probably, but she
had no secrets from him.

She could hide nothing in the wonder, the intense pleasure, of his mouth pressed to hers. She rested her hands
on his chest, let the wild racing of his heart throb up her
arms and match the rhythm of her own. Then she slid her
palms upward, relishing the touch of his neck, the feel of
skin-on-skin. She stroked the edge of his jaw.

A growling sound murmured from his throat as he deepened the kiss, and she wove her fingers up into his hair,
pulling him closer. The fire inside her wanted to consume
him. Wanted him to consume her.

But then something seemed to shift, and his kiss gentled. She nearly whimpered for more, but the aching sweetness of this new touch swept through her, weakening her knees. She slid her hands down to his shoulders for support.

He pulled back an inch, and his breath caressed her the way his mouth had done before. She gulped in deep inhales, struggling to refill the air the fire had scorched out of her.

When she opened her eyes, he was there, his gaze so full of . . . something wonderful. Her mind was too befuddled to decide what. His hands cupped her shoulders, then he slid them up to her jaw, cradling her as his eyes roamed her face.

The glance at her lips was her only warning before his mouth came down to brush hers again. A single, gentle caress, yet it reignited the flame she'd been trying to bank. When he pulled away, her body tried to follow him.

She forced her eyes open once more. She had to take control of herself, else he'd think her . . . well, who knew what he already thought of her, the way she'd given over so completely to that kiss.

He drew back more this time, and his mouth curved at the corners as he studied her. He ran his hands down the length of her arms, taking her hands in his and lifting them to his chest. His thumbs stroked the backs of her fingers, then he raised one hand to press a kiss to its tips.

She could only grin like a simpleton.

He started to say something, but his voice came out in a high-pitched rasp. He cleared his throat, then tried again. "You take away my ability to speak."

If only she could think of a witty response, but her benumbed mind wouldn't form anything coherent. This giddiness bubbling inside her clouded out every clear thought.

Did he . . . really? Could he want there to be . . . something . . . between them?

He studied her, not speaking again. She had to know what he was thinking, but would it be too forward to ask?

His mouth parted—that mouth that drew her attention so easily—and this time he cleared his throat before trying to talk. "You've taken me by surprise."

She raised her brows, waiting for more insight.

He met her look, earnestness marking his expression and tone. "I didn't think you would . . ." He seemed to struggle for words as much as she did. "I didn't think you would consider me. That you would find me . . ." The corners of his mouth pulled upward again. "I didn't think you'd have any interest in kissing me."

Heat flushed through her as he put into words what they'd done.

But then the pleasure slipped from his face. "I understand if you'd rather pretend it didn't happen. I don't mean to tie you to something—to me—if you had no intention or wish to pursue anything more than friendship."

As he spoke, tightness pressed in her chest, twisting her middle into a knot. Had he changed his mind about her and was trying to find a kind way out? He was waiting for her answer, so she had to say something.

She swallowed down the lump clogging her throat. "Is that what you want?"

He made a noise that sounded almost like a snort, then stepped back and lowered her hands. But he didn't release them. His mouth curved once more, yet this time only sadness glimmered in his eyes. "I won't hold you to something you don't wish to continue."

Realization slipped through her, and her jaw might have dropped open a little. He thought she didn't desire him. Hadn't he *felt* her kiss? How could he not realize she'd been drawn to him in so many ways since that first day he'd showed up at the ranch with news that he had a milk cow? She straightened and turned her hands in his so she could hold them tightly. His brows rose, his expression turning to something like a mix of surprise and wariness.

She took in a breath for courage. "I won't deny I didn't . . . I mean, I wasn't expecting that . . ." She just couldn't bring herself to say *kiss*.

She raised her chin for a bit more courage. "You took me by surprise too. But that doesn't mean it's an unwelcome one. I . . ." Did she dare reveal how inexperienced she was in matters of the heart? Papa and her older sisters had always kept her so sheltered, and she'd been content focusing on her animals. She could always find a new creature in need. She'd never worried overmuch about the men of their acquaintance. In truth, there'd never been a man worth worrying about.

Not until Tanner.

His gaze softened, and his thumb stroked the back of her hand. "I'm glad." Then his gaze slid to the side, taking in their surroundings. A line formed across his brow. "We need to take care with your reputation. Perhaps I should see you back to your sisters' ranch, especially with White Horse gone."

She choked out a laugh. "I'm not sure my reputation matters out here. Most people don't know me at all. And of those who do, half already think we're man and wife."

He looked back at her, worry in his eyes. "I'm sorry about that. I shouldn't have presumed . . ."

She shook her head. "Safety is more important than reputation in this land."

Before he could answer, a distant call sounded from the direction of the trade room. "Halloo, the fort."

Tanner released her hands and stepped back. His eyes crinkled at the edges. "Once I finish up with these customers, I'll ride you to the ranch."

Disappointment pressed in her chest as he turned and strode toward the trade room, his long legs covering the ground quickly. She didn't need to retreat to her sisters for protection from him. She was a grown woman, perfectly capable of handling herself with propriety, even when alone with a man.

Yet that kiss. Even now, the memory swept a flood of warmth through her.

She'd responded with every part of herself. How could Tanner have possibly been uncertain about her feelings after that? He was a handsome, intelligent man. A business owner. Someone who'd experienced far more of the world than she had.

Was it his father's actions that made him so unsure of himself? Or had he been spurned by a woman too?

A smile curled inside her. It seemed impossible any woman would refuse Tanner Mason, but whoever she was, her loss was Lorelei's gain.

White Horse didn't return until midmorning the next day. Curly was the first to alert Lorelei of his approach, as the calf lifted his head toward the exterior gate and bawled. The familiar nicker of White Horse's stallion answered from outside the fort walls.

She'd been sitting against the rear wall, enjoying the sunshine and the animal's company, especially since Tanner seemed bent on depriving her of his companionship. Hopefully now that White Horse had returned, he wouldn't hole himself away in the trade room like he had since their kiss.

When she'd insisted she had no need to return to the ranch while White Horse was gone, he'd looked worried. Was it himself he didn't trust, or her? They were both adults; they could act with propriety.

But apparently Tanner's form of propriety included locking himself away, only opening the trade room door when she knocked with his meal the night before. His demeanor had been guarded, though he'd acted friendly and thankful for her delivery.

But she'd not seen him since, and as much affection as Curly showered on her, he simply didn't fill her longing for the man on the other side of that door.

She pushed up to her feet and headed toward the gate. The barrier opened before she reached it, and White Horse's face appeared, scanning the interior before he stepped in fully.

His gaze settled on her, but no grin flashed. His eyes slid down the length of her, as though checking for injuries. His expression showed no sign of whether his journey had been a success or not.

"Did you find her?"

White Horse's attention flicked toward the trade room as Tanner stepped outside and approached them. He glanced her way, and her heart stalled for an extra beat as she met his look. There was the warmth from yesterday. Maybe he really had been avoiding her simply to protect her reputation.

When Tanner reached them, White Horse finally spoke. "I found valley and creek and animal trail. I did not find cave." His brow lowered as he shook his head. "No cave on that mountain, I am sure of it. If my mother there, she would call to me."

She knew his expressions so well now that the disappointment was easy to make out, though a stranger might not have recognized the blankness in his eyes as such.

She searched her mind for something that might encourage him. "Maybe she left that place and hid the opening to the cave. Perhaps she went to gather berries or roots. Maybe she'll be back. We can try again in a week or so."

He shook his head. "No cave on that mountain." Was he trying to convince himself? Or did he really believe this had been a false lead?

Adams had sounded so certain, though his idea of a specter couldn't be right. That might simply have been his mind playing tricks on him, trying to understand what he saw. In truth, it was more likely Steps Right had become adept at hiding. They might have caught her off guard that one time, but she managed to slip away.

Yet why wouldn't she come out for her son? Was there a danger she protected him from?

Lorelei studied White Horse as that new possibility unfurled in her mind. "Is there anyone else who might be searching for your mother? Someone who means her harm?"

His eyes narrowed as he returned her look. "Not safe if

she returns to village of Son of Owl. But they would not go to find her. They do not want her to heal their people, but they have washed their thoughts of my mother."

She didn't miss the fact he no longer called Son of Owl's band *his* people. Clearly he'd also washed his thoughts of the village he'd grown up in. How must it hurt both him and Steps Right to be rejected by the only family and friends they'd ever known.

And now, the thought that his own mother might be hiding from him must be even worse. No wonder he wouldn't even consider the idea.

From everything Lorelei had heard of the woman, both from White Horse and from her own father, Steps Right wouldn't do anything to bring pain to those she loved. She was a healer, with a generous heart even to a white stranger she'd found nearly dead on the plains two decades before.

Well, no matter what his mother or his former village might do to him, White Horse had a family in the Collins sisters.

She gave him the brightest smile she could manage. "I guess we'll have to keep looking. We should tell my sisters what's happened." She glanced from one man to the other. "I think we're overdue for a family dinner."

When Rosie came for her daily visit, she would let her sister know to set three extra places at the table tonight.

NINETEEN

Lorelei slipped an arm around Juniper's waist as she strolled beside her sister toward the gate. "I'm so glad you were able to come tonight. I hope it wasn't too much for you." They'd opted for her sisters and Riley to come to the fort for the family meal so Curly and the trade room weren't left unprotected.

Juniper leaned her head against Lorelei's. "I've missed you a great deal. I was just about ready to come here on my own."

"She was." Riley's voice sounded warm on June's other side. "She's been talking about riding out here for days."

Juniper didn't usually waste time *talking* about an idea; she simply did it. The fact that she hadn't already come, either during one of Rosie's daily trips or with her husband, must mean she'd been feeling even worse.

Please don't let anything happen to my sister or this baby. She sent up the silent prayer even as she tightened her hold around June's waist. Her body seemed more frail than usual. Certainly less padded than before, save for the bump at her middle that now protruded enough to flounce out her skirt in the front. The baby must be growing, but was it using nourishment June needed to keep herself healthy?

A niggle of guilt pressed through Lorelei's middle. She should be there, making soups and whatever food her sister could keep down. Providing care Riley might not think of. Sure, he loved Juniper and had already proven he would give all he had for her. But men simply didn't have the nurturing instinct women possessed.

She moved her hand to rub Juniper's back as they reached the gate and had to proceed single file. "I was thinking to make some soup from the last of the salted pork in Tanner's larder. I'll bring some for you tomorrow."

Outside the gate, Juniper turned and took her hand, the moonlight glimmering off her sweet smile. "I would love for you to come visit, Lor. But don't feel you have to nurse me. Faith and Rosie and Riley are all taking excellent care of me. And the baby's growing well. These movements I started feeling are such a relief." She rested her free hand over her middle as she squeezed Lorelei's fingers. "I would treasure your company, but I don't want you to feel obligated. I'm well cared for."

Lorelei squeezed June's hand, then released it. Rosie may not have a gentle bedside manner, but she would ensure Juniper lacked nothing that would help her grow healthy and strong through this pregnancy. Riley too. And though Faith didn't relish time over a hot cookfire, she'd developed a fair amount of skill in that area.

"I'll come for a visit," Lorelei promised. "Soon." And she would still bring them soup. All her sisters deserved a taste of the final bit of salted pork they'd have until Mr. Burke returned with the next load of supplies.

After all had mounted, Lorelei stepped back to wave farewell from the gateway. Tanner moved beside her as the group turned their horses westward toward the pass. Was traveling through the dark dangerous for them? Certainly not with Rosie leading the way. Her sister had ridden the route between the ranch and the fort dozens of times since she and Curly had come. Rosie and her mare could likely travel it safely in their sleep.

Speaking of Rosie, she hadn't yet moved to take the lead. Her horse still stood where she'd mounted, White Horse next to the animal, stroking its neck as he and Rosie appeared to be deep in conversation. With shadows concealing both their faces, Lorelei couldn't tell what they spoke of. Their tones were low enough she could only catch the intensity of their murmur. What could they be discussing? Something to do with her and Tanner? Had White Horse realized something had changed during his absence?

Tanner leaned close. "I think they're discussing riding back to the mountain where Adams found the cave. I heard your sister say she planned to go, but White Horse didn't look happy about it."

Ah. That would certainly inspire the tension that marked their rising voices. An impulse washed through her, and she leaned up to speak into Tanner's ear, slipping her hand around his arm for balance. "If she goes, I want to go with her."

He drew back enough to study her face, but she kept her grip on his arm. Would he think her too forward to touch him? Would the others notice her hold? Rosie and White Horse were definitely too preoccupied, and the other three had already disappeared into the shadows of the pass.

Tanner must have seen her determination, for he gave

a reluctant nod. "I'll take care of Curly. Will White Horse go with you both?"

She slid a look at the pair just as Rosie spun her mare away from the brave and loped to catch up with the others. White Horse stayed where he stood, watching her go. Though she could only see the black form of his silhouette, pain seemed to rise up like steam from his profile.

Was it worry over his mother? Or had Rosie said something that hurt him? She would never do so intentionally, but their words had certainly been heated.

"Do you think there's something between those two?" Tanner's low question cracked through her thoughts like iron piercing a thin layer of ice.

She studied his face to figure out what exactly he was asking. "Something like . . . ?"

Were his ears turning red? Maybe it was just the shadows cast by the moonbeams.

He raised his brows. "Something like what's come between us." The darkening of his eyes couldn't be only from shadows.

Now it was her turn for her ears to burn. She shifted her body to study White Horse, doing her best to shift her thoughts as well. With Tanner so near, and the way his hand slid up to wrap around her back, settling at the small of her waist, her mind struggled to think of anything other than him.

Besides . . . White Horse and her sister? He was a brother to them. Rosie didn't think of him in any other way.

Did she?

Lorelei adjusted the men's trousers she wore as she stepped outside in the dim light of early morning. White Horse had said he and Rosie were leaving at first light to go search for the cave again, so she had to be ready.

The courtyard stood empty, except for Curly, who only lifted his sleepy head to study her as he lay nestled by the fence.

She moved toward him. "Don't you recognize me, boy?"

Perhaps he hadn't known it was her without the skirt he liked to nuzzle, for at the sound of her voice, he scrambled to his feet and started toward her. His steps were awkward, as though his legs hadn't awakened as much as the rest of him, but he managed a gangly trot by the time he reached her.

He sniffed her pants, and she stroked his neck as she usually did. "Tanner's going to feed you this morning, and tonight too, if I'm not back in time. He'll take good care of you." This would be the first day Curly would go without having the abscessed hoof soaked in salt water, but she'd been planning to stop anyway. He should be fine. "You behave for him, do you understand?" The calf took a piece of her trouser cloth in his mouth and began sucking, as he did with her skirts sometimes.

She stepped away and turned toward the gate. Men's voices sounded outside, so Tanner and White Horse must already be out with the horses.

When she passed through the opening, both men held the reins of a saddled horse, Tanner gripping her own mare. He was speaking to White Horse, but he glanced her way as she approached. His gaze stalled, and his eyes widened a little.

White Horse too looked her way, and his mouth twitched.

It must be the trousers. She really hated these things, but setting off into the mountains would be much easier wearing them.

As she neared, Tanner blinked, then looked from her to White Horse as his throat worked. Was he trying to remember what he'd been speaking of before?

Finally, he turned back to her and motioned toward the saddle. "I packed a satchel of food. Just a few extra things in case you're gone longer than you expect." He gave a weak smile.

"Thank you. I hope we're out no more than a day." She moved around to tie on the bundle she'd been carrying. What if something happened to keep them longer? What if Curly needed her? Perhaps she shouldn't go on this search.

"I'll take good care of the calf. Don't worry about him." Tanner must have read her mind. He'd been doing that often of late. "You haven't fed him this morning, have you?"

She should have. Why hadn't she risen earlier to do that before she left? "No, but maybe I have time before Rosie—"

"Lorelei." He broke through the weight of her guilt. "I'll feed him. This morning, this evening, and every morn and eve until you return. You don't have to worry about him."

The directness of his gaze held her, helped slow her breathing. She took a deep breath, then released it, allowing her worries to seep out with the spent air.

The edges of his eyes crinkled. "Shall I soak and rewrap his hoof each day?"

She shook her head. "I was going to stop today. The hoof seems healed. You can take the wrapping off if you'd like, but it's fine to stay on another day."

"I'll take care of him." He spoke the words with a firmness that sounded like a promise.

She worked for a smile of thanks, even as that knot of guilt for leaving tried to rear its head again.

A rider appeared at the northern pass. Rosie. Her sister sat atop a horse the same way she traveled through life—with competence and determination that made her a natural leader. Riley had once joked that she would make a good army general, and he'd not been wrong. But though she didn't wear a uniform, those same qualities made her an excellent leader of the Collins clan.

She scanned them as she approached, and she didn't wait to reach them before she called out, "Mount up. We have ground to cover."

Lorelei's mouth twitched at her sister's lack of greeting. As she moved to her mare's side to comply, she couldn't help saying, "Good morning to you too, Rosie. Sleep well?"

When Lorelei landed in the saddle, she glanced over to see her sister's expression. Rosemary had found her own grin, acknowledging the reprimand. "I did, though not as long as I might've wished. I want to make sure we have time to search all those mountains before we need to get back."

With a quick farewell to Tanner, they headed out. Just before they crested the rise that would hide the trading post from view, Lorelei glanced back.

He still stood where they'd left him, a short distance from the fort. He raised a hand to her, and she did the same. From this distance, she couldn't see his expression, but she could feel the connection between them.

Her heart squeezed. He cut a fine figure standing there, but it was more than the broad strength of his shoulders and the perfect symmetry of his features that drew her. His steadiness. His thoughtfulness. Even his shrewdness in the trade room made her smile. He possessed a great deal of business savvy and intuition that made him more than a match for any man.

Yet she'd also seen his fairness. The times she'd stood at the trade room door waiting for customers to leave before she entered, she'd watched him add trade goods to a stack when he felt furs offered him were worth more than the patron requested. How could she not be drawn to a man of such integrity?

TWENTY

As Lorelei turned away from Tanner to face the trail ahead, she caught a look from her sister. She fought the heat that rose up her neck under Rosie's scrutiny. Did her sister suspect anything? Perhaps Lorelei should be the first to speak of her affection for Tanner.

But the thought of confiding in her eldest sister made her breath grow short. As much as she loved Rosie, she could be a bit daunting at times. Faith or June might be the ones to tell first.

Rosie's brows lowered. "Are you worried about Curly while you're gone?"

Maybe that's all Rosemary had read into what passed between her and Tanner. She let out a sigh. "Tanner promised to take care of him. I think they'll be all right for a day or two."

Rosie nodded, then silence settled again for another minute. Her sister pointed toward the Sioux village. "Have they given you trouble of late?"

Lorelei glanced at White Horse to see if he wanted to answer, but he remained silent. Not unusual for him. So, she answered, "They've been good neighbors for the most part. They were curious at first, and it seemed there were always some watching through the gaps in the fort walls. But White Horse made sure they didn't enter. Most days now, only a handful come to watch, and they don't stay long."

Curiosity marked her sister's expression. "Have you spoken with any of them? Are they friendly?"

"I tried in the beginning, but it's hard when I don't speak their language." She turned to White Horse. "Will you teach me more of the hand talk? I should have asked before now." They'd begun learning signs and some of his Peigan tongue during the winter, but as soon as the weather cleared, ranch work had consumed most of their time.

He nodded. "I will."

Their conversation waned as the terrain turned steeper, the rocky ground a challenge that required more focus. By the time the sun rose a quarter of the way to its zenith, they finally reached the pass, and White Horse halted them. He pointed down to a thin line of trees in the narrow valley below. "Camp is there." His finger traced the slope of one of the mountains on their right. "Animal trail climbs to top."

Rosie nodded. "Should we start in the valley?" White Horse was one of the few people Rosie looked to for advice. And rightly so, for he possessed innate skills in this land. Too, he'd already searched this place once.

He nodded, then nudged his horse forward to lead down the slope.

The trappers' camp had been in one of the only flat spots in the small valley, nestled among the trees beside a tiny trickle of water that could barely be called a creek. The stream was likely only snowmelt from the mountains and would dry during the hottest part of summer. Though even July and August in this land were nothing compared to the stifling heat of a Virginia summer.

After exploring the evidence of the men's camp for a few minutes and letting the horses drink, they hobbled the horses to graze and studied the slope.

"Animal trail there." White Horse ran his finger up the pale line that tracked back and forth up the mountain.

Rosemary started forward. "Should we spread out so we cover more ground?"

They divided the mountainside in three vertical sections, then started up. Lorelei had been given the center area. Was that because the route was easier? Or maybe that was simply the way the lot had fallen as Rosie issued orders.

Either way, she wouldn't leave a stone unturned. White Horse had likely already covered this exact ground, so she needed to be creative and thorough with the places she looked.

She moved back and forth, peering behind rocks and nudging shrubs and tree branches aside to make sure they weren't covering an opening in the mountainside. Adams had made it sound like the cave was up near the top of the peak, but she searched everywhere.

The others moved upward faster than she did, but she didn't dare allow speed to make her grow lax in her search.

By the time she reached the area where the cave would most likely be, based on Adams's description, the others had finished their sections and come to join her.

She glanced from one to the other. "Did you find any sign of a cave?" Both wore grim expressions, and White Horse shook his head.

Rosie glanced back at the area she'd searched. "There was an indention in the rock, but I don't think anyone would call it a cave. It certainly wasn't deep enough to sleep in, and I saw no sign that a person stayed there."

White Horse nodded. "I see this too. Not what the white man told."

Lorelei turned back to the route she'd been taking and brushed aside the thin branches of a scrawny evergreen no taller than her waist. There was no way a cave could be hiding behind that lonely tree, but she had to look anyway.

Rosie and White Horse searched the rest of her section ahead of her, but Lorelei still made sure to inspect every bit of it.

Yet, by the time they gathered at the peak, no sign of the cave had revealed itself.

Rosie braced her arms across her chest as she stared out at the mountains around them. "I suppose we should search that one next. Then maybe this one to the south."

Lorelei followed her gaze from the peak on their left to the one on the right. Both rose nearly as tall as this mountain, and they were already several hours into the afternoon. She nodded and held in her sigh. Even if they hunted until it was too dark to see any longer, they wouldn't finish here today. They'd have to set up camp and explore more tomorrow.

She could only hope she'd be back home to Curly—and Tanner—by tomorrow night. *Lord, keep them safe.* Things had been quiet lately, at least where Curly was concerned, so surely all would be well for one extra day.

Lorelei should have been back by now.

Tanner stood at the fort wall, staring through one of the larger cracks. No wonder White Horse chose this place to stand guard, though the brave usually positioned himself on the outside of the wall. From this vantage, he had a perfect view of three directions.

Pressure on his leg made him look down to where Curly nuzzled his trousers. That long wet tongue snaked out to lick the cloth, then he drew a bit of it into his mouth to suck. This must be what he did to Lorelei's skirts, and why she often had round wet spots at the calf's tongue level.

He eyed the animal. "I'm only letting you do that so you don't miss Lorelei too much." The calf had moped all day yesterday, only showing life last evening when Tanner brought the bucket of milk for his feeding.

With damp trousers still in his mouth, Curly eyed him.

Tanner shook his head. "You rascal."

He lifted his focus back between the logs and stared in the direction Lorelei, Rosemary, and White Horse had disappeared. They'd been gone nearly two days now, or at least a day and a half. Far longer than White Horse had stayed away last time. Tanner had told Lorelei he and Curly would be fine no matter how long she was gone, but he hadn't really expected her to test those words. What might be keeping them?

A motion from the south caught his gaze. A Native woman rode toward the fort on a bay horse. The animal moved at a quiet walk, its head lowered as though it had been riding a long distance. Was she coming to trade? He'd never had an Indian woman come by herself. Sometimes a few of the Sioux squaws shopped together, but usually they brought a brave with them. Trappers occasionally came through with their Native wives, but never a woman alone.

When she reined to a halt in front of the trade room, he started toward the back door. Best he take up his position behind the counter.

A few minutes passed before the front door cracked open, allowing in a stream of daylight. He'd left the rear door ajar to light the room so his customer wouldn't be fully shadowed as she entered. He didn't like to do that when Lorelei might be in the courtyard in case his visitors caught a glimpse of her. But this time, he'd like as much light on their exchange as possible.

Was she in need of something specific? Or had she simply come for general goods? The latter didn't seem likely. Only an urgent need would propel a woman alone to his establishment.

She carried in a rolled fur that was wider than she was, a buffalo hide from the looks of it.

He gave the sign of greeting, though she wasn't looking at him. When he stepped forward to help with the load, she startled and backed away from his outstretched arms, as though he planned to steal the fur.

He forced his frown to shift into a friendly smile and made the sign for *hello* again. She gave no hint whether she understood, which was strange. He'd seen the Sioux women use sign language as well as the men.

He motioned toward the pelt, then made the sign for *trade*. He swept his hand around the room to point at all his supplies.

Her gaze followed where he motioned, and she turned hesitantly toward the wall of clothing. She still carried that heavy fur curled in both her arms, which meant there was no way she could even pick up what she wanted to trade for.

He moved to the trade counter and tapped the wood surface. When he had her attention, he motioned to the hide, then tapped the counter again. She looked hesitant, or perhaps that was worry. She clearly didn't trust him. But he couldn't blame her for being leery of a strange man.

He dropped his hands and let her make the decision about whether or not to bring the fur to the counter.

She chose not to.

Watching her brush her fingers over the flannel shirts while maneuvering that heavy load made his hands itch to help. But he couldn't, not without making her fearful. The best thing he could do to help was let her shop in peace. She didn't seem like she'd come in search of one particular item, so maybe this was simply a special outing for her.

Did Native women treat themselves to shopping excursions like white women did back east? They likely didn't have much chance for this kind of browsing, but perhaps they enjoyed visiting when they searched for roots and berries.

This must be a special event for her.

Curly's urgent bawl drifted from the courtyard, and something in the sound tightened Tanner's belly. The calf didn't usually call like that unless he heard Lorelei's voice. Had she finally returned?

Tanner strode to the doorway and glanced toward the gate she and White Horse would come through. Rosie would probably head straight for the ranch instead of stopping at the fort.

Sure enough, the gate began to open. The wall was too

tall to see the person on the other side, but Lorelei would be eager to come check on her young charge.

Tanner barely breathed as he waited for her to appear. She'd filled every other thought since she left, and he hadn't been able to get the image of her in those trousers out of his mind. He loved that she wore skirts like the beautiful lady she was, but he hadn't let himself imagine how she would look in the pants her sisters usually donned.

Even now, his mouth went dry at the image that slipped in. If she wore those revealing trousers often, he'd have even more trouble keeping his vow to protect her virtue.

The slender figure in trousers who slipped through the gate was *not* Lorelei.

It took Tanner's mind a moment to interpret what his eyes saw. A man scanned the interior of the fort walls, then his gaze locked on Curly. A determined expression settled as he crept toward the calf.

Tanner spun back to the interior of the trade room, lunging the two steps to the counter where he kept his rifle and shot bag. He would only have one chance to surprise the thief, but he needed a weapon.

When he whirled back to sprint toward the courtyard, a squeal from behind nearly made him pause. He'd forgotten about the Native woman.

He couldn't worry about her now, though. He had to protect Curly.

TWENTY-ONE

As Tanner charged out the rear door, he tugged the bag's strap over his head and raised the rifle to firing position. The stranger had already wrapped his arms around the calf and was turning him toward the open gate.

"Get your hands off him!"

The man jerked his head up at Tanner's shout. He didn't stop, though, just shoved the buffalo harder.

Tanner sprinted toward the gate to cut him off. He could put a well-placed bullet in the thief, but he'd much rather stop him without bloodshed.

When he'd almost reached the gate and had a clean shot at the intruder, he halted and sighted down the rifle barrel. "Let the calf go. He's not worth your life."

The fellow finally looked up, and though his collar concealed the lower half of his face, something about his eyes struck a familiar chord in Tanner's chest. But it wasn't until the man flicked a glance toward the open door to the trade room that awareness sluiced through him.

The guns.

This was one of the lackeys who'd been with that Purcey fellow who tried to steal the rifles the other night.

Tanner tensed to sprint back to the trade room, but he couldn't let the man abscond with Curly. What a time for White Horse to be gone.

He had no choice. He'd have to waylay this man, then get back to the trade room and see if he was too late to protect the rifles and ammunition.

He adjusted his aim down to the man's lower leg, the fleshy part at the back of the calf where he wasn't likely to hit bone. At this range, the bullet would go all the way through and bring enough pain the fellow shouldn't be able to hobble out with Curly.

Just as he squeezed the trigger, a woman's scream radiated through the air. Tanner flinched. The man holding Curly cried out, then dropped to his knees and clutched his leg. The buffalo bawled and stumbled away from the thief.

Tanner didn't have time to stay and inspect the fellow's injuries, but it looked like his bullet had done what it needed to, even with the distraction.

As he spun toward the trade room, he reached into his shot bag and grabbed a bullet and premeasured wad of powder. All those years of practice served him well now, even more than when he'd been part of the Day Police. He reloaded the gun as he ran and positioned the set trigger as he reached the trade room.

Even with the rear and front doors open, it took a precious moment for his eyes to adjust to the dim interior. No movement stirred, but a glance at his bedding in the corner showed someone had jerked a fur out of the stack. Looking for the rifles he'd pretended to keep there, no doubt.

The rest of the room showed some of the supplies had been ransacked, with blankets and shirts spread across the floor. He moved to the trade counter and reached to where he kept the rifles.

His hand touched only the empty wood shelf.

A knot clenched in his gut and forced out a word he hadn't used in years. He'd brought in extra rifles this morning, more than usual since there had been a deluge of customers yesterday and he was manning the place himself.

He sprinted toward the front door.

That Native woman. Had she been part of the ruse? A distraction to alert Purcey as soon as Tanner was out of the space? She might have been the female he'd seen when the group rode away that night they tried to steal the weapons. Maybe married to Purcey.

When Tanner reached the doorway, two men were frantically loading their stolen goods on pack animals. Purcey was tying a crate of rifles on a mule, and Quigley was strapping a barrel of gunpowder on his horse. The woman had already mounted her bay and looked panicked as she saw Tanner aiming his rifle at them.

Her flurry of speech made Purcey turn to look, and Tanner caught the man's gaze down the length of his gun barrel.

Tanner kept his voice hard and even. "Set those rifles and ammunition on the ground, or this bullet finds its home in your heart."

Hesitation flashed across Purcey's eyes. Surely he wouldn't be foolish enough to reach for a weapon.

Tanner adjusted his focus so he could also watch the other man's actions. Thankfully, that fellow hadn't moved. If Purcey forced Tanner to shoot him, Tanner would have to duck back into the trade room quickly to reload before the other fellow could get a shot off.

A flash of light to his left jerked his focus just as a bullet jolted into his shoulder. The gun's explosion came a heartbeat before the pain.

Tanner ignored the burning as he fought for balance and scrambled to see what was happening. The woman who'd shot him now held an empty gun.

The men yelled as they ran to their mounts and scrambled aboard.

Tanner had to do something fast or he'd lose his most expensive and needed merchandise. Even more, who knew what these scoundrels planned to do with the weapons.

He aimed at Purcey as he did his best to steady the trembling in his injured left arm. The pack mule that carried the rifles didn't seem eager to shift into a gallop, dragging behind Purcey and slowing his mount.

A new idea slipped in. Tanner couldn't bring himself to kill an innocent animal just because he had a lousy owner, but he could wound the mule enough to keep it from running away.

As he shifted his aim to the thin crest of muscle at the top of the animal's neck where the mane began, his injured arm finally steadied. He squeezed the trigger, then plunged his hand into his pouch to reload.

The mule screamed as though it had been mortally wounded, then spun and bucked in a wild circle. It must have broken its tether strap with the first pull, for Purcey's horse surged forward, finally free of the beast dragging behind it.

The big man reined his horse in and looked like he would

come back for the mule. But Tanner already had his gun loaded again. He'd be content with keeping the rifles the mule carried if these men would just leave. And he still had the one around back to contend with.

He aimed just beside Purcey, where he and his horse would hear the bullet whizz by, then fired.

The scoundrel jerked his focus to Tanner, maybe surprised he'd been able to reload so quickly. Tanner was already forcing the ramrod down the barrel, and that might've been what finally convinced the blackguard he'd stolen all he'd be able to. He had the barrel of gunpowder on the other packhorse, after all.

With a shout, Purcey spun his horse and kicked hard to catch up with the other man. He must not care about the fellow he'd sent to take Curly. Maybe he thought the man dead from Tanner's first rifle shot.

Tanner turned and headed back to the courtyard. The man wasn't dead—he had no concern about that, even though the woman's scream had shifted his aim.

Was there a chance that fellow had gotten away with Curly? Tanner's chest tightened and something like panic welled in his throat.

No. Tanner's flinch had been to the left, which meant the bullet might have penetrated bone. At that range, the limb would've shattered. The wound would be agonizing, but not deadly yet. If it wasn't treated right, though, the injury could fester and spread poison through his body. Death might come eventually.

Tanner pushed that thought aside before it could plant pain in his chest. He had to deal with all the threats first.

The courtyard was empty.

He scanned the area once more, slowing his gaze in the corners to make sure he didn't miss anything.

Frustration plunged through him. How had he let the man get away with Curly?

He sprinted toward the open gate, then skidded to a stop just outside.

The man—Anderson, he remembered—was struggling to pull himself up onto a horse. A howl strangled from his throat as he finally draped his injured leg over the mount's side. He slumped forward over the horse's neck and slapped the reins on its shoulder as he kicked his good leg.

The spooked horse needed no more prodding, leaping forward into a canter in the direction the others had gone.

Tanner finally managed a breath, though not a very deep one as he searched the area for the calf. Curly's bawl drew his attention to the right, nearly to the corner where Lorelei's cabin stood. The calf huddled against the fort wall, looking impossibly scared.

Tanner looked around once more to make sure no other threat remained. Then he finally released a long breath that made his chest hurt.

He kept the rifle secure in his good hand and allowed the arm where fire shot down from his shoulder to rest atop the gun.

He had to get Curly inside, then catch that mule and return the rifles to a safe place before he could see to his injury and the mule's.

But as he approached the calf, the matted crimson on the animal's haunches made his own blood run cold. The closer he came, the more the calf trembled. Could the blood be only a smear from Anderson's wound?

When he had nearly reached the animal, Curly darted sideways with a fearful bawl. Tanner forced himself to slow and hold out a hand. "Here, boy. It's all right. I've come to help."

Curly let him approach this time, and Tanner slipped his arms around the calf's chest and hindquarters, though the rifle in one of his hands made the grip awkward. A deep gash on the calf's rump clenched his belly. The cut ran about the length of Tanner's hand and looked too much like the crease of a bullet.

His bullet.

He couldn't tell for sure how deep the wound ran, but it looked to be into the muscle, and drops of blood leaked in a steady trickle.

Don't die on me. Lorelei would never forgive him for not only allowing the calf to be hurt but actually causing the wound himself.

But the only way this injury could be fatal was if the wound festered, or if the calf bled to death, though that didn't seem likely with the slowing drips.

Still, he had to get Curly in and doctored.

The calf allowed himself to be guided back inside the fort walls, though he let out a pitiful bleat that sounded more goat than buffalo.

As soon as Curly was safe inside, Tanner patted him on the shoulder. "I'll be back soon. Rest now."

He stepped back outside the gate and settled the latch securely, then turned and headed around to the front of the fort to find that mule.

Hopefully the animal had settled down, and maybe even begun grazing. Losing those rifles would be terrible, not only because of how much Tanner had paid for them, but who knew what man might get his hands on them? The weapons were meant to provide the people here with hunting tools, not start a war between whites and Natives.

When Tanner reached the front of the fort, the area proved empty, save for the Sioux camp down in the valley. Had the mule gone that way? The Sioux had moved their horses one valley over, so maybe the animal had followed the scent of the other. Or perhaps he'd gone after his master and the horses he was familiar with.

Tanner's gut pulled a little tighter at that thought. That would make him much harder to find. But if the mule was dripping blood, Tanner should be able to track him.

As he jogged toward the place the animal had broken free of its tether, the pain in his own shoulder began to radiate. He needed to move faster. Push aside this discomfort. His wound was only a graze of the bullet. Just like Curly's.

Buck up, Mason. You're stronger than the calf.

A noise from his right broke through his thoughts. Behind a cluster of cedars, he could just see a patch of brown fur exactly the right height to be a mule. He started that direction, and as he neared, the animal let loose a bray.

The knot in his chest eased a little. Now if he could just catch the beast.

But as soon as the mule caught sight of him through the trees, he blew a skittish snort.

Tanner slowed even more and extended the hand on his injured side since the other held his rifle. "Easy there, fellow. I'm here to help." His head and shoulder throbbed, but he worked hard to keep his voice level.

The mule must not have liked the sound, though, for

it spun and darted away, bucking out its hind legs toward Tanner as it ran and brayed.

A dozen strides away, the animal slowed and halted, dropping its head low. From this angle, the blood dripping down its neck could be easily seen.

Tanner had caused that injury too. Just like Curly's. Both had been to stop something worse from happening, but why did it seem he was always the villain, even when he tried to protect?

The bile churning in his middle felt too much like that last day in his father's home. He believed he'd been saving his father and their entire family when he presented the case against Cameron. But Pa hadn't viewed the news that way. He'd seen Tanner's efforts to collect all those documents as a traitorous act. Deliberate sabotage against the cousin who he'd always been jealous of.

And maybe Pa had even thought Tanner was trying to bring down the business his father had worked most of his life to build into a massive empire.

Of course Michael Mason wouldn't let his kingdom fall apart so easily. The reputation of Mason Mercantile would be easy enough to rebuild. Even the lost money could be regained, despite the additional schemes Cameron had been planning with his merciless business partners.

Tanner fought to pull out of the memories, out of that bitter place he'd left behind when he rode out of Massachusetts.

The mule eyed him warily as he approached once more, with his hand trembling, but his step slow and steady. He'd not speak this time, for it might've been his voice that scared the animal before.

When about three strides separated them, a noise from the left jerked the mule's attention. That sounded like the heavy tromping of an animal, perhaps more than one.

The mule brayed again, its entire body quivering with the sound. Then it spun and kicked out once more as it ran away.

A new bout of frustration swept through Tanner. He had to catch that mule.

He glanced back over his shoulder to see who approached. Hopefully Purcey hadn't returned for the animal and the rifles. Though Tanner's gun was loaded, he was in no condition to resume the battle.

Three horses emerged from the trees, all familiar, though his pain-fogged mind took a second to register how he knew them. Only when his gaze tracked upward to the riders did a weight finally lift from his chest.

Lorelei had returned.

TWENTY-TWO

The horses cantered toward Tanner, Lorelei in the lead. The moment she reached him, she leapt from her mount, worry clouding her face.

"What happened?" She touched the elbow of his injured arm, her wide eyes locked on his shoulder.

Her concern sent a stab of guilt through him. She wouldn't be worried about him when she learned he'd shot her young charge.

He nodded toward the mule. "I'm all right, but we have to catch him. The animal has the rest of my rifles strapped to him. He's injured too. Shot through the neck."

"White Horse and I will catch him. Lorelei, take Tanner back and get him doctored." Rosemary's voice took on a tone of command, and she and White Horse started their horses toward the pack mule.

Would they be able to catch him without help? Maybe with the two of them working together. And the Collins sisters had grown up on a ranch, so Rosemary likely possessed better instincts with animals than he did.

And just now, the thought of collapsing onto his bed

pallet and letting the fire in his shoulder rest held more appeal than Tanner was able to resist. Once he'd told Lorelei about Curly's injury, she'd be focused on the calf.

Tanner would offer to help her, but maybe she would have mercy on him and wave him off. He was a selfish man, but just now, the pain had worn down the last few threads of his resolve.

Lorelei touched his elbow again. "Come back to the fort so I can clean and bandage your shoulder. How did it happen?"

Now was his chance to scare her off from worrying over him. He slid a look at her. "Rifle shot." Then he turned toward the fort and started trudging.

She kept up with him, her horse trailing behind them. "I assumed that from the blasts we heard. Who was it? Were they trying to get the guns?"

He kept his focus straight ahead. "It was Purcey, the man who broke in the other night. He sent a Native woman into the trade room to distract me, then another man went around back to steal Curly. While I was trying to stop him, the others made off with a barrel of gunpowder and probably all the bullets. He would've got that box of rifles too, except the mule broke free when I shot him in the neck. I also shot Curly in the rump. I think he'll survive, but he needs tending."

It took what little self-control he had left not to look over and see her reaction, especially when a gasp slipped from her throat. He had no doubt of the horror in her expression. Nor did he have the desire to see the hurt in her eyes.

She didn't speak. And as her silence lapsed on, it became easier to hide himself in the cocoon of numbness.

He knew this place well. He'd first discovered it as a boy, any time Cameron would come around and prove himself superior in whatever game they were playing. Then at sharpshooting, the one place Tanner's father had shown any pride in him. Until Cameron's marks formed a tighter circle in the target than Tanner's.

Then when Pa brought Cameron on as managing partner over the Boston store, this cocoon had given him the strength to quit his job as clerk in that very store. He had no need to work his way up the chain now that Cameron stood at the top.

He'd retreated into this shell when Jessamine walked away, once she saw he wouldn't be heir to his father's empire.

And that last day when Tanner had revealed Cameron's plans in court, it was this cocoon that had strengthened him to face his father's anger. Tanner hadn't been the turncoat . . . his father had been. Turning against his son to favor the nephew who'd planned to steal the Mason fortune.

But his father had chosen Cameron long before then. He could see that now, looking back.

Just as Lorelei had chosen the calf long before any tender feelings might have developed toward Tanner. Even before she met Tanner. He couldn't hold that against her.

She wasn't his father. But neither was Tanner naïve enough to let himself be hurt the same way again.

He had to put space between him and Lorelei. Allow her room to tend to this calf she loved so well. He'd be the gentleman and offer help when she needed it, but he wouldn't let his emotions get involved.

When they reached the gate in the fort walls, he turned to Lorelei. "I'm truly sorry Curly got hurt. I aimed only for the man's leg, but a distraction when I pulled the trigger made my bullet stray." He reached for the gate latch, trying not to see the glistening of pain in her expression. "I'll hold him while you tend the wound."

"Tanner." Lorelei's voice was soft. Gentle. Calling to him.

He wrapped the cocoon tighter around himself. "I'll get a bucket of clean water." Then he headed toward the trade room, leaving her behind.

Lorelei poured another cup of water over Curly's wound to flush out the last of the blood and hair. The calf shifted, but White Horse tightened his hold.

"Are you sure you don't want me to doctor the mule before I leave?" Rosie finished tying off the long-eared beast, then turned to Lorelei.

She shook her head and reached for the salve she used for injuries like this to keep them from festering. "White Horse is here to help." She glanced up at the man, and he offered a solemn nod.

Rosie still sounded hesitant. "I'll just go check on things at the ranch, then I'll be back."

Lorelei rested her free hand on the calf's rump to keep him from flinching when she touched the gash. "You don't have to ride all the way back here. We'll be fine. I'm sure they need you at the ranch."

"I'll be back." Her tone took on that rod of steel that said argument would be futile.

Normally, that would make Lorelei smile, but the weight

pressed too heavily on her chest. After delivering the bucket of water, Tanner had offered to hold the calf while she cleaned the gash.

But she could see the exhaustion around Tanner's eyes, and that wound that created that circle of blood at his shoulder must be painful. The ring of crimson hadn't grown larger during their walk back to the fort, so she was pretty sure the bleeding had stopped.

Perhaps she should have seen to his wound first, but with Curly still dripping blood, this had seemed the more urgent need. She'd not expected Tanner to disappear into the trade room and close the door like a barrier between them. Should she check on him before helping the mule?

And was he speaking the truth when he said he'd been the one to shoot both animals? Just the thought made her belly clench into a tight knot.

She knew Tanner, and he would never intentionally injure an animal unless that was the only way to stop something far worse from happening. It sounded like Curly's wound had been accidental. Tanner had been one man against four others. It was a wonder he'd come away alive and able to save the precious stock of rifles.

She leaned back to study her work with the calf. This injury would heal in a couple weeks with regular care. There would likely be a scar, but no lasting damage.

She pushed up to standing and glanced from the mule to the trade room door. "I'm going to check Tanner and see if he'll come out for us to doctor him." As if he were another animal for her and White Horse to tend. But she knew better than to go into the trade room alone in a situation that could be seen as far more intimate than usual.

Her knock on the rear door didn't receive an answer at first. Had he fallen asleep?

She pressed her mouth near the barrier. "Tanner? Are you in there? Can you come out so I can clean and bandage your shoulder?"

"No need. It's just a scratch. I already washed it off." His voice sounded muffled.

Maybe he *had* been sleeping. He'd looked tired enough to collapse. And if it was only a light scrape, washing would suffice for now. When she brought him the evening meal, she would insist on applying salve and bandage to keep it from festering. Bullet wounds could turn inflamed and feverish so easily.

"All right then. I'll send White Horse over to help with any customers. We put the rifles in the storage room for now."

"Give him my thanks. I can see to any who come to trade." His voice did sound a little stronger now.

Should she take him at his word? He was a grown man, after all. She'd have to learn to trust him, even when her nurturing instincts wanted to help.

She leaned close to the door once more. "Thank you for handling things so well here, Tanner. I don't know how you managed it. Curly and the mule will be just fine."

Only silence answered her. Finally, after too many heartbeats passed, she turned away.

After getting some rest, Tanner would be himself again. All would be right between them, and her heart wouldn't feel like she'd failed this man when he needed her most.

203

Lorelei stirred the stew with her big wooden spoon, careful to loosen any chunks that stuck to the bottom. She couldn't let even a single dumpling scorch. This meal had to work two different miracles—to nourish Juniper and give her something she would *want* to eat, and to break through the wall Tanner had erected around himself.

She still couldn't quite figure out why he kept himself distant. Was it his injury? Did he not want her to know how badly he was hurt? But why not when she could help him?

She'd portioned out some of her salve and asked White Horse to give it to him, since Tanner was working so hard to avoid her. Even White Horse seemed to be intentionally acting as a barrier between them, offering to take meals to Tanner and almost standing sentry in front of the trade room door.

This reminded her a little of that night White Horse had been gone, after she and Tanner had kissed. He'd kept himself holed up in the trade room then, but it was to protect her reputation. At least that's what he'd said. Did he think he was protecting her now? From what?

Sometimes men made no sense.

A knock sounded at the door. As she turned, voices drifted through the thin wood partition. Tanner's deeper tones were easier to pick out, but that other voice wasn't White Horse. The words came too quickly, a little high-pitched. Had Riley come? Her pulse leapt. Was something wrong with Juniper?

She strode to the door even as her mind registered that the voice didn't sound like Riley's either. She pulled the latchstring and opened just a crack. Perhaps she should have reached for her rifle just in case. But Tanner and White

Horse wouldn't have let someone inside the fort walls who wasn't safe.

The first face she saw was lined with deep grooves and had a smoky, almost-bluish tint. The familiar grin that flashed in his eyes eased the knot in her chest.

She pulled the door wide and smiled. "Ol' Henry. Dragoon." She couldn't help but slide her gaze over to Tanner, who stood a little behind them. He met her look for the first time since they'd walked back to the fort yesterday. His eyes were clearer than she'd expected, though there still seemed a distance in them.

She forced her focus back on her old friends. "What brings you to the fort?" She should have better manners than to keep them standing in the doorway. The cabin behind her was so small, and they only had one barrel for a seat, but she couldn't simply leave them standing on the stoop.

She stepped to the side. "Will you come in? I have soup cooking. It's not done yet, but we can visit."

Dragoon shook his head, his hat clutched in both hands. "Thank you, Miss Lorelei. We've just come from the ranch to tell you Miz Juniper's doin' poorly."

Her pulse surged again, and a lump lodged in her throat. "My sis—" She cleared her throat to bring her voice back. "What happened? What's wrong now?" She knew she should have gone to help Juniper instead of trekking off with Rosemary and White Horse. Her instincts had told her June needed her. Why hadn't she listened?

Ol' Henry shook his head. "Miss Rosemary said it's just the baby. She said she doesn't think anything special is wrong."

She searched his weathered face for what he wasn't saying. "But you *do* think something is wrong." Why else would they have come to get her?

He lifted a slow shrug. "She looked a bit worried. And ol' Riley is beside hisself."

Dragoon's mouth lifted at the corners. Riley had trapped with these men for many months before she and her sisters met them. These two likely knew him better than she did.

She spun and struggled to think of what she should take with her. "I'll go there now. Did they ask me to bring anything?"

"No, ma'am. They didn't actually ask you to come. Miss Faith just thought you'd want to know."

Of course she would go. She gathered up her extra pair of underthings and her clean apron. She'd take stock of Juniper, then decide whether she should stay the night at the ranch.

"How can I help you?" Tanner's voice hummed low behind her.

She glanced back at him. He'd entered the cabin, and the sight of him standing there, concern marking his features and softening his eyes, made her want to fling herself into his arms. To absorb some of his strength. If Dragoon and Ol' Henry weren't standing at the doorway, she might have done so.

But instead she picked up her pack and turned to face him fully, using the satchel as a buffer between them. "I'm going to see what I can do for Juniper. Once I know what's needed, I'll be back. Either tonight or tomorrow morning at the latest. Can you and White Horse see to Curly and Frisco?"

His brow lowered in confusion. "Frisco?"

Another pain pressed on her chest. She hadn't even had a chance to tell him what she'd named the mule. "That's what I'm calling our new friend, after a mule we used to have on our ranch when I was younger." She turned to the soup still simmering over the fire. "White Horse knows how to doctor them, I think, but he'll need help holding each animal. Just make sure you scrape the scab off and pour water over her wounds before putting fresh salve on."

A new thought slipped in, and she spun back to him. "Your shoulder." She searched out the place where the circle of blood had been. There was no sign of that stain on his shirt now. She looked up at his eyes to gauge the pain. "Maybe you'd better not help with the animals. Are you putting on the salve I sent you?"

That distant look appeared in his eyes again, but his throat worked. "I'm fine, Lorelei. It's only a scratch. Don't worry about us. White Horse and I can manage the animals. Take care of your sister."

The burn of tears surged, so she turned away. Why was she getting emotional *now*, of all times?

She reached for the leather pads to protect her hands from the heat of the pot. "I'll be back as soon as I can."

"I'll carry that." Tanner stepped up beside her and reached for the leather pieces.

As he took the pot from her, her mind finally recalled her former plans. "Here, pour some in this kettle for you and White Horse to eat tonight. I planned to split it between us and my sisters."

"Just take it all with you."

Would he really refuse this offering too? She spun on

him and bit out her words. "Eat the stew, Tanner. Let me do this one thing for you. Please."

He blinked and drew back. "If you're sure."

"I'm sure." She reached for the kettle again and picked it up this time. The man was harder to care for than a skittish horse.

And far more stubborn than that mule in the courtyard.

TWENTY-THREE

Dragoon and Ol' Henry rode with Lorelei back to the ranch, and as they neared the buildings, she scanned the yard for any sign that something awful had happened. She would've run her horse this last stretch, but she couldn't let the stew slosh. Nothing seemed out of place, though.

A mare and a young foal stood in the corral attached to the barn, the place they'd kept Curly. The memory of the trapper who died there tried to raise its awful images, but she pushed them down. That sweet colt must have been born yesterday, for it wobbled a few steps on shaky legs.

As she neared the house, the door opened, and Riley stepped out. He strode toward her with a purposeful step.

"How's Juniper?" She slid to the ground, then turned to unfasten the pot Tanner had strapped behind her saddle.

Riley reached for her reins. "She hasn't thrown up in the last hour or so. She's resting now."

When she had the pot free, she turned to her brother-in-law. His face looked pale, with lines fading away from his eyes. "Is she still feeling the baby move?"

"I think so. She said she did this morning." He looked back toward the house and ran a hand through his hair.

Poor man. He must be wrung out with worry.

She started toward the house. "That's good. We'll get her eating and feeling better, and they'll both be fine."

Lord, please let that be true.

Faith met her at the door with a hushing finger to her lips. "She's finally sleeping, I think."

Lorelei looked toward the bed pallet that Juniper had taken over from her first moments back in the cabin. Her sister barely seemed to raise the covers as she lay on her side, turned away from the door.

Faith lifted the lid from the soup pot in Lorelei's hands and sniffed deeply. "Is that ham I smell?"

"Ham soup. It needs another hour to cook. Can you hang it over the fire?"

As Faith took the load from her, Lorelei scanned the room. The floor didn't look like it'd been swept in a week, but Faith and Rosie had probably had their hands full with Juniper and the horses.

She moved to the corner to grab the broom and kept her voice low so she didn't wake Juniper. "Has Riley been caring for June while you help Rosie with the horses?"

"He was at first, but Juniper started to get bad right after you guys went to look for Steps Right. I thought I'd stay here in case he needed help. One of us rode out mornings and evenings to see if there were new foals, but otherwise we kept close."

Lorelei paused in her sweeping to study Faith. "Were there times Juniper needed you both?" Had they thought something awful was about to happen that would require two people to handle?

Faith's gaze moved to Juniper, and Lorelei followed her direction. June's face seemed completely devoid of color, maybe even a little gray. Was that a trick of the dim light?

When Faith finally spoke, her voice came far softer than its usual blunt tone. "It was just . . . scary. She cast up her accounts every hour at least, sometimes every quarter hour. There wasn't anything left inside her to come out, but I knew she had to keep sipping water, even if she couldn't keep it down."

Faith looked more vulnerable in that moment than she had in years. Lorelei would have drawn her into a hug, but Faith usually shied away from affectionate touches. Probably because she'd been pinched too many times when they were little.

So Lorelei settled for laying a hand on her arm. "That must have been awful for all of you. I'm sorry I wasn't here to help."

Faith's eyes shimmered as the corners of her mouth pulled up a little. "I'm glad you're here now."

Once more, her eyes stung. Should she move back to the ranch? At least for tonight, she would stay and see if the worst was over or if Juniper still needed her.

Juniper didn't stir for more than two hours.

Lorelei had sent Riley and Faith out to help Rosie with the herd, for it was clear both of them had been holed up in this cabin too long.

She was kneading cornmeal batter to make johnnycakes when Juniper's weak voice broke the quiet. "Lor?"

She spun around to see her sister's eyes had finally opened, the blanket lowered a little. Lorelei's heart lightened, and a smile came easily. She dipped her hands in a bowl of water, then dried them on her apron as she moved to Juniper's bed and knelt beside the mattress. "How are you feeling?"

Juniper gave her a weak, sleepy smile. "Much better."

A cup of water sat beside the bed, and Lorelei reached for it. "Can you sip this? I have ginger tea ready as well."

A look of pain crossed Juniper's face, but then she dutifully raised up on one elbow and reached for the cup. Lorelei kept hold of it to help lift. Her sister seemed so frail. So fragile. Like skin draped over bones that might crack any moment.

Lorelei's own body ached as even the small act of sipping water seemed to exhaust her. Juniper sank back onto the mattress, her eyes closed as she recovered from the effort.

"Has your stomach settled?" In this condition, Juniper didn't look capable of eating even ham stew. If only they had a chicken for broth.

"A bit." Juniper kept her eyes closed as she murmured the words, which meant they may not be true.

Lorelei brushed loose tendrils of hair off Juniper's brow, then rose. She would start with ginger tea, then once that had time to perform its calming magic, hopefully Juniper could keep down the ham broth. They'd work up to bites of the salty meat.

One thing was certain: Juniper needed special care and focused attention right now. As important as Curly had become in Lorelei's life, her sister mattered far more.

And Juniper needed her.

Tanner's insides had been coiled tight for nearly a full day now. The longer he stared at the ledger, the more the numbers blurred. At least this new worry about Juniper had pushed his other pain to the background, both the redness ringing the gash in his shoulder and the weight constricting his heart as he forced himself to place distance between him and Lorelei. The shoulder would be easy enough to fix if he'd be more faithful to apply the salve Lorelei gave him.

But his heart . . . He couldn't get his thoughts to linger on anything other than her.

What was happening with her sister? So many times he'd nearly placed the bar across the trade room door and saddled his gelding to head toward the ranch. White Horse could protect the calf and other animals. The man was far more capable than Tanner had proved to be. And maybe those at the ranch would appreciate if he showed up with supplies for them.

But he'd promised Lorelei he would stay here and watch over things. Whether he was the right man for that job or not, he'd given his word.

The rear door to the trade room opened, and White Horse appeared in the frame. A little of the tension in Tanner's chest eased, especially when the man stepped inside. White Horse had become a welcome companion during his stay here. His movements now seemed almost casual, as though he was simply killing time. Did he realize how much Tanner needed a friend right now? Probably not. But even still, his presence felt like a gift.

White Horse moved to the open doorway and stared

out toward the mountains where he'd gone to search for his mother. Was he thinking of her now? Did he wonder if he'd missed something in their search?

Tanner worked for a casual tone. "Do you plan to go search for your mother again soon?"

White Horse didn't answer immediately but kept his gaze on the distant peaks. "She will find me when she's ready." Then he turned back to Tanner. "She gave to her people everything she had. Healed them. Loved them." He pressed a fist over his heart. "When they turned on her . . . made her leave when she could not save one man. She grieved what she has lost." His gaze turned back to the mountains, and his voice softened. "When she has done with her sadness, she will find me."

Tanner swallowed down the heat clogging his throat. He knew well the feeling of being abandoned by a mother, though his own hadn't chosen to leave him. She'd died when he was five, and his only memory was of standing beside her sickbed, sobs shaking his chest as he begged her to get better. She'd only given him a sad smile and patted his hand.

For years, he'd wondered why hadn't she fought to stay with him. She could have overcome the chest cold that turned to pneumonia if she'd tried. Didn't she know how much her little boy would need someone on his side? Someone willing to love him? To fight for him?

He pushed the memories away. He was a grown man now. She'd taken ill and died. He knew now there was nothing she could have done to save herself. Yet no matter how many times he told himself that, he couldn't shake the loneliness, the panicked feeling he had no one left who cared.

White Horse turned to face him again and stepped forward. The friendship in his eyes showed clearly as though they shared a similar pain.

But then the brave stopped and turned, his head cocked. Tanner strained to hear. Was that hoofbeats?

White Horse returned to the doorway and peered out. "Lorelei has come." He charged outside. Tanner dropped his pencil onto the ledger and bolted after White Horse.

He reached the two after Lorelei had already dismounted by the side gate. She stood there, reins in hand, exhaustion creasing the edges of her eyes and darkening the hollows beneath them. Her sister must be even worse than they'd thought. The knot in his middle twisted tighter, and he touched her arm.

She allowed him to tug her inside, and once White Horse took the reins from her, she looked weary enough to blow away in a strong wind. Had she slept at all since she left the fort? Tanner slid his arm around her to guide her toward the cabin.

She slid into the crook of his arm, moving where he guided her. White Horse followed along on the other side, the horse trailing behind him.

"How is your sister?" Tanner kept his voice gentle but loud enough for both to hear.

"A little better, but still very weak. She can't keep anything more than a few drops down, and she barely has the strength to stand."

The weight pressed harder on Tanner's chest, especially when Lorelei pulled from his arms and turned to face him. She cast her focus from him to White Horse, then back to him. "I need to stay at the ranch to help. Juniper needs special care right now."

He swallowed down the lump that rose up. He'd expected that. Thought about recommending it. But if taking Curly back to the ranch brought that other danger back with her, which would be the lesser problem?

Lorelei had surely considered all and must believe her attention was needed more than anything. If anything could bring her sister back to health, Lorelei's care would do it.

Still, she was leaving him. He'd told himself this was what he wanted. For her. She needed to focus on her family and the creatures she cared so much about. The injured animals who needed her devotion.

He would be fine on his own. And far better he protect his heart now than after becoming too involved.

He turned to look around for the calf. Curly stood nose to nose with Frisco in the corner by the storage room. "I'll help you take the animals over. I think Curly might be too big to ride across your saddle, but I suspect he'll come along willingly."

"Tanner."

At the weight in her tone, he turned back. Did she not want his help? He could understand that, but moving the animals with only her and White Horse would be more of a challenge. She must really distrust him now.

She seemed to be struggling to meet his gaze. He should make it easier for her and step back without forcing her to request it.

But she spoke again before he could offer. "I was hoping to leave Curly and Frisco here with the two of you." She glanced between him and White Horse again. "Is it too much to ask you to care for them both? I'll come over each day and help clean and salve the wounds. But I think they're safer here than at the ranch."

His mind struggled to make sense of her first words, but the more she spoke, the harder his heart began to pump. She trusted him to keep both animals safe without her here? Indefinitely?

He studied her face to see if she really meant the words. Her look was earnest. "I know it's a lot to ask—"

"We will." He darted a look back at White Horse. "I mean . . ."

White Horse nodded. "I help."

Tanner turned back to Lorelei, and the relief easing her features pulled some of the weight from his chest.

"Thank you." She glanced toward the pair of injured animals. "How are they?" Her voice sounded hesitant. Maybe she dreaded the possibility of hearing more bad news about those she loved.

At least he didn't have to add to her worries on that score. "No sign of festering with either one. The mule isn't fond of us poking in his wound, but we've managed to follow your instructions."

A soft smile curved her mouth. "And Curly?" She looked back at Tanner, and the intensity of her beauty washed over him anew. Even in this fragile state, she possessed a strength that made his chest ache.

He swallowed to bring moisture back into his mouth. "You've trained him well. He stands like a gentleman."

Her eyes warmed, and the way she looked at him made

every part of him long to pull her into his arms. To kiss her the way he had three days ago.

Except this time he would be gentle. He would give only, not take. He would lend her his strength and savor the moment.

He forced himself to look away. There wouldn't be another kiss. Lorelei Collins deserved a man far better than him.

As Lorelei turned and started toward the animals, he could feel the weight of disappointment she left in her wake. Or maybe that was his own disappointment.

White Horse followed her, but Tanner stayed where he was, putting distance between them.

The hum of their voices drifted across the courtyard as they looked at Curly's gash first. Lorelei motioned and must have asked a question, for White Horse answered with a shake of his head and a few words.

They moved on to the mule, and White Horse held the animal by the rope halter they kept on him as Lorelei stroked its neck and inspected the wound.

The wound *he'd* caused.

He could turn away, escape back to the trade room and pretend he'd not inflicted this pain. He could even pretend Lorelei wasn't here, was out of his reach. He could save himself the pain of watching her gentle touch heal where he had caused damage.

But he deserved every twist of his gut, every knife blade in his chest.

Lorelei spoke a few more words to White Horse, and he again shook his head. If only Tanner had moved closer so he could hear. But this extra bit of torture in not knowing what they said seemed appropriate.

Lorelei patted the mule a final time, then turned and began walking toward Tanner.

His breathing hitched, and his mind barely registered the fact that White Horse had released the mule and was striding toward the trade room.

His gaze roamed over Lorelei's face, searching for a hint of what she would say when she reached him. Was she angry? After examining those wounds he'd caused, she should be seething.

Her expression carried no sign of frustration, though he couldn't decipher exactly what was there. Determination, maybe?

As she stopped in front of him, White Horse disappeared into the trade room, eliminating the last minor distraction so he could focus fully on Lorelei. She must be coming to give final instructions for the animals.

"I'd planned to tend their injuries, but White Horse said the two of you would do it this evening?" She spoke the words as a question, so he nodded.

"We'll take care of them. Should anything be done differently?"

Her expression lightened as she shook her head. "They're already beginning to heal. Thank you for handling their treatments so well."

He had to work to keep the compliment from penetrating. He'd only done what she said, and if he'd protected them better in the first place, there wouldn't be injuries to tend at all.

She seemed to be waiting for him to say something, so

he scrambled for anything he needed to tell her. "I set the last of the flour and cornmeal on the table in there." He motioned toward the cabin. "Take it with you."

Her brow furrowed. "Are you certain?"

He nodded. That way he wouldn't be tempted to come visiting. "Is there anything else that would help? Milk to make butter?"

Instead of answering, she studied him, as though trying to see deep inside. Did she suspect some diabolical motive?

He cleared his throat. "I just want to make sure you have everything you need to help your sister."

She still didn't speak, and if anything, her expression turned wary. Had he said the wrong thing? Perhaps she thought of the offer as charity.

Before he could clarify, or even decide if he should say more, she finally responded.

"Have I done something to offend you?"

Her question stole all the words from him. Offend *him*? Did she think he'd been trying to insult her?

But she clearly wasn't finished, so he held his tongue. "Ever since we returned from looking for Steps Right, you've acted as though you want nothing to do with me. Did I do something wrong? Are you angry with me?"

He blinked. The way her words lashed out wasn't like her at all. And why in the world would she think he was upset with her? *He'd* been the one to fail *her*.

He shook his head. "You've done nothing wrong."

She pressed on before he could say more. "Then why have you . . . Why are you avoiding me?"

He swallowed down the lump in his throat. If he could avoid this *question*, he would. But he couldn't. Perhaps she didn't fully realize the truth yet. If not, he needed to speak it.

He didn't look away from her, but he couldn't quite meet her gaze, so he focused on her chin. "I was giving you the freedom to . . . carry on. To focus on what's most important. You don't need to feel obligated . . . especially after I was the one to wound both of them." He motioned back to the calf and mule.

She studied him, her brow lined with confusion. "Obligated? You didn't mean to shoot Curly or Frisco. Did you?" She tacked on that last part as though suddenly questioning what she'd thought before.

He locked his jaw. "The calf, no. The mule, it was the only way I could stop Purcey from getting away with the rifles."

"The wound wasn't mortal, though. I'm guessing you aimed for the crest of his neck? That place would do the least amount of harm to an animal, yet still have a good chance of stopping it. And you kept that thief from getting away with weapons he had no business taking. That many guns could hurt a lot of innocent people."

Tanner frowned. He couldn't let her think so well of him. She would find out eventually he was nowhere near good enough for her. Better he convince her of it now than later when splitting ways would be so much harder.

"Lorelei, I'm no saint. I've lived a hard life. You could do far better than getting mixed up with the likes of me." She still studied him, the look a mixture of gentle reproach and something that felt like affection.

Did he really have to unveil all his failings to make her see? If it saved them both heartache later . . .

He swallowed hard. "I'm not good enough for you, Lorelei. You need to believe me. Everyone who gets close enough to see my failings realizes it quickly enough. That's why my father brought on my cousin to run the family business instead of me. That's why he took Cameron's side when the evidence I brought against him showed Cameron had practically handed the company over to a group of thieves. Even the woman I was supposed to marry only wanted me for my family's money and connections. Once those were gone, so was she. If you don't already see my failings with what's happened to Curly and Frisco, your eyes will be opened soon enough. Better you not have any regrets on that point."

He took a step back to make it easier for her to do the same. She would leave now. Standing here with her, baring his flaws, hurt too much.

"I'm so sorry, Tanner." Her voice came out quiet. Gentle enough to take the sting out of her words. They were the right words, though. Lorelei had the ability to see what others missed. He'd realized this about her early, and it was one of the things he loved. At least she was using the skill for her own good now.

But instead of moving back, she stepped forward. Close enough to rest her hand on his arm. His entire body tensed, and he finally met her gaze to see what she could possibly be doing. Being so sweet didn't make the parting easier. Didn't she realize that?

She looked at him with a glossy sheen over her eyes. "Tanner, I don't know your father, so I don't understand how he could possibly choose your cousin over you. But I know the man who's been protecting me and Curly and my whole family these past weeks. I know how hard you work and how fair you are in your trades. I know what a sharp business mind you possess, and I've seen the strength of your integrity. I don't need to hear about others' poor choices to make my own decision."

He'd been bracing himself against her good-bye, so it took a moment to hear her words. But when she began stating so many sterling qualities, so many things he wanted to be good at, areas he worked so hard in, a lump rose up to his throat.

As she finished speaking, her hand slid down his arm and captured his own, wrapping her fingers around his palm.

Her voice pressed in. "Don't pull away from me. Let me choose what I want." Then her expression shifted into a hint of shyness as she shrugged a shoulder. "And you might find things you don't like about me." She gave him a gentle smile, a hopeful look. "We won't know for sure if we don't try. Don't give up on me yet."

His throat was so full, he couldn't speak. A good thing, for his mind scrambled to find the right answer.

Every part of him wanted to say yes. To draw her all the way to him and wrap their intertwined fingers behind her back, to hold her to him. To say yes, both with words and with a kiss that gave her no doubt of his agreement.

He couldn't rush into this. . . . But maybe he didn't have to push her away just yet. After all, she would eventually see for herself what his own father had known.

Until then, Tanner could enjoy her beauty a little longer. Both the stunning image she made looking up at him as she did now and the richer loveliness of her heart.

So instead of pulling her close, he lifted their joined hands and pressed a kiss to her knuckles. "I won't pull away, but you're free to do so at any time."

A smile curved her beautiful lips, though moisture still glimmered in her eyes. "I suppose I can live with that. For now."

Then she reached up and did what he'd not allowed himself to, pressing her warm sweet mouth to his for a kiss. A kiss that ended far too soon.

TWENTY-FOUR

Knowing where she and Tanner stood eased some of the weight from Lorelei's chest as she rode back to the ranch. She'd not even realized how that uncertainty had pressed on her.

It still seemed hard to believe he would think himself not good enough for her. Everything Tanner had told of his past broke her heart, but there had likely been even more. Perhaps a lifetime of disappointments, times his father hadn't been there when Tanner needed him most, or a multitude of situations where his father chose the cousin over Tanner. His father must be blind not to realize the exceptional man he'd raised—or rather, the exceptional man Tanner had become in spite of his upbringing.

What had his mother been like? Tanner never spoke of her. Not even a passing mention. Lorelei would find the chance to ask. Her heart longed to know more of his history. To understand the events and challenges that made him the man she knew today.

As her mare crested the final pass and the ranch came into view in the valley below, her middle clenched again.

As much as she'd like to think about Tanner for hours, she had a far greater challenge at hand with Juniper.

When she reached their cabin door, the sounds of retching inside made her own belly twist tighter. She left her horse in the yard and slipped through the door, meeting Faith's worried gaze where her younger sister knelt by Juniper's bed.

Lorelei strode to Juniper's other side and began to rub circles on her back as her shoulders convulsed again. Nothing came as she gagged, and only a scant bit of liquid lay in the pot.

Poor thing. She must have already tossed up the broth Lorelei had helped her sip that morning.

When Juniper finally finished, Lorelei wiped her mouth, then wrung out a clean cloth from the bowl of fresh water. Juniper sank against the mattress and took the cloth to wipe her face. A sheen of sweat covered her brow, and her bright red lips stood out against the pallor of her skin.

Lorelei swallowed down the worry that tried to rise up. "I'll get more ginger tea."

Juniper's eyes were already drifting shut. These episodes exhausted her. *Lord, keep her and the baby safe. Bring her through this quickly.*

Juniper managed several sips of the ginger tea before slipping away into a weary sleep. Faith had begun to pace the cabin by the time Lorelei left their older sister's side and carried the used dishes to the washpot.

She turned to Faith. "Do you need to go check the foals in the corral?"

Faith darted a glance at the door as though it was a forbidden pleasure. "I probably should."

"Go then, and bring me some wood when you're done. After that, Rosie and Riley could probably use help with the herd."

Faith had already reached the door but turned back. "Are you sure? I told Rosie I'd stay here and help you."

Lorelei turned to look at their sleeping sister. "I think she'll rest for a while. I'm going to cook and clean, and I'd rather have you out of the way." She tried for a teasing smile, but Faith didn't stay long enough to notice.

Juniper woke twice through the afternoon and managed to finish the ginger tea and sip a cup of broth. Riley returned once to check on her, but Lorelei sent him back out so he didn't wake his wife.

When the three of them rode in at dark, Juniper was sitting up on the bed and had a little more color in her cheeks. Conversation bounced around the small cabin as relief showed on every face.

"Whatever you're cooking smells good." Faith approached the pot over the fire. As she peered inside, her nose wrinkled. "What is it?"

Lorelei pulled bowls from the shelf. "Buffalo with cornmeal dumplings."

Faith raised both brows at her. "Never would have put those together myself, but I'm hungry enough to eat it."

Riley's chuckle rumbled across the room as he dropped down to sit beside his wife.

Lorelei quickly spooned out the meal and handed dishes to each. Juniper accepted another cup of broth and raised it to her mouth for a sip. As Lorelei settled into her usual chair, the food in the bowl held no appeal. Still, she forced herself to take the first bite.

"How were things at the fort today, Lor?" Rosie's question offered a welcome distraction, and Lorelei shifted her focus to her sister.

"Good. Tanner and White Horse seem to have everything in hand with the animals. Both are recovering as well as I would expect."

Rosie nodded, but she kept her focus on Lorelei even as she took a bite of dumpling, chewed, and swallowed. The way she lowered her spoon and raised her brows before she spoke made something tighten in Lorelei's belly.

"So, Lor. What do you think about Tanner Mason now that you've spent time with him?"

Heat flushed up Lorelei's neck before she could stop it. Though her ears were likely bright red, she did her best to act casual. "I, um, think he's a good man. A very good man. Honest. And hardworking. And . . ." Her mind stalled. No other words would come.

She closed her mouth and struggled for a smile to show Rosie all was as it should be.

But her response had been suspicious enough that every one of her sisters now eyed her. Even Riley's eyes had rounded, a bit of a shocked look on his face. He must not have suspected anything, but the girls had. Juniper's knowing look and Faith's smirk showed that fact clearly. And Rosie was studying her as though if she looked hard enough, she could see the secrets of the pyramids in her eyes.

Lorelei turned away and took a bite of dumpling. The mushy corn bread tasted awful, even with the buffalo gravy, but at least with her mouth full, her tongue couldn't get her in trouble.

"Does he feel the same way?" The quiet intensity in

Rosie's voice drew her attention, and she swallowed the wad, though it lodged in her throat.

Rosie didn't look angry, just . . . concerned. More like their mother than ever before, with the glimmer of worry softening her eyes.

Lorelei thought through the question. Did Tanner feel what way, exactly? Attracted to her? The memory of those two kisses swept in, and another round of heat flooded her face. Even as Lorelei struggled to hold Rosie's gaze, Faith's giggle penetrated her efforts.

"I never thought I'd see the day Lorelei turned swoony over a man. An animal, yes. But not a fellow." Their youngest sister's teasing sparked her ire. "Has he kissed you?"

Lorelei spun to tell Faith to mind her own molasses, but Juniper raised a hand to stay her. "Faith. That's not a question we ask, dear." She sent a sly look toward Lorelei. "But if she wanted to tell, we'd certainly be willing to listen."

She could take no more. Her feelings for Tanner were too new. Too precious to take the teasing yet. Setting her bowl aside, she rose and started for the door. "I'm going to check the horses in the barn."

As she stepped into the fresh evening air, she closed the door on the chuckles inside. She walked the short distance to the barn, letting her mind wander.

If she were at the fort, this would be the time she would go out to milk Elsa and feed Curly. She would have already delivered Tanner's and White Horse's meals to them and stayed to visit if they weren't busy. It seemed a customer often arrived just as Tanner was bringing in the latchstring for the night. Had that happened today too? How late would he be out milking and tending wounds?

She'd said she would come every day, but she couldn't leave Juniper if she was too weak. Maybe her sister had turned a corner this afternoon, and Lorelei would be able to ride over to the trading post tomorrow to check on things.

Playing with the new filly eased a bit of the tension in her. Its silky soft muzzle caressed like kisses as it nuzzled her face. By the time she headed back toward the house, the weight on her chest felt far lighter.

But as she reached for the latchstring to enter the cabin, the sound of retching met her ears once again.

Lorelei hadn't come that day. Tanner could stand the strain no longer, so he milked Elsa early and left the milk for White Horse to feed the calf. He'd set the bar in place on the trade room door, then saddled his gelding and headed toward the mountain pass.

Full darkness had nearly settled by the time he descended into the valley where the Collins ranch nestled. No lantern lights shone in the yard, but as he drew nearer, he could make out a glow emanating from the cabin walls. They wouldn't be expecting company. Should he alert them of his presence?

As he reached the yard, he let loose a friendly whistle. A heartbeat later, the door cracked open, and Riley peered out. He didn't appear surprised to see Tanner.

The doorway widened as another figure appeared behind the man. That flash of burgundy skirt had to be Lorelei. Riley didn't seem eager to concede the doorway, and the shadows hid much of his expression.

But then Lorelei slipped around him, and Tanner could look nowhere else.

She smiled at him. "Tanner."

He slid to the ground to meet her, and when she came into his arms, he clasped her tight.

Only for a second, though, for he could feel the weight of Riley's scrutiny. Had she told her family about their . . . courtship?

As he pulled back, she gripped his upper arms and studied his face, the shadows forming deep grooves around her features. "What's wrong? What happened?"

He shook his head. "Nothing. The animals are fine. I just came to check on you." He glanced toward the house. "And your sister." Did that sound like an afterthought? He did hope Juniper fared better, but it was Lorelei's absence that had twisted his insides all day.

She stared at him a moment longer, as though deciding whether he spoke the truth or not. She must believe him, for she finally seemed to relax. Maybe even wilt, as she released one of his arms and turned to walk with him toward the house. "She's better. Mostly. When I'm here, she'll drink the ginger tea and broth, and she's even been eating biscuits. But every time I leave the house, she takes a turn for the worse."

His chest tightened, but he tried not to show the tension. "You're good medicine. We all know that."

She slid him a look that she probably meant for a smile, but the light through the cabin doorway illuminated her worry lines. "We have to get her strength up. She's lost a great deal of weight."

If only he could better help them. Just now, all he could

do was reach up and place a hand on Lorelei's upper back. He rubbed a little to show his support, and the flash of a true smile lit her eyes.

Riley still watched them from the doorway, so Tanner gave her a gentle nudge. "Let's get inside. White Horse went out today and found some of the root he's seen his mother use for women in the family way. Maybe it will help."

As he followed Lorelei into the cabin, the wash of light made him blink at first. But the glow held a warm coziness as his eyes adjusted. Miss Juniper sat on a mattress near the back wall, propped against pillows. She gave him a weary smile. "Tanner. Do come in. We've been enjoying the delicious food you sent."

He nodded, his gaze sliding over to her husband, who'd moved to stand like a guard beside her mattress. "All I sent were supplies, so if anything was tasty, you've yourselves to thank." Probably Lorelei, for she could make any dish remarkable.

"We love having johnnycakes again." Miss Faith piped up from over near the hearth. "Lorelei made them tonight. Do you want a plate?"

He eyed the stack on the platter in her hand. "I can't stay long." He had to force the words through the hungry rumble in his belly.

She turned to plop some onto waiting plates. "Take some with you then."

Lorelei moved toward the fire with the pouch of roots he'd brought and began chipping bits into a kettle. "June, White Horse sent a root he found that Steps Right uses for expectant women."

From her seat in the corner, Rosemary looked up. She'd

been working on a leather halter, but now she looked from Lorelei to him. "Has he seen his mother?" The sharpness with which she regarded him made him want to step back.

He shook his head. "He's gone out several times searching for the root ever since he got back from your trip. He only found one plant, but he said he'll be looking for more." He nodded to Juniper. "Hopefully it will help you feel better."

She gave another weak smile. "Please give him my thanks." She hadn't lifted her head from the pillow since he entered. Her face held some color, but he could understand why Lorelei was worried.

"Have you heard anything more that might tell us where Steps Right is?" Rosemary no longer studied him as though seeking out his innermost secrets, but she still watched with a keen eye as she waited for his response.

Tanner shook his head. "Nothing."

She dropped her gaze back to her work, and her voice lowered, almost as though she was speaking to herself. "I've half a mind to go back to that mountain. We had to have missed something."

"I know what you mean." Lorelei frowned at her older sister as she stirred the liquid in the kettle. "But we were thorough in our search."

Rosemary didn't answer, but as she focused on buckling the leather, the furrow in her brow showed her thoughts probably hadn't left the subject.

Faith carried plates to Riley and Lorelei, then to Rosemary, receiving murmurs of thanks from them all. Then she approached Tanner with a dish holding two johnnycakes.

He didn't want to overstay his welcome, and he'd left White Horse to guard the fort alone. "I'll just take these with me. Thank you." He lifted the food from the plate. "I'd best head back now."

Rosemary set aside her halter and rose to her feet. "Take this to White Horse." She reached behind a stack of blankets and pulled out a small satchel, then used long strides to bring it to him. "We made cinnamon crisps the other day. They're his favorite." She didn't meet his gaze as she handed the pack over, as though it mattered little.

But he didn't miss the way Lorelei watched her sister, brows raised in curiosity.

He couldn't deny a bit of interest in its contents himself, but Rosemary didn't offer an explanation, so he didn't ask for one.

Besides, Lorelei was walking toward him, stealing all his focus. She gave him a shy smile. "I'll walk you out."

He forced himself to glance around the room. "Good night, all."

He nodded to accept their farewells and didn't miss the knowing grins from Faith and Juniper. Lorelei must have spoken of him to her sisters, especially if she was bold enough to escort him outside.

She motioned for him to precede her, then she closed the cabin door behind them.

The calmness of the night settled over him as they strolled to his horse. One of the animals from the corral nickered softly, and Lorelei sighed. "I love peaceful nights like this, when the animals are content and all is calm."

Peaceful, yes, but with Lorelei so close to him, his body felt nothing like calm. Were they at a point where he could reach for her hand? She had her fingers clasped in front of her, so that might be awkward.

They arrived at his gelding, and he stroked the animal's neck. Lorelei moved to the horse's head, letting him sniff her hands. Domino knew her and lifted his head in pleasure as she scratched his jaw and the flat part between his eyes. "You're a good fella, aren't you?" As she cooed the words, the horse's eyes drooped shut.

Tanner could watch her magic way with animals for hours, but this would be his only moment alone with her. If she didn't return to the house soon, one of the others would likely come to add a chaperone.

He secured the pouch for White Horse and laid the johnnycakes atop a saddle pack, then turned to Lorelei, doing his best to keep his tone light. "You're making me jealous of my horse." He nearly winced at the words. That came out far less chivalrous than it had sounded in his mind.

She gave the animal a final pat, then turned to Tanner with that shy smile she'd worn before. He reached for her hand and tugged her closer.

She came to him and rested her hands on his chest. Did she feel the thunder of his heart?

He placed his hands at her waist, holding her far more loosely than he would have liked. A part of him—a large part—wanted to take her mouth with his now. But the way the moonlight shimmered on her face as she looked up at him . . . Her beauty made it hard for him to breathe.

He needed to tell her what she did to him. But would she think he only appreciated this lovely outer packaging? "You're so beautiful . . . it hurts. But not just the outside of you." He dipped his forehead to rest on hers and secured his hold at her waist. "Though every part of that is remarkably lovely. Even if you hadn't captured me with your looks, your heart and your goodness would have caught my attention anywhere."

Should he say the other that still weighed on him? "I know I'm not good enough for you, but I'm now hoping you won't realize it." But that was selfish. He should be encouraging her to use wisdom.

He drew his head back a little. "If you do decide I'm right, though, all you have to—"

She rose up on her toes and pressed her mouth to his, halting his words in a blessed mercy.

TWENTY-FIVE

Tanner relished the taste of Lorelei, the way she gave of herself and seemed to expect nothing in return.

But of course he gave. He would put his very soul into the kiss if he didn't know exactly where that would lead.

As it was, he forced the connection to stay gentle, then ended it far before he wanted to. Though his gelding concealed much of them from view of those in the house, he didn't want her family to worry.

He pulled back enough that he could see her face. The moonlight shimmered off her cheeks, making them appear porcelain. Her eyes were too shadowed to see their emotion, but her lips were red and a little swollen from his own. He'd been gentle, hadn't he?

Her hands had moved up to his shoulders, and they now gripped him as though she didn't plan to let him leave. That would be fine with him, if only he wasn't needed at the fort. Her family might have something to say about it if he stayed much longer. Between Rosemary's assessing gaze and Riley's wary look, they intended to protect their little sister.

He softened his hold on her sides. He would protect her too—from himself or anyone else.

"Tanner." Her voice came out a little hoarse, and she cleared her throat. Her thumb reached up to stroke the edge of his jaw, sending a tremble through him. He should have taken time to shave away the stubble before coming over.

She opened her mouth to speak again, and he forced himself to look in her eyes, not down to her lips. "I realized something. But before I tell you, I need you to promise you'll stop saying you're not good enough."

He wanted to respond, to tell her he was only speaking the truth. But she touched a finger to his lips, halting his speech before he could begin. She was right. It was her turn to say what lay on her heart. He pressed a kiss to her finger.

She moved her hands back to his shoulders. "God hasn't rejected you. You are good enough exactly the way He made you. Better than good enough—you're perfect. Exactly the way He wants you." The corners of her lips twitched. "The man I see, the man I've come to know, is strong and good and wise. And so much more. I can't even list all the things I love about you."

His heart stalled on that word. Why would she use it so lightly?

Her mouth curved as she must have seen his reaction. "That's what I realized these past days I've been home. Perhaps it's too soon to say such, but you've secured my heart, and I think the Lord wanted me to tell you."

His mind struggled to keep up with her words, to make sense of them, even as part of him wanted to lift her high and swing her around as he hooted.

She *loved* him? How could she say that?

He opened his mouth to tell her she shouldn't, but again she touched his lips with her finger.

"Think before you speak. In fact, don't answer at all. You've no need to respond if you don't feel the same."

How could he not feel the same? She was . . . perfect. For him, anyway, and every man who met her seemed to agree, even before they got to know her beautiful heart.

But he couldn't let the two of them move so fast. She needed more time to see all the things she'd clearly missed.

He raised a hand to grasp hers, pulling her finger away from his lips as he wrapped her hand in his. "I won't answer yet, except to tell you I'm honored." He couldn't say more, but he didn't want her to feel bad.

A kiss might help with that, so he pressed his lips to her knuckles, then lowered his mouth to hers. She responded timidly at first, as though she wasn't sure of his reaction.

But soon she came alive as usual, and within a few seconds, he'd fully accomplished the distraction.

He left her with one final brush of his lips, then pulled back, taking both her hands in his. "I need to get to the trading post, but I'll see you tomorrow. If you aren't able to ride over, I'll come to you."

She nodded, and he pulled away, moving to mount his gelding. Before he turned the horse, he drank in the sight of her once more.

He had much to think about before he saw her again.

He did love her. Tanner hadn't allowed that idea to form before she said it, even in his mind. Yet all through the night and this morning, the thoughts pounded him. Now, he was standing in the open rear doorway of the trade room, staring out at the mule that grazed contentedly with Curly.

Lorelei would love this scene.

And that thought once again brought him to the ideas swirling in his mind.

"God hasn't rejected you. You are good enough exactly the way He made you. Better than good enough—you're perfect. Exactly the way He wants you."

He'd gotten so distracted with the word *love*, he'd not fully captured the first part, and he let it settle deep within him.

God had rarely been a thought for him before meeting Lorelei. Sure, people spoke of the Deity sometimes—one of his university professors, another of the clerks at the mercantile, and a few parents of his school chums. And yes, there had been a number of churches marking street corners in Boston.

But attending services was simply an activity the elite did to be seen. Even his father had done so on Easter and Christmas. But God had not held a place in their lives. His father had never spoken of the Almighty, except during an occasional bout of anger.

But Lorelei was different. She spoke of God as though she knew Him. As though she had actual conversations with Him, like the prophets of old.

Had God really told her He thought Tanner was good enough? Certainly not. That idea was preposterous. The thought that God would waste half a second on Tanner, when Tanner had never done the same for Him . . .

He lifted his eyes to the wide blue expanse above. A few small clouds decorated the sky, but for the most part the blue spread as far as he could see. Was God up there, peering through those clouds, watching him?

How did Lorelei speak with Him? Out loud?

He moistened his lips. "Are you up there? Can you hear me?"

No audible voice responded, though had he really expected a boom from the heavens? A bird twittered outside the fort walls, and Curly snorted as he nibbled grass. He'd begun doing that since watching the mule graze. Having an older animal to teach him would be good for the little fellow.

Tanner raised his gaze heavenward again. "I don't know if the things Lorelei said are true, if you care anything about me at all. But if you do, could you show me a sign or somehow let me know it?"

Why was he even asking this? He'd done well enough on his own without involving God in his life. Why did he feel the need to seek out the Almighty now? To raise questions that might very well bring disappointment if Lorelei wasn't right.

If Tanner hadn't been good enough for his own father to choose him, there was no way he could please the God who reigned over the entire earth.

The sound of horses in front of the trade room pulled him from his thoughts, and he stepped back into the building. White Horse had gone out to find more of the root to help Juniper, so Tanner had to be more on his guard than usual.

Having White Horse here was like a breath of fresh air, a friend who possessed an uncanny ability to be in the right place at the right time. If someone came to peer at Curly through the fort walls, White Horse sensed it and would leave the trade room to stand guard near the calf. Or if

Tanner was in the midst of a trade with one of the Native men, White Horse would step inside just as Tanner's frustration with his limited language skills began to grow. The man's quiet presence always made things better.

The rare times he wasn't here, Tanner couldn't help but be on edge.

The front door opened, but no one appeared. He moved to his position by the trade counter and waited. Perhaps the fellow had started to come in but went back to secure his horse better or retrieve something he'd meant to bring.

Usually Tanner could see the animals tied to the hitching post through the front door, but the newcomer must be allowing his mount to graze instead of fastening him to the rail.

He cocked his head. He couldn't even hear the sound of horses anymore. Had the customer decided to ride on?

Tanner strode to the open door and looked outside. No one.

Had the door blown open on its own? Sometimes the latch failed to catch on the first try, so that could be possible. But what of the noises he'd heard? The jingle of metal and even what sounded like a soft nicker. Had that been a trick of the wind?

He stepped outside and scanned the area more fully. The Sioux village stretched out in the valley to the left, and all seemed quiet there. A few children played on the larger boulders while women scraped hides nearby. None of their sounds reached him.

A glance at the passes to the left and the right showed the trail empty, and far too many tracks layered the ground in front of the fort for him to pick out any that had just come near. He'd had a number of customers throughout the day.

A glimmer of movement caught his attention, and he spun toward the pass leading to the Collins ranch. The motion wasn't at the pass. Something shifted just beyond the corner of the fort wall.

Tanner strode that way as apprehension knotted his belly. He should have grabbed the rifle from behind the trade counter. He had his knife, but his aim wasn't nearly as good with that weapon as with a gun. Maybe he should investigate from within the fort walls. That way he could keep an eye on Curly and the mule.

But he would just sneak around the corner and see who had come. It might be Lorelei, and then he would have no need for weapons.

The thought loosened some of the tension. He hadn't really expected her to come today, not as weak as her sister had looked last night. Perhaps the root White Horse sent hadn't helped a great deal.

He reached the corner and eased his head out just enough to see. Two horses stood near the gate. No riders.

He studied the animals. Neither looked like the mares Lorelei or Rosemary usually rode, but sometimes they came on young mounts from the ranch that needed exercise. Since there were two, her sister must have come with her. Probably thinking he and Lorelei shouldn't be allowed much time alone. And rightly so.

The visitors had already entered the gate, so he strode quickly to catch up with them. If by chance this wasn't Lorelei and her sister, he needed to get inside there and clear out whoever it was.

His empty hands clenched into fists. He should have gone back for the rifle. Better to be prepared for every possibility.

He had another rifle in the cabin that would be closer to grab now, but he would have to go inside the fort walls to get to it. That fusee wasn't his faithful Hawken, but it would get the job done if he had to fire a warning shot.

As he neared the open gate, the knot in his belly tightened. Lorelei would not have left the gate unlatched so Curly or the mule could escape. And she usually removed her horse's bridle so it could graze instead of leaving the animal to stand. Perhaps she only planned to stay a few minutes. She might have only come to lay eyes on the wounded animals and see if anything different should be done with them.

At the opening, he eased around the frame far enough to see.

Two men stood in the courtyard, their arms around Curly, trying to lift him onto a horse.

Panic swept through Tanner. "Hey!" He pushed off the gate post and sprinted toward them.

One of the men spun toward Tanner, and recognition dawned. Anderson, one of Purcey's men. The skinny one. The fellow he'd shot in the leg.

Clearly the man had recovered.

Anger surged through him. Would these scoundrels not leave him alone? They must have realized how valuable Curly was and taken their sights off stealing the rifles.

As he covered the ground between them, the men scrambled to heave the calf up onto the saddle. Amidst Curly's bawls and kicking hooves, the horse sidestepped.

As he reached the horse, he stretched up to grab the calf's back legs. Something slammed into his side, knocking his feet out from under him and toppling him onto one of the men. Quigley, the bald man, grabbed his legs, locking them in a tight hold.

Tanner's hands were free, though, and he turned to slam his right hook into the man's temple, a place that should knock him senseless. His fist collided with flesh-covered bone, sending a shot of pain through his hand and wrist.

The grip around his lower half loosened, and Tanner scrambled to crawl away. The other man had climbed aboard the horse behind Curly, and they were galloping through the gate.

He stumbled to his feet and sprinted after them, but by the time he reached the opening, the man, horse, and buffalo calf were galloping westward—the same direction they'd gone the last time.

He had to go after them. The man here might regain consciousness any minute, and for that matter, Purcey, the leader, was probably searching for the rifles.

But he couldn't worry about those. He had to get Curly back.

Spinning, he covered the two strides to the horses and grabbed the reins of a bay. The animal stood quiet while he swung up into the saddle.

He dug his heels into the animal's sides, and the horse lurched forward. Tanner was a decent horseman, though not as skilled as Lorelei. He'd never leapt on a strange mount and kicked for all he was worth.

The horse tottered forward at first, and Tanner gave another hard nudge. The bay finally broke into a trot, and with more encouragement, he pushed into a lope. Perhaps Tanner had chosen the wrong mount, but he was on his way now.

Anderson and the calf had a strong head start on him. The pair was just disappearing into the trees in the distance. Tanner kicked his horse harder and managed to work him into a full canter.

He had to catch up with the man. This buffalo calf meant the world to Lorelei, and to a great many other people too. He couldn't let it remain in the hands of men so unscrupulous. Who knew what they would try to do for money or power? They could have entire Native villages groveling at their feet in exchange for the calf. One wrong step and Purcey could start a battle with the Natives that would shed far too much innocent blood.

He couldn't let them get away with Curly. If only he'd thought to stop for his rifle.

TWENTY-SIX

Why hadn't she gone to the fort?

Lorelei stared out into the darkness between the slats of their cabin wall, straining for any sign of movement. Any sign that Tanner had come.

Juniper had grown so much better this afternoon, even rising from bed and going out for a stroll with Riley. Lorelei had almost saddled her mare and headed over to the trading post then and there. But by the time she'd determined it was safe to leave Juniper, dusk had settled. She expected Tanner any minute.

But he hadn't come.

Why didn't he come? Maybe something had happened with Curly. Or perhaps customers stayed late and he decided to wait till morning.

Her heart knew neither of those was the reason. It had been too soon to tell him her feelings. She'd thought so, but in that moment, she'd felt so strongly the Lord's pressing in her spirit, she'd said the words.

But maybe it hadn't been God's leading. Perhaps only an effect of moonlight and emotion.

Now she'd scared him away.

She would go to the fort first thing in the morning. At daylight, so she could catch him before the trade room grew busy.

But that meant she'd have to endure a sleepless night of this panic welling in her chest. And Tanner would have more time to think without her correcting her error. Had she ruined things between them?

She couldn't let this linger. She had to fix it now.

She spun to face the others, and three pairs of eyes lifted to her. Juniper had already fallen asleep, her face peaceful, with a bit of color returned to it.

Lorelei focused on Rosie. "I need to go to the trading post tonight. Tanner hasn't come here, which means something is wrong. I have to go help. One of the animals might need me."

Rosie released a long sigh and looked down at the buckskin strips she'd been braiding into a rope. With another sound that came out like a harrumph, she pushed the leather out of her lap and stood in a smooth motion. "I guess I'll go with you."

No surprise she'd be coming along.

Rosemary brushed the tiny pieces from her hands as she looked from Riley to Faith. "Hopefully we'll be back in an hour or two."

Faith jumped to her feet. "I want to go too. I'm tired of being left behind."

Lorelei scanned the interior of the cabin while Rosie argued with Faith. She'd take her rifle of course. They never left without a gun. Anything else? Nothing that she could think of. She simply needed to see Tanner and talk with him.

Faith was still pleading to accompany them as Lorelei slipped outside. Hopefully Rosie would be right behind her.

They traveled quickly through the mountain passes with Rosie in the lead. She and her horse had maneuvered this ground so many times, nighttime probably mattered little to them.

When they finally reached the open ground where the trading post stood like a silent shadow in the darkness, she scanned each of the buildings for light from a cookfire or lantern.

The entire place was dark.

A frisson of worry snaked through her. Could something else be wrong? Maybe her words weren't the only thing that had kept Tanner from coming tonight.

She nudged her mare into a trot to cover the last of the distance to the fort. As she reined in, she called out into the smothering silence. "Tanner? White Horse?"

No one answered as she dismounted, and the worry twisted into something more. "Curly? Frisco?"

Not a single sound drifted from the place.

Then the low sad moo of the milk cow rose from behind the fort. She eased out a breath. Elsa was here. But where were the others?

"Something's not right." Rosie's voice hummed low with tension as she dismounted. "Let me go in first."

The knot in her chest tightened as she slipped from her own horse. *Lord, where did they go?* Maybe Tanner had left a note.

Lorelei strode toward the gate. Part of her wanted to call out again, but the weight of the silence nearly pressed out her breath.

As she reached for the latch, Rosie caught up with her and grabbed her arm. "I said let me go in first."

Lorelei shook away her grip and pulled the gate open. Rosie could be far too protective at times. And in this moment, they needed to focus on finding any clue about where the men had gone.

Rosie entered the gateway at her side, and as they paused to take in their bearings, the stillness inside seemed to close around her.

Lorelei gripped her sister's wrist. "Tanner?" Her voice sounded small amidst the darkness.

"White Horse!" Rosie's tone held more gumption.

But still no one answered.

They needed a lantern to check each of the buildings. Perhaps the men were sleeping, but that didn't explain where the animals were.

She started toward the cabin. "I'm going to find a lantern. We should see if their horses are out back. I heard the milk cow. Maybe Curly and Frisco are with the horses." Tanner wouldn't allow them outside the fort walls, especially not at night. But it was the only option she could think of that didn't mean something bad had happened here.

Rosie followed her to the cabin door. "I'll help you search the buildings before we look for the animals."

As she reached for the latch on the cabin door, a thought made her pause. If Tanner was asleep inside, she should knock first.

She pounded on the door with her knuckles. "Tanner? Are you in there?" They didn't have time to waste, so she didn't wait long for him to answer. At least he'd been warned.

When she pushed open the door, the darkness was even

thicker in there. No light glowed from coals in the hearth. He must not have lit the fire all day.

She reached for the lantern from the hook and started toward the hearth where they kept the flint and steel. "It doesn't look like there's any live embers left. It'll take me a minute to light this."

Rosie turned out of the open doorway. "I'll go check the other buildings while you do that. There should be enough light from the moon to at least see if things are amiss."

Panic shot through Lorelei, and she spun away from the hearth. "No! Can you wait just a minute? We need this light to see by." The thought of Rosie walking into the murky darkness of the storeroom nearly cut off her breath. What if someone was in there?

But Rosie didn't stop striding, just called over her shoulder. "I can see good enough with the door open. I only want an idea of whether the place has been rifled through."

Lorelei set the lantern down and lifted her skirts as she ran after her sister. She couldn't explain this panic, other than she had to be there to see what might have happened. She'd much rather see it with the warm glow of a lantern, but she wouldn't be the last to know.

She caught up to Rosemary as her sister pulled the latch-string on the storage room door. Rosie pushed the wood open, and the leather hinge rustled. The moonlight lit a triangle on the dirt floor inside, but everything beyond was a black cavern.

Rosie, in her typical fearless fashion, stepped forward, planting a foot into the unknown. "If I can get my eyes to adjust to the—" She loosed a bloodcurdling scream and jumped backward, slamming into the door as the wood bumped against the wall behind her.

Lorelei yelped and reached for her sister, though most of her wanted to turn and sprint far and fast from whatever was in that building. But she couldn't leave Rosie to its clutches.

Rosemary stumbled from the room and grabbed Lorelei's hand. Lorelei tugged her away from the place. Now they could run.

Rosie pulled like an anchor, though, forcing Lorelei to stop as she released her and turned to face the open doorway. "Who's in there? Show yourself." She raised her gun and aimed, the light click of the set trigger whispering in the quiet.

A shuffle sounded from inside, and a new knot of fear gripped Lorelei's throat. There really was someone in there.

She edged backward. "Rosie, let's—"

Before she could pull them both farther away from the door, the shadows shifted, and a figure stepped out.

A scream rose in her throat and would have plunged out if she could have breathed.

"Stop." The familiar voice registered even before the figure, whose features were distorted in the shadows of the pale moonlight.

"White Horse?" Rosie voiced the name before Lorelei could fully comprehend that this was their friend.

He raised a hand and stepped forward. "Do not shoot." He reached for the gun Rosie still aimed at him. Apparently, she wasn't fully in control of her faculties either.

Rosie lowered the gun and eyed him. Lorelei turned her focus to the man too.

This really was White Horse, though his hair was more disheveled than he usually allowed it. He looked a little . . . sleepy?

Of course Rosie took charge of the situation. "What's happened here? Why didn't you come out when we called?" Lorelei couldn't help adding her own questions. "Where's Tanner? And the animals?"

White Horse reached up and touched the back of his head, and a flash of confusion crossed his features. Had they thrown too many questions at him? And was that pain forming wrinkles at the corners of his eyes?

Lorelei took a step forward. "Are you hurt?"

He dropped his hand and straightened, his expression donning the strong warrior look he usually showed to strangers. He was hiding something.

She moved to his side and touched his arm, looking behind him at the back of his head. His hair rose in a bump near his crown, and realization made her gasp. "Were you hit with something?" She peered at his face and waited for his answer. They would be going nowhere until he told them what happened.

He started to nod but stopped with a flinch. "I think. Yes." His eyes drew into a squint as he stared into the distance. "I go find more root for Juniper. When I return, Tanner not here. I search. Go there." He pointed into the storage room. "Hit on head." He reached up to touch the lump on his crown again. "Nothing more."

Rosie had moved closer, her voice dropping its hard edge. "Someone was here? Someone hit you?"

"Yes. Hide there." He pointed to the building again.

"Do you think that same person took Tanner and Curly

and Frisco?" Lorelei asked. This was far worse than she'd let herself imagine.

"Not know." White Horse seemed to be taking care not to move his head.

She glanced around the courtyard. "The trade room is the only place we haven't looked yet, but I think we need to search everything better." She turned a glare to Rosemary. "I'm going to light the lantern. Don't move from this spot until I come back with it. We're not doing another thing without proper light."

Rosie nodded, and Lorelei lifted her skirts to hurry back into the cabin. Where could Tanner be? Had the men knocked him out as well? Was he lying in the trade room unconscious . . . or worse?

Her hands trembled as she stepped into the cabin and gathered the lantern and flint case to take them back out into the moonlight. Every second might matter for Tanner's life.

She sat on the stoop and pulled out the flint and steel to begin striking sparks into the tinder. The faster she hurried, the more her fingers fumbled.

By the time Rosie came over to help, she had only managed one spark.

"Let me help." Rosie crouched beside her and reached for the flint and steel, but Lorelei pulled it back.

"I can do it." She had to be stronger. She had to steady her nerves. For Tanner.

After two more tries, she lit a spark strong enough to make the tinder smoke. Rosie blew to form a tiny flame, then Lorelei opened the lantern door, and they lit the wick. She eased out a breath as Rosie snuffed out the tinder and put away the tools.

She carried the lantern toward the trade room, Rosie and her rifle on one side and White Horse and his tomahawk on the other. He owned a rifle too, but he must not have had it handy now.

When they reached the door, she gripped the latchstring before the others could.

What time I am afraid, I will trust in thee. Her mind whispered the verse on a silent prayer. *Help us find Tanner.*

As she pushed the door open, the lantern's light flooded the interior, casting shadows that made her mind slow to form the image of what she saw.

The place had been ransacked.

TWENTY-SEVEN

L orelei's gut coiled as she stared at the trade room. Furs and blankets lay twisted in heaps around the space. As she lifted the lantern, hundreds of tiny crystals glittered back at her. The bead necklaces had been tossed everywhere. Or perhaps they'd been ripped apart and the individual beads spilled among the mess of everything else.

She swung her gaze into the corners, searching for a form that might be hiding amidst the chaos. "Tanner?"

White Horse stepped farther in, and she forced herself to follow right behind him, moving the lantern so its light would help him see too.

Though her mind expected to find Tanner in every dark corner she lit, he wasn't there. The three of them moved around the room, stepping over the piled goods.

White Horse went to the front door and opened it, walking outside to look in all directions. He returned a moment later, drawing the latchstring as he pulled the door tight and set the bar across to secure it.

She looked from him to Rosie. "We should search the

storage room and the cabin better. But what if he's not here?"

Rosie started toward the back door. "We'll answer that question if we have to."

She had to hurry to catch up with her sister's long stride, and as they reached the open door of the storage room, she held the lantern out for them to see inside. As before, White Horse entered first, but this time Rosie followed on his heels.

A strange dread pressed on Lorelei's chest, and under her own strength, she might not have followed them inside. But once more, a verse slipped through her spirit. *Not by might, nor by power, but by my spirit, saith the Lord of hosts.*

Go ahead of us, Father. She took a step in, then another. This room looked mostly undisturbed, except for one crate that had fallen over on its side.

She pointed to it. "Is that what hit you?"

He hesitated, studying the box. "I do not know." His voice sounded almost as though he was disappointed with himself.

Or maybe he thought *they* were.

But then he moved to the scant stack of crates that still lined one wall. "Rifles gone."

The words sank like a stone in her belly, and she focused on the patch of barren dirt. She and White Horse had laid the crate of rifles in that very place after they unloaded them from the mule. She hadn't been in here since.

She turned to search the room. "Maybe Tanner moved them. Would he have taken the box to the trade room so he could access it better?"

Or had this entire awful event been carried out by Purcey

and his cronies, the ones who'd come to steal the rifles before? Now that she thought about it, the situation did sound like something they would do. Ransacking the trade room and carrying off Curly, the rifles, and even the mule that had been theirs to start with.

"I don't think so, Lor. We can . . ."

Her thoughts drowned out the rest of Rosie's response as certainty crept through her. Either those men had injured Tanner and taken him captive along with the calf and mule, or somehow they'd stolen the animals and rifles, and Tanner went after them. Either way, Tanner needed help.

She turned and marched outside toward the cabin.

"What are you doing?" Rosie strode after her. "Lorelei. Answer me."

Her sister's sharp bark was one Lorelei would never have ignored before, but she didn't turn around this time, just called over her shoulder, "I'm getting food and supplies from the cabin. Tanner's gone after those men, and he needs help."

"Do those tracks look fresh enough?" Lorelei motioned to a set of hoofprints pressed into the ground on the other side of White Horse. They'd been searching from the moment the sun rose enough for them to see.

They should have found the tracks last night and be caught up with Tanner now. But White Horse and Rosie had both insisted they would never find the prints in the dark, not among so many others on this well-traveled path away from the trading post.

The two were probably right, for they'd been searching at

least an hour so far, leading their horses behind them, and still hadn't found tracks recent enough to be from Tanner or Purcey's crew.

Nor had they found tiny buffalo prints. Had Curly been carried on one of the horses? That seemed most likely, though he was nearly a size that would be too large to hoist.

White Horse bent over the tracks and studied them but then shook his head as he straightened and moved forward. He must've located another likely possibility, for he paused to study a new spot.

She held her breath as she waited, scanning the area around him. So many horses had traveled the stretch coming to and from the trading post. How could they know exactly which ones belonged to Tanner's mount and the men who'd ransacked the fort and stolen the animals?

Rosie was tracking on White Horse's other side and had moved ahead a little. She bent over the ground, then crouched even lower. Had she found a likely suspect?

Lorelei needed to focus on her own section of trail. Just as she turned to the ground ahead of her, Rosie's voice sounded. "Look at these."

The words were clearly intended for White Horse, so Lorelei kept her place as the brave moved forward. They would let her know if they found tracks promising enough to follow.

She scanned the rock-and-grass-strewn path ahead, searching for any sign of a recent horse print or the more oval shape the mule might have left behind. White Horse had said to search for deeper indentations, especially deep at the toe, which would mean the tracks were both recent and made from horses on the run.

"This might be them."

She jerked up at Rosie's call. Her sister waved her forward.

Lorelei's heart surged as she tugged her mare into a faster walk behind her. *Lord, let these be the right ones.*

The tracks Rosemary had found ran slightly off the main path and fit both qualities White Horse had said to watch for. It seemed several horses and one mule had ridden through here.

White Horse moved quickly as he followed them, his long strides covering ground. Rosie stayed just behind him with little effort, her own quick steps almost a match to his.

Maybe it was Lorelei's skirts that slowed her down. She'd not had her trousers at the fort to change into for this search and hadn't thought to have Rosie bring them when she went home in the night to let the others know what they were doing. But she should be able to manage anything in skirts the others could in trousers or leggings.

Perhaps she should mount now, for she certainly wasn't adding to the hunt by keeping on foot. If anything, she slowed them down.

Just as she made up her mind to do so, White Horse turned and motioned to the horses. "Ride now."

Once in their saddles, they moved faster. A faster walk, anyway.

White Horse seemed certain of the path, so she focused her attention on the terrain around them. They would need to be able to return the same route—with Tanner and the calf and the rifles, Lord willing. And maybe even the mule, if they could manage it, though its ownership was questionable at this point.

At first, they took the same route they'd traveled when the three of them went in search of the cave Adams told them about. But after riding about an hour, their path shifted farther north. Still westward bound, but at least one, maybe two mountains over from the valley with the tiny stream.

The sun had burned away the morning mist and dried the dew from the grass, though much of the mountain slope they traveled now was littered with small rocks, and the horses even trekked across solid stone at times. How White Horse could continue tracking in this terrain showed the depth of his skill.

She reached for the leather pouch containing her drinking water and lifted it for a sip—not too much, for she could already feel the call of nature pressing in her middle. Surely White Horse would pause to let the horses rest. They'd brought enough food for two days, but it was mostly smoked meat and a few biscuits that could be eaten while they rode.

But as they descended the slope and began to travel up and around the next mountain, White Horse never stopped them, only pushed harder.

The pressure within her pressed stronger too. Maybe she shouldn't have taken so many sips of water, but the sun and her worries had made her mouth impossibly dry.

This section of the mountain had no trees to hide behind, and all the rocks came up no higher than her ankles. But she could go no farther without a private moment.

"Rosie." She tried to keep her voice quiet enough to reach only her sister, but both turned to look at her, though neither slowed their horses.

She motioned vaguely to the area around them. "I need to stop and, um, answer nature's call. You two keep riding and I'll catch up."

Rosie glanced at White Horse then back to Lorelei, her expression uncertain. "Are you sure? We can wait."

Lorelei shook her head. The last thing she wanted was White Horse there as she took care of private matters.

Rosie seemed to understand, for she faced forward and nudged her horse as she waved White Horse onward. "Catch up with us as soon as you can."

Lorelei halted her mare and dismounted, her inner need growing stronger by the second as she waited for the two to ride out of sight around the curve of the mountain.

When at last she was alone, it didn't take long to take care of concerns. She breathed a long sigh of relief as she moved back to her horse and patted the mare's shoulder. "How are you, girl? I'll bet you'd like some water too." They hadn't crossed a creek yet that morning, but they'd find one soon. Small rivers and streams ran in nearly every valley among these mountains.

After remounting, she straightened her skirts and started in the direction Rosie and White Horse had gone. She'd likely see them as soon as she rounded the bend in the slope.

She pushed her mare into the fastest trot they could manage over the uneven, rocky terrain, but as they moved around the mountainside, the sight before her was *not* her sister and White Horse. A forest of low pines covered the bottom of this incline and a good way up the next, concealing her companions. She could have just waited until this section to take care of her personal need. But at least now she felt better.

Except for the pressing worry about Tanner and the calf. How much faster were the thieves traveling than she, Rosie, and White Horse? Did they have Tanner as a hostage, or was he following the bandits too? White Horse hadn't been certain from the tracks.

When she reached the edge of the tree line, the rocky ground turned to needle-covered soil. The path Rosie and White Horse took was easy enough to find, and even a novice tracker like her could tell these prints were very recent. She could call out for her sister, but better to follow their trail and keep quiet. If the thieves were nearby, the last thing she wanted was to alert them of their presence.

The tracks wound through the pines, moving down the mountain, then tracking along the base of the next. At times, the prints of the two animals split apart as they maneuvered the trees, but they always came back together. One horse seemed to take more steps than the other, for there were more hoof tracks on that one's path when the two separated. Perhaps that was White Horse's stallion? His slightly shorter height might mean he had to move his legs more often to account for the speed White Horse pushed him to.

As much as she could, she kept her mare at a trot unless she lost sight of the tracks. Shouldn't she have caught up with them by now? Maybe she should call out to make sure she was on the right path.

She had to be. Even the pine needles the horses kicked up still showed wet on their undersides. These tracks had been made that morning. They had to be from Rosie's and White Horse's mounts.

She must have ridden a quarter hour now, and she'd been

moving at a good clip for most of it. Her sister and White Horse wouldn't have sped up while they waited for her to catch them.

The weight in her chest pressed harder. Something else must be wrong.

She reined her mare down to a walk and raised her hands to cup around her mouth as she called out.

But before she could make a sound, another noise drifted to her.

A man's voice.

TWENTY-EIGHT

L orelei strained to hear better. Was that White Horse speaking? The voice definitely belonged to a man, but the tones were far harsher than he normally used. Unless they'd found Purcey and his crew.

Lord, let it be. That might account for why Rosie and White Horse would have hurried ahead. If they'd spotted the men, they wouldn't have let the chance slip away.

She eased back on the reins to slow her mare's walk as she strained to see through the trees ahead. The voice had stopped.

Should she halt and leave her horse here, then proceed on foot? She might not be close enough to do that yet. She should have her rifle at the ready, though.

She pulled the weapon from its scabbard and settled it across her legs, checking again that the gun was loaded. She would need to pull the rear set trigger before she could fire, but she didn't dare risk an accidental gunshot by doing that part now.

The voice sounded again, louder now, and she halted her mare to see if she could make out words. That definitely wasn't White Horse's clipped accent, but the only thing she could make out clearly was *shut* and *ride*. The tone sounded harsh. Was that Purcey yelling at one of his men? Or maybe at Tanner?

An image flashed through her mind of Tanner sitting at the base of a tree, his hands and feet tied, and a rag binding his mouth. Had they hurt him? Her mind added blood dripping down his face, his head lolled to the side, and an eye swollen shut, bruised an ugly black.

Oh, Tanner. Hold on. We're coming.

She nudged her mare faster, straining for any sight or sound of the strangers. Daylight appeared between the trunks ahead. Was she nearing the edge of the woods?

This would be the right time to leave her horse here. The men talking might be just beyond these trees.

Taking care with her rifle, she slid to the ground and tied her horse, then started forward as soundlessly as she could manage. The more light that filtered between the trunks, the more she tried to hide herself from one step to the next. Was someone else tucked behind one of these trees watching her?

The thought sent a shiver down her spine, and she paused to do a thorough sweep around her, searching for any movement in the shadows.

Nothing. She couldn't let unfounded fear slow her down.

Ahead, the man spoke again, and she froze to listen. "That's enough. Now tie that thing tighter, and let's get a move on. We wasted too much time here."

The voice didn't sound familiar at all, nor did it sound amiable. Through the trunks ahead, a blur of movement flashed.

Horses. And they were leaving.

Should she run back and get her own mount to catch up with them, or hurry forward and see who it was? The latter, and there was no time to waste.

Clutching her rifle in both hands, she sprinted forward, dodging the trees in her path. At the edge of the woods, she slowed enough to focus on the three horses trotting away.

Behind the saddle of the one on the left, a white-tan mound was tied on, a head lolling from one side. Her heart clenched.

Curly. Was he alive?

She scrambled to make out the forms of the three men. Neither the one carrying Curly, nor the burly fellow riding in front looked familiar. But the figure riding the mount just behind him struck a chord of panic in her chest.

Tanner.

He was slumped over—from pain, maybe. Or perhaps he was tied to the front of the saddle. His horse rode close enough to the one in front, the animals might be tethered together.

She started to turn for her mare. Should she call for Rosie and White Horse? Who knew where they were at this point. There might be Purcey's other lackey or the Indian woman around too. She didn't want to alert them to her presence until she had to.

But the chance to save Tanner and Curly was slipping away. They'd already ridden half the distance a rifle shot would carry. She'd only have time to fire once. Was there a way to use one bullet to save both Tanner and the calf?

No. Several strides separated the two kidnappers. She would have to choose whether to save Tanner or Curly.

It was no choice. She would save Tanner if it took her last breath.

She raised the rifle and focused down the barrel. Should she aim for the big man or his horse? Shooting the animal might stop him for a minute, but he could easily cut Tanner's horse free, then climb aboard and ride away while she reloaded.

Or worse yet, he could turn his gun on Tanner.

She inhaled a calming breath. She had to stop the man. And now. Before he moved out of range.

She steadied her hands and focused her aim, pulled back the rear set trigger, then breathed a prayer. *Lord, save Tanner.*

She fingered the front trigger, sighted once more . . . and fired.

Tanner worked the rope against the exposed wood of the saddle, back and forth. He might be cutting only one fiber with every scrape, but this was the only way he would get loose.

After he freed his hands, he'd have to figure out how to cut the bonds at his feet. Purcey had tied them underneath the horse's belly. Heaven forbid the horse tear off in a bucking spree. That would likely be the end of Tanner.

But perhaps that would be a swifter way to die than whatever Purcey planned. In the man's fury when Tanner found the group holed away in a ravine with the calf and rifles, Purcey had nearly choked him to death as they wrestled. His greater brawn had gained the upper hand, especially when Anderson and Quigley stepped in with their rifles.

Rifles they'd stolen from Tanner's store.

He'd spent much of the night awake and working at his bonds, but the smooth surface of the tree he was tied to hadn't broken through the rope much.

The saddle felt like it was making better progress, though still so slow. How far would Purcey take—

An explosion ripped through the air. Tanner ducked low. One of the other men screamed, and Purcey leaned sideways in his saddle. No, not leaning. The man toppled headfirst down the side of his mount, landing facedown on the ground with a thud.

Tanner's pulse pounded in his chest as he jerked his head to see where the shot had come from.

Had White Horse found their tracks and followed him here? That had felt impossible with all the other prints marring the ground leading away from the trading post, but perhaps he'd underestimated the brave's skills.

Or maybe Quigley had turned on his boss and shot him in the back while he had a chance. Neither he nor Anderson seemed to like their leader, even though they fought for him and followed his orders readily. There must be quite a stake in it for them.

For half a heartbeat, the figure standing at the edge of the trees looked like a woman in a burgundy dress. A woman who looked so much like Lorelei, he couldn't breathe.

But then she disappeared. The vision must have been his eyes seeing what his heart wanted.

The horse beneath him jerked forward, spinning Tanner's focus back to his mount. The mare he was tethered to had no rider, and Purcey lay moaning on the ground.

Anderson looked over at them, his eyes almost wild as he stared from his boss to Tanner, then down to the two horses who could take off running at any minute. If they did, Tanner would have no way of stopping them. Anderson would probably grab up Purcey's reins, and Tanner would still be under their control.

The skinny man looked behind him, to the woods they'd camped beside last night. Curly let out a tiny pitiful bleat through the rope they'd tied around his muzzle to keep him quiet.

The sound seemed to make a decision for Anderson, for he sent a final determined look toward Purcey, then plunged his heels into his horse's side. The mount leapt forward, and the fact that the calf didn't fly off its back with the sudden motion showed just how well they'd tied him on.

Anderson kicked the horse into a canter down the slope, and realization finally swept through Tanner's exhausted mind. He was leaving with Curly. After all this work to find the calf, the animal was being carried off again.

Panic welled in his throat, and he turned back to see if the person who'd shot Purcey had showed himself yet. If it was White Horse, he would've come by now.

No movement showed near the trees.

Wait. Was that—?

A horse charged from the shadows, the rider's burgundy dress flowing out behind the pair.

Lorelei.

Warmth swept through Tanner. How had she gotten here? She must've come with White Horse. It shouldn't surprise him that she would come after the calf.

A glance ahead at Anderson showed the man and calf were still in sight. If Lorelei kept up her galloping pace, she would reach them.

But she couldn't follow him by herself. Where was White Horse? He scanned the trees again, searching for any sign of another person.

The approach of Lorelei's horse made his own mount skitter sideways, bumping once more into the horse they were tethered to. Thankfully, that animal stood squarely beside Purcey's body.

The man still moaned. Could he sit up and take a shot at Lorelei as she approached? How could he protect her with his hands tied? Helplessness nearly choked him.

Lorelei reined her horse to a walk just before she reached him, and he turned back to face her. Maybe she had a knife she could use to cut Tanner's ties. He could secure Purcey, then go after Curly once more.

"Tanner! Are you hurt?" Her eyes scanned the length of him, then focused on his face.

Those beautiful eyes made his heart swell even now. He had to get her to safety.

He shifted so she could see the ropes at his wrists. "I'm not hurt, but do you have a knife?"

She nudged her mount forward as she reached to unfasten her saddlebag. Her gaze slid over the two horses, then she must have caught sight of Purcey on the ground. Her eyes widened, and her hand flew to cover her mouth.

He had to keep her attention on getting him free. They had no time to lose. But he kept his voice gentle as he repeated, "The knife?"

She jerked her attention back to him, then scrambled to open her pack. A few seconds later, she pulled out a hunting blade and moved her horse closer to his as she reached out to cut his ropes.

He used the opportunity to ask questions. "Did White Horse come with you? Who shot Purcey?"

Her brow furrowed as she sawed at the multiple layers of cord. "Rosie and White Horse came, but I don't know where they are. We were separated." She looked back at the man on the ground, who'd fallen silent. "I shot him." Her voice dropped a bit with those last words, but she returned her focus to the rope.

His heart plummeted as he stared at her. She'd been the one to aim her rifle at a man and pull the trigger? He knew well how that act could wrench a person's gut, no matter how necessary. She must be desperate to get the calf back. Why had she aimed at Purcey instead of Anderson, who had the calf? Maybe she didn't want to risk hitting Curly with a bullet.

The knife finally sliced through the last strand of rope, and he jerked his hands free as the coil fell away. "Let me cut my feet loose too." He reached for the blade.

Instead of handing it over, she slid to the ground and bent to cut the rope under the horse's belly. "Are you hurt anywhere? What did they do to you?"

"I'm fine. I'll take Purcey's gun and horse and go after Anderson. He has Curly."

"I know. We can go together. Maybe Rosie and White Horse heard the shot and will come this way to help." She cut through the rope, and the pressure on his ankles gave way.

Pain shot up both legs, and a prickling sensation began in his calves, moving downward. He might not be able to walk, but he had to try.

Lorelei straightened and looked up at him as she rested

her hand on his lower leg. "Can you feel your feet? I suspect they're numb. Should I rub them to bring the feeling back?"

How could she even suggest that? He had to go after Curly before it was too late. He shook his head and leaned forward to lift his right leg over the saddle and dismount. "I need to get down so I can ride that other mare to catch Anderson."

"Tanner. If you're hurting . . ." Her voice came out with a tinge of frustration, but she stepped back to allow him room.

He gripped the saddle with both hands as he lowered himself to the ground. Knives shot through his legs, and he had to clench his jaw to keep from groaning at the thousand beestings burning his feet. But he forced himself to release the saddle and take a step toward Purcey.

That foot would barely hold his weight, but he made the other leg move anyway.

"Tanner." Lorelei's hand settled on his shoulder with enough pressure to slow him down. "Stop and let yourself recover. I don't even know all you've been through. We can wait a few minutes to see if Rosie and White Horse come, then we'll go after Curly. Together we'll catch him, I pray. But *you* are more important."

The earnestness in her voice drew him, made him really listen to her words.

He was more important? More important than getting Curly back? That couldn't be what she meant.

He studied her face. The sincerity from her tone furrowed her brow and shone in her eyes. His heart squeezed. He loved this woman more than he could put into words.

Which meant he had to return her precious calf to her. "I have to go now. I'll bring Curly back to you."

She shook her head, almost glaring. "Did you hear me, Tanner? I said you're more important to me than Curly is."

Maybe she did understand what she was saying. But could she mean that?

She moved directly in front of him, then reached up and took his face in her hands so he could only look directly at her. "I had the choice back there to save you or Curly. And I chose *you*. I would choose you every time. Over an injured animal or another person or anything, save God Himself." She slowed her words, letting each one penetrate his heart like an arrow. "*I choose you.*"

Warm peace like he'd never felt crept over him, and emotion clogged his throat, rising up to burn his eyes. She meant those words. *God, is this what happiness feels like?*

His entire life had been bringing him to this point. Could it even have been a journey orchestrated by God? Lorelei's choice wouldn't mean nearly so much without the host of disappointments that had come before. He might not even appreciate her—much less *love* her the way he did now—without knowing how the loss of love could slay him. *Thank you, Lord.*

He reached up and cupped his hands around her jaw, sliding his fingers into her hair. Then he lowered his forehead to hers. "You are the best gift God's ever given me." His voice rusted with the emotion thick within him.

Lorelei's smile shone even through her glassy eyes.

He wanted to say more, so much more. But the thunder

of hoofbeats sounded behind him. They would have to finish this conversation later.

He spun around, keeping himself between Lorelei and the oncoming riders, just in case. But the sight of White Horse and Rosemary had never been so welcome.

They reined in hard by Lorelei's horse, and both took in Purcey's body with grim expressions. Then Rosemary looked to her sister. "Lor, are you hurt?" She seemed to just then realize Tanner was there too. "Either of you?"

He almost smiled. Rosemary would always be a protective older sister, no doubt about that. And she'd done well getting Lorelei to this point. He aimed to do his part from here on out.

"I'm not hurt. I don't think Tanner is, at least not that he's said." Lorelei looked to him.

He shook his head, then pointed the direction Anderson had gone. "There's another man, Anderson, who has the calf tied on his horse. There might be two others in the area still, a man named Quigley and an Indian woman. They left camp this morning, but I couldn't hear where they were going."

White Horse motioned the direction they'd come from. "We find them. Tie to trees."

Lorelei spoke up. "So that's where you went. I was following your tracks, I thought, but they brought me to Tanner and these two men."

Rosemary's horse began to shift impatiently, probably feeling the anxious energy of its rider. "We'll go after the one with the calf."

Tanner tensed. "I'd like to go also. Let me make sure Purcey isn't going anywhere."

"I'm coming too." Lorelei's voice rang strong with determination.

It would be hard to make her stay here. But she'd proven herself brave and capable, and she'd definitely earned the right to see this adventure through.

TWENTY-NINE

Anderson had a good start on them, but White Horse's tracking skills allowed them to move quickly. Rosemary rode at his side, with Lorelei and Tanner just behind.

Lorelei eyed the terrain around them. "It looks like we're headed back toward the trading post, doesn't it?"

Tanner's gaze did the same sweep hers had. "I was thinking that too."

"Where do you think he's headed?" Rosie raised a hand to shield her eyes from the burning midday sun.

Tanner squinted, but it was hard to tell if from the sun or from his line of thought. "This is one of the routes back east. He must have something in mind to do with the calf."

Poor Curly. Her heart ached for the sweet boy who'd been such a good friend these past weeks. He must be frightened and miserable, tied on the back of the horse. Had they at least let him stretch his legs and drink water in the night? Tanner hadn't said, and she hadn't gathered the nerve to ask him.

She'd been hoping they would catch Anderson right away,

but at least an hour had stretched on, then longer. Her belly tightened with every half hour since then. Before long, they would be back at the trading post.

During one of the stretches where White Horse slowed them to a walk as he searched for tracks, she glanced from Rosie to Tanner. "What about the other man and woman who are tied back there? And the . . . other one." She still couldn't bring herself to say *the body*.

By the time Tanner had approached Purcey to tie him up, he'd passed. She'd killed a man, and the single glance she'd caught of his motionless form made her want to cast up her accounts even now. At least he'd been facedown. Seeing his lifeless eyes might have been more than she could bear.

She let her gaze settle on Tanner. It had been to save his life. She would get the full story later, but as they were remounting back there, he'd said they hadn't planned for him to come out of this alive.

Purcey would have to answer to God for his choices. She'd done what she had to, and the Father had given her strength.

Rosie shot a look over her shoulder. "They're secure. We'll go back for them and bury Purcey once we find this last one." Then her expression softened as she looked at Lorelei. "I'm not turning you loose again."

Warmth eased through her. She'd proven she could manage just fine, but Rosie's protectiveness came from love. And having so many people around who loved her was a gift from God.

They continued on. And on. The land around looked far too familiar.

She called up to White Horse. "Can you tell how far ahead

he is?" Could they possibly be gaining on the man? Surely not, since he would be able to travel at a faster clip than them, as they searched for tracks. The only way they could catch him would be when he stopped to rest. And that could be hours. Maybe even tonight.

At last, the trading post appeared in the distance.

Her chest tightened, though part of her was a little relieved. This would be a chance to restock supplies. But they couldn't stop for long.

As her mind wandered through what they might need to grab at the fort, her heart hitched. They hadn't told Tanner about the trade room being ransacked. Maybe he'd already seen it. But if this was news, it would be a blow.

She slid a glance at him. "Tanner, when we searched the fort looking for you, we found the trade room in a bit of . . . disarray."

He raised his brows. "Could you tell what was taken?"

She nibbled her lower lip. "Things were strewn everywhere. I think some of the bead necklaces were broken. It's quite a mess."

He nodded and turned forward, as though he'd expected as much. Nothing about his demeanor showed distress, or even anger.

"Have you seen it already?"

He leaned forward to help his horse maneuver up the incline. "No, but I figured they'd take as much as they wanted, or at least as much as they could carry. Getting Curly back was more important to me." He sent her a look soft enough to warm her through. He'd left his entire livelihood behind to be stolen or destroyed to go after what he knew she valued.

She waited till they reached a more level stretch of ground, then nudged her mare close to his mount. She reached out and grasped his hand. "You're a good man, Tanner Mason, but you don't always have to sacrifice yourself to make me happy."

Before he could respond, a sound drifted over the distance. Quiet and familiar but . . . different. She looked toward the fort, straining to hear.

"Is that . . . ?" Tanner's words drifted away as certainty pressed through her.

She plunged her heels into her mare's sides and charged toward the fort. Was it possible Anderson had come back here for refuge? Maybe he wanted to steal more from the trade room.

The others had pushed their horses into a run as well, gathering in a pack around her. She had them for safety, along with her rifle.

But Rosie raised her hand and called out, "Slow down. We need to plan our approach." She motioned for Lorelei to rein in.

Aargh. She could see the wisdom in slowing, but though the cry sounded weak and hoarse, that had definitely been Curly. She could feel it with every bit of her insides.

And he needed her.

She reined her horse to a walk along with the others, but slowing her thoughts proved much harder. At least Curly was alive, though he might be in dire straits. Perhaps dehydrated and starved, and he might have sustained injuries from flopping around on the horse's back for hours.

But the urgency that overshadowed every notion pressed harder. "We can't let them get away again."

Tanner kept his voice low. "Anderson might be holed up

in the fort, rifle trained on us. We have to be careful with our approach. I'll go first. The rest of you stay here and wait. I'll try to get him to fire his rifle, then close in before he can reload. He only had one gun, as far as I could tell." He moved his horse around Rosie and nudged the gelding faster.

Her heart surged up to her throat. "Tanner, no. It's too dangerous."

He turned back to her with a look both gentle and determined. "I'll follow the tree cover as far as I can. Pray God protects me."

Though her chest ached, she nodded. She'd never heard Tanner speak of God, and she needed this reminder. *Lord, hide him under the shadow of your wings.*

As Tanner turned his horse toward the trees that spanned half the distance to the fort, she did her best to watch both him and the walls ahead. No sign of motion flashed among the logs. *Lord, protect him.* She sent up a steady litany of prayers.

The trees grew sporadically, so they didn't fully conceal Tanner, but at least they would make him harder to aim at. Especially since he kept his mount to a faster trot.

But no blast of gunfire sounded.

Tanner reached the end of the tree line and halted. The knot in her throat made it impossible to swallow. He studied the fort for a long moment, then glanced back at them. Should she tell him not to go any farther? *Lord, give him wisdom.*

Tanner turned back to the fort, and a second later, his horse leapt from the brush and charged the log walls at a gallop. Such a quick-moving target would be hard to hit.

But still, no gunfire sounded. Was the man lying in wait until Tanner entered the gate?

She kept her gaze fixed on Tanner, but from the corner

of her eye, she caught White Horse nudging his stallion toward the same tree cover Tanner had used.

She had to go with him. When Tanner needed reinforcements, she intended to be there for him.

Pushing her horse forward, she followed White Horse's path.

"Lorelei." Rosie hissed at her, but she ignored the call. Seconds later, the rustle of Rosie's horse trotting through grass sounded behind her.

Tanner had reached the fort walls and jumped from his horse's back, pressing himself close to the gate. He seemed to be pausing, but she couldn't be sure from this distance and with her horse moving.

White Horse left the last of the trees and kicked his horse into a run. She reached the same spot seconds later and bent low over her mare, urging the horse with body and voice. "Come on, girl."

The horse responded, stretching her legs into a near gallop, covering the ground as the landscape on either side blurred. At this speed, she couldn't tell if Tanner had entered the fort yet or not. *Protect him, Lord. Guide him to the calf and shield him from Anderson's bullets.*

As she neared the fort, she sat up and reined her mare down to a lope, then a trot. The horse's sides heaved as she walked the last few strides and halted beside White Horse's and Tanner's mounts. Neither man was here, so they must have entered the fort already.

She grabbed her rifle from the scabbard and jumped to the ground as Rosie halted beside her.

"Wait for me." Rosie leapt to the ground, her own rifle in hand, and together they approached the gate.

No sounds came from inside. Was that good? Tanner and White Horse must not have found Anderson yet.

But not even Curly cried out anymore. Her chest pressed harder. Had the physical and mental deprivations been too much for him? Or had they left this place already once they heard them coming? Her poor boy. *Protect him, Lord. All of them.*

Rosie reached the gate first, and as her sister pulled the wood open, Lorelei peered inside.

At first, nothing moved within. But then Tanner stepped from the door to the trade room. His face held grim lines, and he caught sight of her almost immediately and started her way.

She stepped inside the walls, with Rosie coming just behind. As soon as Tanner reached close enough to hear, she whispered, "Have you found anything?"

He shook his head and stopped in front of them, as though to shield them. His body was even half turned away as he spoke, his gaze roaming the area. "Nothing in the trade room. White Horse is looking in the supply building. I'm going to the cabin now."

He started that direction, and she followed him. If there was danger, they would face it together. But would Anderson really hole up in there? It didn't seem likely, but perhaps he'd wanted a place to sleep for the night. Evening would be on them soon.

But where were his horse and Curly? Maybe tied behind the fort with the milk cow.

As they reached the cabin door, White Horse stepped from the supply building and strode toward them. He shook his head to show he'd found nothing.

Only the cabin remained.

Tanner pulled the latchstring, and the click of the bolt releasing sounded from inside. She and Rosie aimed their guns, as did White Horse behind them. Tanner readied his own rifle, then pushed the door open. Woe to the scoundrel at the other end of all these weapons.

The cabin's dim interior sat motionless, and the earthy smell of disuse lingered in the air. It had only been that morning since she'd left the place, but it felt like weeks. There was almost nowhere the man could be hiding inside, except perhaps crouched behind the barrel they used as a seat or tucked behind the door.

Tanner stepped inside and checked behind the door first, then made a sweep of the room. His face formed troubled lines as he approached them. "I guess he's not here." He looked to White Horse. "Let's see if we can find his tracks outside. Maybe he left the main trail long enough for us to pick out his prints."

Her belly sank at the thought of starting over. The man had been here less than a quarter hour before. She'd heard Curly, but he must have been riding away even then. Now they'd lose any distance they'd gained on him as they tried to find his trail again.

The sound of Elsa's low moo drifted from behind the fort. Lorelei had to keep busy, and since she wouldn't be any help with the tracking . . . "While you guys look for his tracks, I'm going to milk Elsa. It might be tomorrow before we return, and she can't wait that long. I'll hurry, but if you pick up his trail, start after him and I'll catch up."

"Oh no. I'm not leaving you to do that again." Rosie grabbed the pail from the wall and started out the door.

"You're likely to take the wrong trail and end up in front of the man. I'll help milk while the men search, then we'll catch up with them together."

If Lorelei wasn't already fighting the burn of disappointment, she might've smiled at that. She followed her sister into the courtyard, then out the gate and toward the back corner where she'd staked the milk cow that morning.

As they rounded the corner, a weak bawling made her stop short. Elsa stood over a mound on the ground. A white, hair-covered mound that lifted its head and released another pitiful sound.

A sob slipped from Lorelei's throat, and she surged forward.

Curly seemed to sense her presence, though she approached from behind him, for he let out another cry, this one stronger.

"My boy." She dropped to her knees at his side and ran a hand down his neck and along his ribs. Her fingers wove through the coarse hair. Warmth pressed into her palm, and the rise of his breathing lifted her hand. "Thank you, Father." Her voice broke as tears leaked down her cheeks. God had brought him home, alive and wonderfully whole.

Curly cried again, the sound distorted through the cord binding his mouth. The effort shook his body. She had to get the ropes off his muzzle and legs.

Tanner appeared beside her, crouching at Curly's head. "I'll cut these off." He used his hunting knife to loosen the knot under the calf's jaw.

As soon as the binding fell away, Curly lifted his head again and released a full-blown bawl. The sound nearly burst her ears, but her heart was too full to care.

"My precious boy." She ran her hands over his muzzle, clearing away the marks left by the cord. The threads had created an open sore on one corner of his nose, but that was the only injury she could see. A week of salve would heal that wound completely.

Tanner moved to cut the bindings from his legs, and within a heartbeat, all four hooves pulled free.

She ran her hands roughly over each limb, working the blood flow back into them. They would be numb and stinging as Tanner's had been. But Lord willing, the calf would scramble to his feet in a minute or two.

At last, Curly started to move his legs on his own. He sat up, tucking them under him.

She scooted back to stand, and Tanner gripped her elbows to help her rise. As they stood waiting, watching Curly gather his strength for the next effort, Tanner slipped both arms around her waist, clasping her in front of him.

She leaned back against him, relishing his strength. Relishing the connection stronger than she'd ever imagined. God had blessed her more than she could have hoped for with this man.

THIRTY

Curly lifted his head from the bucket of milk and bawled toward the gate leading outside the fort. Lorelei spun and faced that direction. He must have heard something important enough to distract him from his evening meal. The calf had certainly been uneasy in the day since they'd found him tied behind the fort. Though except for stronger-than-usual hunger and thirst, he didn't seem physically injured.

They might never know for sure why Anderson left him at the fort, though Tanner and Rosemary both figured the man simply wanted to escape and leave Purcey's sordid business behind. Regardless of his thinking, she'd thanked God a hundred times for bringing everyone through it safely—including Curly.

The sound of horses approaching drifted through the logs. She strode toward the gate, slipping her rifle strap over her head so she could aim the weapon if she needed to.

Rosie stepped from the cabin and fell into stride beside her, rifle already positioned against her shoulder.

"It might just be Tanner and White Horse." They'd hoped

to be back before dark, but they could have run into any manner of delay as they buried Purcey's body and brought Quigley and the woman back with them.

Rosie peered out first as she opened the gate. "It's them. Or . . . it's Tanner and that Quigley man. White Horse and the woman aren't with them." Her voice tensed with those last words.

Lorelei pushed the gate wider and poked her own head out. When Tanner saw her, his teeth flashed in a grin. "He's smiling. There must not be anything wrong."

Rosie made a sound that came out like a growl as Lorelei stepped out and started toward Tanner.

About thirty strides separated them, and Tanner pushed his horse into a trot. Since Quigley's animal was tethered to his gelding, the bald man bounced along behind him.

Tanner reined in as he reached her, then slid to the ground in a smooth motion. She couldn't help it, she flew into his arms.

He accepted her willingly, his strong grip closing her in, wrapping her in the security of his hold. He pressed a kiss to the top of her head. "I missed you."

She squeezed her eyes shut as she burrowed into his shirt. Her heart was too full to do much more. Though he'd only left early that morning, she'd missed him every moment since.

"Where's White Horse? And that woman?" Rosie's voice bit through the warmth hugging Lorelei. Was she worried the Indian woman might have overpowered White Horse?

But her tone didn't sound so much like worry as . . . Lorelei pulled back from Tanner's arms and turned to her sister. He kept one hand on the small of her back.

The dark lowering of Rosie's brows looked an awful lot

like anger covering jealousy. Perhaps Tanner had been right. Was there really an attachment growing between the two of them? As much as she loved White Horse, life married to a member of the Blackfoot tribe might be harder than Rosie realized.

"After we buried Purcey, White Horse took Singing Crow back to her village." Tanner's voice rumbled from behind her, and she turned a little so she could see him as he spoke. "She said Purcey had traded for her, and she always feared him. I think she wants to be done with white people and return to her family. Their camp is about half a day's ride to the north, from what we could tell, so we figured it'd be best to be done with that part."

He looked from Rosie to Lorelei. "I hope you both don't mind. I didn't think that maybe you'd want to question her. She was Flathead and didn't speak much sign, so even White Horse struggled to communicate with her."

Lorelei turned to Rosie to see her reaction and whether she would respond. She did look a bit relieved. Surely she hadn't thought White Horse ran off with the girl.

Rosie pointed to the man behind Tanner. "Did he have any idea where Anderson was headed?"

They all looked to Quigley.

The man's mouth pinched in a sullen look, as though he would refuse to answer. But he shook his head. "Don't have no notion."

Lorelei turned to Tanner. "What should we do with him?"

Tanner brushed his thumb across her back, then pulled away and moved around his horse to Quigley's side. "For now, he needs food and water. He hasn't answered my questions, so I'd like to hear his full story before we decide his fate." He cut a rope loose, then pulled the man down from his mount.

Rosie took charge of the horses and nodded for Lorelei to go with Tanner and Quigley. "Put together a meal for them both."

Lorelei lengthened her stride to enter the fort ahead of the men, then stepped into the cabin and moved to the fire to dish out bowls of the stew she'd kept heating in preparation for their return.

Both men scarfed down the food quickly, finishing just as Rosie came in from staking the horses.

Lorelei reached for Tanner's bowl. "Would you like more?"

He shook his head before tilting it toward Quigley. "Since this one's still not talking, I'll go to the trade room and try to get things cleaned up for business tomorrow."

"Rosie and I worked on that today. I think we put things back where they were before. We made an inventory list too, so you can know what might be missing."

He stilled, his focus moving from her to her sister and back. "You did all that? For me?"

The weight of his regard made heat rise up her neck. "Of course. You might want to rearrange things, though."

"Was anything broken or destroyed?" Tanner asked.

Lorelei shook her head. "We restrung the bead necklaces, and I think the condition of most is good enough to sell." She started toward the door. "I set aside two that are questionable. I can show you which ones."

Tanner looked at Rosie. "Do you mind keeping an eye on him?" He nodded to the man sitting on the floor, his hands and feet still bound. His wrists were tied in front of him so he could still use his hands to lift the bowl to his mouth. They would need to secure him to something sturdy for the night, but Tanner might have something else in mind for him.

Rosie motioned for them to go on. "I'd like a few minutes with this scoundrel."

Lorelei smiled as she reached for a lantern and stepped out the door. She might pity the man if he hadn't been a party to so much thievery and the cause of pain to those she loved.

Darkness had nearly fallen as they strode across the courtyard. This might be a romantic stroll if Tanner walked slower and maybe took her hand, but tension clogged the air between them. Was he worried about what he would find in his store?

Neither of them spoke, not even when he took the lantern from her as they entered the trade room. He stopped in the center of the floor and turned slowly, taking in the stacks of goods she and Rosie had placed on the shelves and empty crates.

His face didn't give any sign of his thoughts. Was he displeased with what they'd done? He'd seen the mess before he'd left, so she would expect him to be relieved. But maybe he felt they'd meddled.

She swallowed down her worries and moved to the counter. "Here's the list we made. The only things damaged were the necklaces. I think we set all to rights, except these two that are now shorter than the others. You can decide what you'd like to do with them." She was rambling, but she wasn't sure what else to do with his lack of reaction.

Tanner strode to her and fingered the two necklaces. He

still didn't speak, not until he lifted his gaze to her face. His eyes turned earnest, softening as they searched her own. "How long did it take you to do all this?"

She couldn't quite hold the intensity in his gaze, so she dropped her focus to the beads as she shrugged. "Rosie and I worked together, so about half the day." She'd also fed and watered Curly several times, but he had slept in his favorite sunny spot most of the day.

Tanner reached to cover her hand with his own, his fingers slipping around hers, drawing her attention back up to his face. "Thank you. This was a great deal of work. I can't remember the last time someone went to such lengths to help me."

An ache pressed in her chest. Did he still think so little of his worth? What could she say or do to convince him?

He lifted her hand to his mouth and kissed the backs of her fingers, then pressed her palm to his chest, holding it there. He seemed to be searching for words, so she waited for him to speak. "You make me believe what you said the other night is true."

Her breath caught.

He kept going. "That I'm good enough for God the way I am. He and I have been talking more about it. Or rather, I talk and He presses a thought in my spirit. Or something happens to show He heard me, like you coming to save me or cleaning and inventorying my trade store." His brow lowered a little as his tone turned serious. "I want to know Him the way you do. I hope this is a start."

The joy overflowing in her chest spread through her entire body. This was far better than words of love. *Lord, I guess you knew what you were doing that night.*

Her cheeks hurt from grinning. "It's a wonderful start. And God speaks so often through His word. Do you have a Bible?"

"I don't. Perhaps when I come see you at the ranch, we can read it together."

The burn of happy tears sprang to her eyes. "I would love that more than you know."

His expression softened. "Speaking of love, there's something else from that conversation I wanted to revisit." His lips curved in a smile. "I didn't tell you then that I loved you because I was afraid. I told myself I didn't want to rush you, but really, I was afraid to let you know how much I'd already fallen for you." He gathered both her hands at his chest. "How much I love you."

So much emotion clogged her insides, she couldn't manage a word. *Dear Lord. This is too much.*

But Tanner seemed to understand, for he pulled her closer, wrapping her in his arms in a hug she never wanted to leave.

THIRTY-ONE

W e'd just as soon bed down under the stars, Miz Juniper."

Tanner leaned against the cabin wall at the Collins ranch as he watched Dragoon and Ol' Henry say good night to the group.

Dragoon gave Juniper a respectful grin. "The nights are so pleasant these days. Come the next few weeks, we'll be sweating no matter where we sleep."

Tanner hadn't experienced a summer in this territory yet, but the days were already hot enough to make a person perspire.

"If you're certain." Juniper offered a soft smile. "But take some of these sweet biscuits out with you in case you get hungry in the night."

Dragoon's grin turned boyish. "Not sure I can say no to that, ma'am."

Ol' Henry tipped his hat as the younger man took the bundle Lorelei offered him. "You folks have made this a right nice visit. We'll be in to say our farewells afore we head to the rendezvous come morning."

"Make sure you do that." Rosie nodded from her usual place in the corner.

Lorelei patted Dragoon's shoulder as she walked by the man to take up the lantern hanging near the door. "I'll walk you both out. There's a mare I need to check on in the barn."

Tanner straightened. As much as he hated to leave this place that felt more like a home than his childhood residence, he needed to get back to the fort. And this would be his best opportunity for a few minutes alone with Lorelei before doing that.

After he and the two trappers said their good nights to the sisters and Riley, he followed Lorelei, Ol' Henry, and Dragoon out the cabin door.

Outside, Ol' Henry turned to him. "It's been right nice comin' to know you, young feller." He held out a hand, and as Tanner extended his arm and shook, the acceptance in the man's act swept through him. Even these two trappers treated him as an equal. As a friend. They seemed to be almost family with the Collins sisters, and now they were including him in the group.

"Thank you." It was all he could manage as Ol' Henry released his hand.

"If 'n there's anything you think of you need from the rendezvous, just send word over in the morning. Now that they have you here, I don't think Riley or them gals are comin' to the meetup. Especially not with Juniper's condition. But we're awful glad to trade for whatever you might need." His teeth flashed. "'Course, I reckon you've got your own suppliers."

Tanner raised his brows. "I don't expect Wally to come more than two months still, but I doubt I'll have many goods left to trade for by then. Might be I get a few days off."

Ol' Henry's chuckle rose into the night, pulling a smile from all of them.

He then turned to Lorelei but pointed to Tanner. "You let this young fella help protect you gals, you hear?"

She started to speak, but Ol' Henry raised his hand. "I know you sisters are as capable as any women I've known, but this here Tanner, I get the feelin' he's a good fella." The man dropped his voice conspiratorially with the last words, as though speaking just to Lorelei.

The sunray smile that spread across her beautiful features would never cease to warm his heart. Especially when she said, "You're right. He's the very best." Then she turned that grin up to him, and he wanted to wrap her in his arms then and there.

Ol' Henry stepped back. "Alrighty, then. You folks have a good night."

As the men shuffled off to the place they'd already set up camp for the night, Tanner turned to Lorelei and raised his brows. "Shall we go check on the mama-to-be?"

She slipped her hand around his arm as they walked, leaning into him. The warmth of her body stirred his senses to life. "She started leaking milk this morning, so I think the foal could come anytime. I'm considering sleeping in the barn tonight so I'll be near in case she needs me."

He glanced down at her, doing his best not to think of all the ways she would be unprotected here. Not to mention how much less comfortable the barn would be than her mattress in the cozy cabin. But he couldn't let himself linger long over an image of Lorelei sleeping anywhere.

One day, she would be sleeping at his side, Lord willing. And that day couldn't come soon enough for him. Was it too soon to ask?

Over the week since they'd returned from their adventure, their lives had finally seemed to settle into a calmer rhythm. Lorelei continued to live at the ranch with her sisters, for though Juniper seemed to be feeling much better, she still needed Lorelei's excellent care. And as much as he wanted her by his side, he wasn't altogether certain she should return to the fort to stay now that they were courting in earnest. Not until he'd given her his name.

She already possessed his heart and knew it well, but he still made sure to tell her every time she came over to check on the calf and the other animals. That was almost every day, and when she didn't make it to the fort, he always closed the store early to come share the evening meal with her and her family. Getting to know Ol' Henry and Dragoon these last two days had been an extra treat, but Lorelei's presence was the real prize.

They stepped into the barn, and she lifted the lantern higher as she moved toward the second stall. He followed as quietly as he could manage, but his heavier tread still drew the attention of the mare inside the enclosure.

She perked her ears, nostrils flaring and wide sides heaving.

"Hello, girl. It's all right. We've come to help." Lorelei's gentle murmur seemed to soothe the horse as much as it did him.

The mare dropped her head and turned in the stall, spinning in a circle and then digging at the ground. She did seem a nervous sort. Lorelei had said some of the horses in their herd were well trained, while others barely allowed a halter.

But when Lorelei turned a wide smile to him and motioned him forward, he obeyed, coming to stand beside her. She leaned close to whisper in his ear, "It's her time. Her labor has started."

The mixture of excitement and fear that stabbed him might have been stronger emotions than the situation warranted. This was a horse, not a woman. Nor was he in charge of the birthing. The horse could likely do the whole thing on her own, but Lorelei would be able to step in if needed. Since her healing touch was second only to the Almighty's, all Tanner had to do was assist if she needed an extra set of hands.

That he could handle. And hopefully he'd be performing that role for the rest of their lives.

They stayed quiet as the mare continued her pacing, sometimes coming to the front corner of the stall to stare out toward the open barn door, then turning back to the interior and spinning circles before weaving along the back wall.

"She's trying to get away from the pain." Lorelei's voice held its own hint of ache, her tender heart so empathetic.

He slipped his hand in hers. He couldn't comfort the mare, but he could be there for his lady.

She squeezed his hand as they watched in silence.

Her explanation of the mare's actions made sense, and through this better understanding, watching the horse made his own insides hurt. Then the mare lay down. This must be it.

But a moment later, the mare struggled to her feet, her overlarge belly swinging with the effort.

"What's happening? Is it here?" A quiet voice behind nearly made him jump.

They both looked back as Rosemary approached. She must've worried about Lorelei since they'd been out here so long. But she didn't send Tanner a glare as she came to stand on Lorelei's other side.

Lorelei spoke in an excited whisper. "Not yet, but her labor started. I believe the sac broke before we arrived."

Rosemary took a moment to watch the mare. "You have towels ready, and the grease?"

"Everything's here."

Silence fell over them again as the mare lay down once more, this time stretching out on her side with a heave. Poor girl. His belly clenched at the obvious pain. How did females endure such?

The next few minutes brought more of the same restless movements, rising and lying down again. Finally, the horse stretched out flat on her side once more, her legs stiff and feet facing them.

Lorelei gripped his hand tighter and leaned forward as she peered into the stall. "There's the bubble. The feet are coming out!" Despite the excitement, she kept her voice to a whisper.

He craned to see where she was looking, then a flash of white beneath the black tail caught his focus. It did look a bit like a bubble. But where were the feet she mentioned?

The white spot grew larger, longer. Then a tear in it revealed a bit of dark wetness. Was that . . . a tiny nose?

Lorelei's grip shifted on his hand, tightening, and he squeezed back. Was she worried? Was anything going amiss? His own heart felt like it had climbed into his throat.

The mare rose to a more upright position, curving her legs under her. She shook her head, then turned and nipped at her belly. He could only imagine how twisted her insides must feel. *Lord, couldn't you make an easier way for new life to be born?*

A minute later, the horse stretched flat on her side again, legs stiff. He tensed as he waited for what would come next.

The break in the white bubble had widened to reveal two glossy black legs and the bottom part of an equally dark muzzle. As the mare grunted and strained, the rest of the head eased out.

The shiny white covering still protected the eyes and ears from sight, and the effort seemed to exhaust the new mother, for her legs relaxed and she stayed in that stretched-out position, her breath coming in heaves. If just getting the head out had been so hard, how much worse would the rest of the body be? Would she have strength for it all?

He glanced at Lorelei to gauge whether he could ask the question. They'd all been silent as the mare worked, and perhaps he should hold his tongue. Lorelei was so focused on the sight in front of them, she didn't notice he watched her. And what a sight she made, with joy illuminating her entire face. The wonder of this new life being born was remarkable, but seeing her complete pleasure in the sight was even better. Oh, he loved this woman.

He forced his focus back into the stall, though he stroked the back of her hand with his thumb.

The pain seemed to grow even worse for the poor mother, for she grunted and strained, her damp coat rippling across her belly as she worked. With a gush, nearly half of the foal's body rushed out all at once, leaving only the hind legs within.

His own breath ceased with the speed of it. How had she managed so much in a single push?

Lorelei's quiet whisper came to him. "Getting those front shoulders out is the worst. She's almost done now."

The mare seemed to agree with her, for she pushed upright, then propped her front feet in front of her and struggled up to standing. Panic washed through Tanner, and he reached for the latch on the gate. The foal was still hanging out of her. If she dragged it, what damage would be done to the babe?

But Lorelei grabbed his arm, and he paused long enough to look inside again. The foal lay on the ground, fully out of its mother. The mare spun to sniff her new offspring. Maybe the effort to rise had helped the final part of the birthing.

The mare began licking her babe, clearing away the white film that still covered all four legs and the rump. The foal's ears flopped, one standing straight up and the other tilted sideways in the cutest pose.

"He's precious." Lorelei's voice finally rose above a whisper, and her tone held the wonder rising in his own chest.

He'd just witnessed a new life being born. Where minutes before there had been only one live creature, a second now lay here, weak and helpless, yet still very much alive, with its future spreading out before it.

The chaos of emotions sweeping through him made a knot clog his throat. One day would Lorelei be given the chance to bring new life into the world? The thought of her enduring that pain made his chest clench, but a life *they'd* started, a babe God blessed them with . . . What could be more wonderful than that?

He wanted so badly to wrap his arms around Lorelei, to hold her and savor this miracle together. But he wouldn't do that with her sister here.

As though she read his mind, Rosemary stepped back. "I'm going to tell the others. They'll want to come meet our newest addition."

As she left the barn, Tanner released Lorelei's hand and slid his arm around her waist. She moved in front of him, allowing him to wrap both arms around her. As she leaned back against him, he cradled her, holding her tight.

This woman. This gift. He would never tire of her look, her touch. And he would do whatever it took to fulfill the trust she placed in him.

For the rest of his life, if she'd have him.

Did he have to wait any longer to ask? He might burst if he didn't tell her everything right now.

He leaned down to speak into her ear, both so they didn't disturb the pair in front of them and because bearing his heart was something he intended only for her ears. "Lorelei, I have something to ask you."

She glanced up at him, but since they both faced forward, she probably couldn't see him well. Her body turned, and he loosened his hold enough for her to face him.

Those beautiful eyes gazed up at him, stirring his heart.

"I know we haven't been courting long, but I also know how much you've come to mean to me even in the short time I've known you. You're a remarkable woman, a delight to everyone who knows you. Your love is one of the greatest gifts I've ever received. There's no way I could keep from loving you in return. And if you'll have me, if you'll agree to become my wife, I can promise my heart and every other part of me will be yours for all of my days."

He couldn't breathe as he waited for her response. Had he said everything he'd wanted to? He should have rehearsed this better in his mind before asking this most important question. But in this moment . . .

Her eyes turned glassy, and her mouth spread in the most beautiful smile he'd ever seen. "Tanner."

But she didn't say anything more. Did she need time to think about it? This wasn't a decision to be rushed. Perhaps he shouldn't have hurried into the question, though he'd known he'd be asking it.

He kept one hand at her back and moved the other to lift his fingers up to her lips. "Don't answer now. Wait until you're certain. But know my heart and mind won't change. I'm yours, now and for always."

A laugh burst from her, then she sniffed as she shook her head, her smile growing even wider, if that were possible. "I know my answer. I was only trying to think of words as eloquent as yours to respond." She turned her hand in his to weave their fingers together, palm to palm. "Yes. Of course, yes. It would be my honor to marry you. You're the man God has planned for me; He's shown me that clearly. Not only that but you hold my heart too."

The relief that washed through him quickly shifted into joy so thick he could barely catch his breath. *Yes? Of course, yes?* How in the world could she be so certain of him? But he had promised God Himself and her that he would stop questioning his worth in her eyes or in the Lord's.

To seal the commitment they were making, he lowered

his mouth to hers and brushed her lips. Her sisters would come in at any moment, so he couldn't give her the kiss he longed for.

The sound of a throat clearing behind him brought his head up. Too late. They'd been caught after all.

Lorelei grinned up at him, her smile showing not a bit of embarrassment. Then she leaned around him and sent the same look to those entering the barn. "Juniper, Faith, Riley. Come in. Isn't it wonderful?"

For a heartbeat, he thought she spoke of their new understanding. His mind had barely caught up with the news himself, and a prickle of disappointment pressed at sharing their announcement so soon.

But she pointed into the stall and motioned for the others to come and look inside. "I think it's a little boy."

The foal. Yes, that made more sense.

He and Lorelei stepped back from the enclosure to allow the others to line the fence. That gave him the opportunity to slip his arm around Lorelei again. She snuggled into his side, clasping her hands around his waist.

With this woman at his side and the God he'd recently given his life to leading them on their journey, he couldn't wait to see what adventures they would discover along the way.

EPILOGUE

I'm sure it's somewhere through here." Tanner studied the rocky cliffside above them.

This looked exactly like the spot he'd seen as he rode tied behind Purcey's mount. If only he'd realized at the time the dark spot he saw on the slope above him was a cave, he and White Horse could have returned here when they'd come back to bury Purcey's body.

The lay of this land, the way a narrow stream ran through the valley below with the camping spot perched on its bank, the way mountain peaks rose on both sides—this could have been the place Adams described. The animal trail they were climbing now could be the one the man had spoken of. After all, this place was only one mountain range over from where they'd searched before.

"Is that it?" Rosemary pointed at a place above and to the right of them.

A bush grew on the slope. Not an uncommon sight at all.

But as Tanner studied the spot, the shadow behind it became clear. Rosemary was already clamoring up the incline at a run. White Horse likely could've passed her, but he stayed just behind, maybe in case she fell or perhaps letting her be the first to reach the place since she'd been the one to spot it.

"Come on." Lorelei started after her sister, and Tanner followed.

By the time they reached the bush, Rosemary and White Horse had already stepped into the opening of a low cave. His heart thudded as he and Lorelei peered in behind them. Had they finally found White Horse's mother?

Inside the cave was only blackness. Dark so thick he couldn't see how far back the cavern went.

"We need a light." Rosemary turned and scanned the landscape around them, as though a glowing lantern might be hanging from one of the shrubby trees or perched on a rock.

Tanner reached for the pocket sewn into his trousers. "I have a tinderbox." He dropped to his knees and pulled out the flint and steel, then prepared the tinder to catch the spark. "See if you can find a stick dry enough to light."

"This might work." Lorelei knelt beside him with a dead branch from the bush.

Within less than a minute, they had the tiny twigs on the branch lit. He eased up to his feet slowly so the wind didn't snuff out the fire. The small flames on Tanner's stick illuminated the darkness, revealing the cave wasn't much deeper than a small room and only as wide as the span of a man's arms.

And it was empty.

White Horse and Rosemary paced the length of the area, examining the floor and walls and even the ceiling.

Rosemary glanced from the crevice she was studying to

White Horse. "Someone stayed here, but can we tell for certain it was Steps Right?"

He squatted down beside the left wall and examined the floor. "She kept medicines here."

Rosemary moved to his side and stooped to scrutinize the spot. Tanner stepped closer to them to give them more light, and Lorelei wandered to the far end of the cave.

"How long do you think she's been gone from here?" Rosemary's question came quiet enough it was clearly directed to White Horse.

He rose and shook his head as he turned toward the ashes of her campfire. "I do not know."

"What is this?" Lorelei dropped to her haunches beside the fire ring. Without taking her eyes from the cluster of burned sticks, she waved them over. "Bring the light."

They gathered around as she lifted something from the ashes. Something that glittered against the dim light of the fading flames.

"Blue beads." The awe in Rosemary's voice was impossible to miss. Both women looked to White Horse, and the expression that passed between the three of them spoke of a certainty.

Then the last of Tanner's flames died, casting the cave into darkness again, save for the faint glow of the stick in his hand.

"Bring it outside." Rosemary's voice initiated a flurry of shuffling as they all moved to the cave entrance.

When they stepped into the daylight, Lorelei was at his side, one hand on his arm and the other holding a string of light blue beads.

The others gathered around her, and she handed the

discovery to White Horse. "They look just like the ones she gave our father."

White Horse let the string drape across both his hands as he nodded. "These are hers." He kept his gaze fixed on the crystals. A fine powder of soot still covered them, but a few shimmered in the sunlight.

Then he lifted his face, his gaze rising above their heads to the peaks on the other side of the valley. "She say treasure is found in ashes." His focus dropped to Rosemary, and the corners of his eyes crinkled. "She hide gifts there for me sometimes. Sometimes they point to others I must search for."

Rosemary regarded him. "Like clues for a treasure hunt?"

He nodded. "Yes, hunt." He studied the beads again, lines furrowing his brow.

The question in his mind was easy enough to guess, so Tanner spoke it aloud. "What clue does the necklace give? Where should we go from here?"

White Horse lifted his gaze to the mountains again. After an extended moment, he murmured, "I do not know."

"Should we start by searching this area more? The surrounding mountains?" Rosemary's voice offered a gentle prod.

White Horse blinked, then nodded.

Rosemary turned to Tanner and Lorelei. "Let's go back down to the horses. We can eat and make a plan."

As she and White Horse started down the animal trail to the valley where they'd left the animals to graze, Lorelei slipped her hand in his. "Do you have time to help search more, or do you need to get back to the fort? Will Riley be able to manage there without you?"

He met her gaze, sinking into those eyes he loved, running his thumb over the back of her hand. "I told him I'd be gone two days, so I can stay here until late tomorrow afternoon. There aren't many trade goods left in the store, so I told him he's free to lock up the fort and go check on your sisters at the ranch anytime he needs to."

Lorelei's sweet smile curved her mouth and lit her eyes, even brighter than the sun's rays shimmering down on them. As she leaned into him, he couldn't help slipping his free hand up to her jaw and lowering his mouth to hers. Just before he touched her lips, he said, "Have I told you lately how much I love you?"

"You should probably say it once more," she murmured.

A chuckle slipped out, and he let his kiss do the talking for him.

As he tasted her sweetness, White Horse's words from moments before slipped through his mind.

Treasure is found in ashes. There was a time in his life, he'd felt that everything good had been consumed by flames, leaving only the ashes of his hopes behind.

Yet he never would have met Lorelei Collins if he'd not endured that fire. The heat had sent him out of Boston and thousands of miles away to this mountain wilderness.

He'd found treasure here, for sure. Far greater than anything he'd dreamed of.

He'd been given the promise of love. The promise of a future he couldn't wait to begin.

Would you like to receive a

BONUS EPILOGUE

about Tanner and Lorelei's
wedding day?

Get the free short story
and sign up for insider email updates at

https://mistymbeller.com/rmp-bonus-epilogue

USA Today bestselling author **Misty M. Beller** writes romantic mountain stories set on the 1800s frontier and woven with the truth of God's love. Raised on a farm and surrounded by family, Misty developed her love for horses, history, and adventure. These days, her husband and children provide fresh adventure every day, keeping her both grounded and crazy. Misty's passion is to create inspiring Christian fiction infused with the grandeur of the mountains, writing historical romance that displays God's abundant love through the twists and turns in the lives of her characters. Sharing her stories with readers is a dream come true. She writes from her country home in South Carolina and escapes to the mountains any chance she gets. Learn more and see Misty's other books at MistyMBeller.com.

Sign Up for Misty's Newsletter

Keep up to date with Misty's latest news on book releases and events by signing up for her email list at the link below.

FOLLOW MISTY ON SOCIAL MEDIA

Misty M. Beller, Author   @mistymbeller   @MistyMBeller

MistyMBeller.com

More from Misty M. Beller

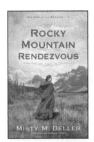

Juniper Collins and her sisters travel west to find the Blackfoot Piegan woman their late father credits with saving his life. Riley Turner became a trapper in the Rocky Mountains to find peace and quiet, but he feels compelled to help the sisters on their mission. But they face more questions than answers as unlikely allies—and enemies—stand in their way.

Rocky Mountain Rendezvous

In a French settlement, hidden deep in the caves of the Canadian Rocky Mountains, three village women face the unexpected peril, rugged country, and handsome strangers who come calling in the treacherous, unpredictable land. With danger threatening their every step, can they risk putting their lives—and their hearts—in another person's hands?

BRIDES OF LAURENT:
A Warrior's Heart, A Healer's Promise, A Daughter's Courage